Samantha David was born in London and now lives in France with her family and a menagerie of animals. She is a journalist by trade, and *I Married a Pirate* is her first novel.

I MARRIED A PIRATE

When Camilla meets the Pirate surfing the Net she refuses to fall in love with him — but the Pirate doesn't give a yard-arm what she thinks. She's beautiful and he's determined. So he inveigles her into boarding his pirate ship in the Caribbean . . . The Pirate is free-spirited, outrageous and irascible, and in Camilla — brave, resourceful and nutty — he has met his match. Together they inhabit a seductive, bohemian world of musicians and artists, buccaneers and eccentrics.

SAMANTHA DAVID

I MARRIED A PIRATE

Complete and Unabridged

ULVERSCROFT
Leicester

First published in Great Britain in 2007 by
Myrmidon Books Limited
Newcastle upon Tyne

First Large Print Edition
published 2008
by arrangement with
Myrmidon Books Limited
Newcastle upon Tyne

British Library CIP Data

David, Samantha
    I married a pirate.—Large print ed.—
Ulverscroft large print series: romance
1. Pirates—Fiction 2. Online dating—Fiction
3. Love stories 4. Large type books
I. Title
823.9′2 [F]

ISBN 978–1–84782–323–6

Published by
F. A. Thorpe (Publishing)
Anstey, Leicestershire

Set by Words & Graphics Ltd.
Anstey, Leicestershire
Printed and bound in Great Britain by
T. J. International Ltd., Padstow, Cornwall

This book is printed on acid-free paper

With love to the WW, Ton-ton R-là,
Lollipop, Dolly, Poodgy-Baby —
and Pirates everywhere.

1

Sunday Night

Dear Philippa

I married a pirate.

Well, that's the short explanation, but I owe you more than just four words. I know I do. You've been so brilliant . . . Look, he was one of my Internet men. I had dozens of them when I lived in France. It was just a late night hobby, emailing nonsense to virtual lovers all over the globe. It's the sort of thing you do when you're as sad and pathetic as I was.

The twins were still little then and I was cursing all men and endlessly struggling to make ends meet. Sounds a bit dire now, but that's how it was and I wasn't alone. The hills were alive with the sound of domestic discord. Every second mother I knew was singing the same song: I got kids, But no cash, Cos Romeo, Done buggered off and left me for his sodding secretary/personal assistant/plumber.

Between the lot of us, we could only

1

muster about one part-time bloke. Two on a good day.

Anyway, I escaped from all this dire-ness by exchanging emails with Internet men. You know the sort of thing: 'Hello kevikof4637, my day was truly dreadful, how was yours?'

Most of them replied: 'Very busy at work today, out playing squash tonite'.

But PirateXXX used to ask me why my day had been so awful, and then come back with: 'Don't panic, the kids are fine, you are wonderful mother, don't worry about roof and above all don't answer letters from tax office. Then they don't know if you exist or not.' (That piece of advice actually worked too.)

He said he lived on a traditional pirate's ship — a 60-foot ketch; double-masted, iron-hulled, equipped with powerful engines as well as sails, radios, global positioning system, electronic charts, radar, computers and generators.

I tell you, Philippa, it's a fabulous boat. There are berths and seating for a dozen people, a large galley, showers, lavatories, teak decks and railings, canvas shades rigged against the sun. He keeps her riding at anchor just off a small Caribbean island because she's too big to sail single-handed. If he wants to go somewhere, he either takes his speedboat or gets someone to fly him.

Oh, she is beautiful, all polished teak and white sails — a real dream boat — unlike the Pirate, who is about as dreamy as a shark.

'Where's yr man?' he demanded.

Me. Well, I've always been alone, apart from those few short months with . . . but you know, I got pregnant by accident and the minute he realised that an abortion was out of the question, he bogged off prontissimo. I haven't seen him since, and I don't suppose he even knows that it turned out to be twins. Charming, huh?

'The last great romantic,' remarked the Pirate. 'Where you living?'

'In somebody else's joke,' I replied sourly.

'Not a tent?'

'That would be luxury. Where do you live?'

'On the Sun,' he typed. That's what he called his pirate ship: the Sun. His personal speedboat is called the Venus, and the rest of his fleet — various other smaller speedboats, a collection of yachts and a handful of catamarans — have matching celestial names: Mars, the Moon, etc.

He doesn't actually fly the Jolly Roger but, believe me, he has a fine selection of dodgy flags to hoist aloft and neither his fleet nor anything else is respectably registered. Because he's a pirate.

Oh God, Philippa. I know! It sounds crazy and no, I've never gone in for bodice-heaving or leaping about with a dagger between my teeth. Nor has he, actually. He doesn't sit in crow's nests, or slide down ropes or swing from chandeliers. He doesn't look anything like Errol Flynn: he isn't dashing or handsome or sexy. He doesn't have flashing eyes or a smile that would amuse Queen Victoria, and he certainly won't ever turn out to be the wronged son of a noble count or the dashing defender of the poor and oppressed.

He's not that sort of pirate. He makes furious sweaty phone calls rather than swinging from the rigging. Frankly, he's short, fat, old and irascible.

What's more, he's as amoral as a cat on heat. He steals, cheats and kidnaps and he only ever does what he wants. He's never motivated by honour or duty. Duty! He doesn't have any duties. He doesn't pay any either. He doesn't give a flying fish about obligations. He runs his personal empire, increases his wealth, and for the rest, unless it's fun, he shrugs his shoulders and lets it fall overboard.

I bet you're wondering why I fell for him, then? Oh, I don't know. He was fun. He was carefree and optimistic and had answers for all my problems; he made me feel that life wasn't that hard after all. I thought he understood me. I felt I'd finally found a soul mate. Ah well. At least he emailed regularly.

'What about you? Where you living? Tell me,' he ordered.

The house was in the mountains, which seemed okay when I first got there. It would. I didn't notice the leaky roof when I bought the place. Because I was pregnant, that's why. Just bursting with hormones and daydreams. And having been born in Paris myself, for some insane reason I thought it would be romantic to have my baby in France.

So I bought the house by cashing in my share of the flat in London — that was from when I was working for the record company — intending to do it up, bask in the sun, learn how to cook and occasionally teach piano in order to pay for the Ambre Solaire.

As you know, it didn't work out like that. For one thing it rained constantly, and for another I didn't have a baby, I had twins.

'What about yr family? Don't they help?' he snapped.

I didn't reply to that one. I wasn't ready to tell him all that stuff. I mean, I hate people being sympathetic about my mother. She was killed in a road accident when I was twelve. But I told you about that, didn't I?

Anyway, I got packed off to boarding

school and at the time I thought the world had ended. I hated my mother for dying, I hated my father for sending me away and I hated everyone else just for good measure. But you know, what else was Daniel supposed to do? He's a musician. He travels all the time. So what do you expect? My mother was dead. I was in boarding school. My father found someone else. Of course he did.

I know what it's like on the road, on tour, gigging in Hamburg, playing sessions in Madrid. I know because Muma and me travelled everywhere with him until the accident. The only people I ever knew when I was growing up were other musos, opera singers, theatre people . . . I mean, even me, I've always worked in the music business one way or another and so has everyone I've ever known.

Perhaps that's why when the Pirate sailed into my life and dropped anchor, he didn't seem so outrageous to me. He wasn't a musician, but he wasn't from civvy street either. I felt at home with him. He made me laugh.

What was I saying? Oh yes, I hate having to explain everything to outsiders, people who can't understand. People who tut and look shocked. You know, even when I had the twins and settled down, I was living on such a tightrope that people still used to give me pitying looks. So when the Pirate first asked me about my family, I didn't trust him not to be sorry for me. I mean, I hardly knew him then. Anyway, I didn't reply.

Two days later he emailed again. 'What? You got no family? They all dead? I gotta dead sister. Fell down the stairs. Tell me.'

So I told him the whole boring saga and he wasn't in the slightest bit sympathetic. 'What? Ain't you got no friends?' he complained. So I told him about Nickie.

My mate Nickie. We met just after the twins were born. Shell-shocked and exhausted on my way home from the French maternity unit, I staggered into the chemist clutching a prescription running into three pages of A4 and there she was, with a toddler screaming on her lap and a wet dog panting at her feet.

When she saw me with the two newborns stuffed into one pram and the rain streaking down my face and the fag I'd forgotten to drop on the pavement outside, she laughed. In fact, she had hysterics: wheezed and coughed, hacked away, thumping her chest, squashing her toddler and intermittently apologising.

All around us, sedate French matrons were raising their eyebrows and tucking their chins into their collars. They take babies very seriously in France. The chemist wasn't amused either, and catching his eye suddenly I collapsed into overdue hysterics as well.

Nickie is a painter, and she'd toshed in her office job to come to France and concentrate on her art.

'Bloody hell!' said the Pirate. 'Don't you know no-one normal?'

'Well, if you think she's mad, it's lucky you don't know Fiona,' I typed back. 'I mean Nickie's practically bourgeois, she's so organised compared to Fiona.'

'Who the fuck's she?'

Well, she was Nickie's friend really, but she was way more outrageous than us. I mean for example, Fiona didn't have special men, boyfriends or husbands, that sort of man. She just had Guys — a succession of mucky, sulky, black-eyed gypsies strutting about her caravan in colourful neckties with pockets full of weed. And a goat.

In fact, I think she's still got the goat. No, don't laugh, Philippa. I'm not joking, she had a pet goat. A stinky mottled creature with broken horns and mad eyes. It ranged around head-butting old ladies in the daytime, but it slept in the caravan at night. Probably even slept in her bed. No, not shagging her! Just farting and trampling and eating the sheets. That sort of goaty type thing that goats do.

You know? No, no. I know. You haven't ever shared a caravan with a goat.

Anyway, so there we were, the three of us, all English, all stranded in southern France. Me, Nickie, and Fiona; all of us with kids, none of us with two centimes to rub together and only Fiona with some sort of male to call her own, even if she did call him Billy.

'Jesus Christ,' swore the Pirate. 'Fucking crazy Englishwomen . . . '

Although I think Nickie was still married then. Not to the father of her kids, to some sex-crazed hunk she met years before and never quite got round to divorcing. Or had he divorced her by then and simply forgotten to let her know? Can't remember. Anyway, she was sort of married. Not that it did her much good.

Not that anything would have done us any good at that point. You have to remember, we were hormonally challenged and deeply disappointed women. To us, men were just fathers who didn't pay maintenance, hopeless cases who turned up demanding food and alcohol, dickheads who could empty a bank account faster than a bar and drank whisky with all meals including breakfast . . . yep, all in all just Standard Issue Class A Bastards.

All except the Pirate. He wasn't a bastard. In fact, he quickly became my best friend.

Apart from Nickie, of course. I could rely on him to laugh at the same things as me and he sent silly cartoons and jokes. He saw the funny side of life, however black it got.

Because apart from poverty and parenthood, we did have comedy. We had lots of that. Addictive, bittersweet comedy, as soft and black as the night. Like when Nickie cut her chin open splitting logs and couldn't go to the clinic because she didn't have the cash.

Me and Fiona had gone over to help cut last year's Christmas cards into new ones, and there she was, rain-soaked and red-faced, with blood pouring from the gash on her chin and the dog going potty trying to lick it off her T-shirt, and Fiona accused her of trying to dye her clothes on the cheap.

For a split second I thought Fiona's life was worthless, but then Nickie choked and we all cracked up. Again.

We stumbled indoors and Fiona cobbled a sweet corn omelette together for the collective kids present while Nickie found cotton wool, bathed her chin and realised she needed stitches. Needless to say none of us had health insurance, so in the end Nickie got her chin sewn up with rough blue string by the vet.

He owed her a favour because she'd taken a litter of kittens off his hands in the summer, but he was afraid someone might see through the kitchen window so having given Nickie a whole handful of useless canine painkillers he did it really quickly, leaving her literally in stitches but trying not to laugh because it hurt too much.

Between hoots she begged me and Fiona to shut up, but we couldn't stop because we were both in the same boat. We all had string in our chins one way or another, and that was about all we did have. None of us had a bean. Blimey, we didn't even have purses, we were so broke.

About a week later when she had to get the stitches out, Nickie went off to find the vet again. Obviously she daren't go to anyone else. But the vet had taken fright and wouldn't have anything to do with it so she had to take the stitches out herself. She says she couldn't keep her hands steady for laughing because it was all so awful. Which is why she still has faint blue lines under her skin: she didn't get all the string out.

So after that if anyone started moaning, we used to chorus 'and I've still got string in my chin'. But mostly we only moaned from laughing too much.

Apart from anything else, we loved being in France. We were addicted to it, to the beauty of the mountains, the poetry of the ancient

11

villages, the rhythm of traditional village life, the warmth of the sun, the colour of the sky.

We were living our dreams.

But I digress. That was my life, and that was why I had the Internet men. I mean apart from the poverty I was too busy with the kids to bother with a real man — even if there'd been one on the horizon, which there wasn't. So I used to flirt with and fantasise about a bunch of unknown strangers. At least that way I wouldn't get pregnant again or find myself facing an irate Frenchwoman wielding a ham-knife. In Cyberland, even the Pirate seemed safe.

But gradually the other Internet men fell by the wayside. They were boring compared to him. I got into the habit of emailing him constantly; to pass on the gossip, bitch about the neighbours, complain about the kids, gloat over my small successes, and drone on about the washing machine packing up, and the house being so glacial all winter.

And he used to come back with all sorts of advice on how to chop wood without amputating your chin, how to mend an oven door with a tin opener, and what to say to morons who asked if I liked being on holiday all the time. He also offered to shoot people I didn't like and it wasn't long before he offered to send me tickets so I could visit him in the Caribbean. He emailed every day. Sometimes twice a day.

'Come here and let me look after you. I send tickets.'

He said he'd lived in the Caribbean for twenty-five years and had a business there — something to do with yachts and T-shirts. And he claimed to have pots and pots of the folding stuff and swore that he wanted nothing better than to squander it on me. Because I am blonde of course. And thin. He saw that from the photo I sent him.

When he got it, he instantly emailed: 'You are too thin. You need me to look after you, come and live on my ship with me. I love you.'

I emailed back immediately: 'Cut the crappy lurve-stuff. You've never even met me.'

So he sent me pictures of his Caribbean island and his boat, and the beaches, and asked yet again if I would go and see him — just for a holiday, no strings attached. I mailed back and said no, I couldn't possibly drag my kids halfway across the globe and anyway I haven't got the money and he declared that money was nothing more than a psychological phenomenon.

'If you wanted money, you'd have it,' he said. 'Think about that.'

Well, I suppose he was right. I didn't earn

13

much because I refused to work during the twins' school holidays, which meant I was constantly scrubbing about teaching piano to the local kids instead of getting a proper full-time job at the sweet factory like all the other mothers.

I didn't really want to discuss that though, so I told him about the French countryside and what it was like to find a bolt-hole from the rat race, and he said he'd done the same thing when he ran away to sea and washed up in the Caribbean.

You see, Philippa! That's what I fell for. He just understood. He never said stuff like 'Oh, aren't you brave?' or 'I don't know how you cope,' or 'Don't you ever get bored living out there on your own?'

He told me tall tales about his life and his adventures at sea and sometimes he'd just write nonsense to cheer me up.

'Darling woman, let me take you in my arms, let me smooth away all your cares . . . my day was boring too, I had to shoot a robber off the deck of my ship, but now I take you in my arms and together we enter paradise.'

His emails warmed and cheered me. He was encouraging and positive, and he made me laugh. He was my refuge. I used to log on every night after the kids were in bed knowing there'd be at least one email waiting for me, knowing that he would offer proper advice and if all else failed, offer to shoot all the Standard Issue Class A Bastards in my life.

He sent jokes, flirted outrageously and incessantly begged me on virtual bended knee to visit him.

'Stop wasting your time with those fuckers and come here. I promise to make you happy,' he said. 'No strings attached. Just come, I am rich man, I send you ticket.'

So in the end I closed up the house in France and caught the bus. The twins were about 10 years old then, and I told myself that they were the main reason I went. They'd been ill all summer with a series of childish stomach upsets and I convinced myself that a Caribbean holiday would put them back on their feet.

Don't bother telling me I'm crazy. I know that. It just seemed like a good idea at the time — I had itchy feet and, of course, I was already at least half in love with the Pirate. Not that I would admit it. I mean look what happened last time. Twins and no twin tub.

I'll skip the flight, Philippa. You know what it was like anyway. Long, boring, dehydrating and exhausting. Still, we weren't delayed, no-one was sick and the boys enjoyed going off to the cockpit to meet the Captain. Yes, in those days you could still do that . . .

When we arrived at the airport — and no, I'm not going to identify any of the places I'm talking about — that would be madness — when we arrived in the Caribbean, the arrivals lounge was heaving with the usual mix of exhausted passengers jostling with taxi-drivers, families meeting travellers, lay-abouts, crooks, officials, rich bitches, foreign holiday makers, hawkers, madmen, nutters, and . . . well, us. Having collected our luggage (one battered suitcase that I'd borrowed from Nickie), hauled it onto a trolley and shoved our way through customs, I hadn't the faintest idea where to go or what to do, so I just stood in the arrivals hall waiting to see what would happen.

The arrangement had been that the Pirate would meet us off the flight but, gazing at the mass of people writhing around us like eels in a fish tank, it was obvious that he hadn't come.

I was stranded, I hadn't a bean in my pocket, knew absolutely no-one, and felt sure that Air France would refuse to change the tickets and fly us straight home. Unless I could find a bar somewhere with a piano but no pianist, we would be doomed to stay in the airport for two whole weeks scrounging for leftovers in airport bins and sleeping on our beach towels behind the vending machines.

The boys were beginning to whine too, which made it worse. I lifted the hair off my shoulders and smiled encouragement at them. I'd nicked a substantial number of mini-bottles of wine off the trolley in the plane and they clanked comfortingly in my bag. I made some sort of joke to amuse the kids and wondered how long I could make my stolen wine last.

'Hey, you Camille?'

I turned my head and found myself looking at a man whose resemblance to the pictures he'd emailed was zip, zilch, nada. Non-existent.

The photos had shown a laughing brown face with flashing eyes and a mop of chestnut hair atop a strong bull neck and a massive, powerful torso. This man was pot-bellied, pallid and covered in liver spots. He was wearing a sweat-stained shirt, dreadful shorts and ancient espadrilles. His hair was greying and since the photo was taken it must have receded faster than the tide because there was hardly any of it left.

The twins shrank behind my skirt, asking, 'Mummy, is this the Pirate?'

Blimey. Trust kids to spit it out un-chewed. But he was unfazed. His eyes flashed amusement at me and he ruffled the kids' hair.

'That's me. I'm the Pirate,' he said looking straight through my eyes into my brain. 'Not what you expected, huh?'

A seriously global understatement. After a year of chatting and flirting and being infatuated with a man who had talked, advised and joked his way into becoming my lifeline, I was horrified. He was so far from anything I'd expected, so ugly, so tatty and revolting. He didn't even look clean.

The hair rose on my scalp. What the hell was I to do? I mean there I was, and there he was, and I just knew I couldn't spend more than ten seconds in his company without being sick. So I did the bourgeois thing: denied it, claimed I was tired after the flight, apologised for being stupid, said I had a headache, we were just hungry . . .

He raised his eyebrows and shrugged. 'I don-cair,' he said. 'Is no problem,' and he seized the handle of the trolley. We followed him. Well, what else could we do? I mean, what else would you have done? And don't give me any crap about credit cards or ringing Muthar. I didn't have those options. I told you, Muma died. Anyway, the guy was just an old fat slob. He wouldn't be a problem.

I grabbed the boys and hurried after him. As he surged through the automatic airport doors ahead of us, the August heat rose up like a hot sponge, flung itself at our faces and clung to our skins. It was late at night but there wasn't breath of air and within minutes we were drenched to the skin and sweating. Finding the car in the dark seemed to take an eternity, the night cracking as palm trees laboured to stay upright in the heat, and faces looming in and out of focus all around us. But finally he unlocked a dusty red Clio, flung the suitcase into the boot, and piled the boys into the back. We got in and sat side by side like yesterday's sardines in a jacuzzi. He rammed the ignition key into the starter and twisted it impatiently.

The heat was intense, and even worse when the engine sputtered into life because it fanned hot air into our faces. I fumbled around to wind the window down.

'Dondo vat!'

'I'm so hot . . . '

'Wait for la fuckin cleem.' His English was fractured, even more so than in his emails, and mixed up with bits of other languages, mainly Greek and French garnished with shreds of Italian. 'La clim' is air conditioning and although it sounds weird to say it now, it was the first time I'd come across an air-conditioned car. You have to remember I'd spent ten years with no running hot water, cutting logs for the stove before I could start cooking, and wearing 'un jogging' in bed over my pyjamas.

I fell in love instantly. No, not with Mr Vomit. Not even with the Caribbean or the bloody car. With 'la clim'. I could hardly believe that such luxury existed, such control over our personal environment. It made me want to laugh and laugh.

I gazed out of the window at scrub grass caught in the headlights, at a murky, sulky sky, great scuds of cloud lurking in front of a dull, moody moon. I gazed at any bloody thing so that I wouldn't have to look at the pale plump hands strangling the steering wheel beside me. In his turn the Pirate kept up a prize-winning stream of muttered abuse and obscenity about the car, the roads, the heat and every other driver on the planet: no hesitation, no repetition, no deviation, and he kept it up for well over twenty minutes. Glancing over my shoulder, I could see by their wide-open eyes that the twins were deeply impressed.

The Pirate mangled his way down to a marina which looked like a Disney film set. The whole scene was lit by thousands of tiny glimmering fairy lights, the palm trees were cunningly floodlit and the reflections danced gaily in the gentle waves. The buildings were covered in ice cream coloured clapboard (vanilla, strawberry and pistachio), the glittering water lapped at white stonework, and shiny chains looped into golden wooden posts to prevent you tumbling into the inky drink. Stunned, the boys trotted ahead with me calling feebly after them not to fall in.

'Leave them, give them some space,' said the Pirate. 'They're okay.'

He took my arm just above the elbow and steered me onto a terrace overlooking the water where tables were laid with flowers and candles and menus. We sat down opposite each other and I hid behind a menu. I didn't agree that the boys were okay, teetering about on the edge of a bottomless pit, but short of starting a stand-up argument there wasn't much I could do about it and in any case, within minutes the twins had come rushing back and clung round the table.

'Can we have chips?'

'Can we have ice-cream?'

'Can I have one of those, Mum?' pointing at a towering knicker-bocker glory being demolished at a neighbouring table.

'Er, I don't know, I'll see . . . perhaps if . . . '

'Yes, you have anything. Order what you like! Camille! Your fucking sons! Give them a break!'

Coming straight after his award-winning swear-fest in the car, they were instantly seduced and I had to swallow back a snappy retort. They looked so happy, their matching faces lit up with enthusiasm and joy, that it was impossible to argue. It was also impossible to correct his pronunciation of my name. Camilla, not Camille pronounced the French way. Milly if you insist, but absolutely definitely not Cam-mee. It smacks of soap scum to me.

Meanwhile the Pirate had ordered mountains of food. Shellfish and salad and chips and chicken wings and milk shakes and a dish of stewed vegetables and a bottle of chilled white wine. Don't ask me what it was, I know nothing about wine, but it was wonderful: dry, cold, light, almost perfumed, and incredibly intoxicating.

What the hell. The boys' eyes lit up, they could barely contain themselves when they saw all this food being loaded on to the table. They sat there gazing at the dishes and shooting incredulous glances at me — and the Pirate got cross again. He's a bad-tempered man.

'Well, what you doing? Mangez! Eat! For Christsake, Camille, what you been feeding dees piccolo uomini? You do feed them don't you? Hey, you, have some chicken, put your fork down, eat with your fingers, and you, whatsyername, take chips!' He piled their plates up and turned to me, waving the serving spoons like cutlasses.

'And you. You eat, too. You too fuckin thin,' he complained.

So we ate. And drank, and ate more. In fact I think he was secretly impressed by our ability to dispose of all food within our reach. Not that he showed it. He was more irritable than anything else, hectoring and lecturing on child welfare and shouting at the staff for more fried fish, more bread, more ice cream, more chocolate sauce, and take this away they don-lie-kit.

Drugged with excess calories, knocked out by a long haul flight and ten gallons of wine . . . don't ask me what happened next. Did he pay that bill or did he slam an axe into the table before we left? Or was it more of a wink and a handshake? I don't know. He doesn't pay restaurant bills, I can tell you that much. Not in cash, at the time, I mean. If he pays them at all, he pays them off in kind; in favours, in protection, in all sorts of nefarious ways. Even now, I'm not entirely clear about all his dealings. The loan of the Clio was definitely a favour though, as were our hotel rooms.

They were air conditioned too, and we had

a marble bathroom. Our room had two double beds in it; one for me, one for the boys. He had a room somewhere else. Don't ask me where. Probably in an even posher bit of the hotel — because although I'd never seen such luxury in my entire life at that time, for the Caribbean it was just the standard stuff. You know, tourist hotel with balcony and bathroom. All these places have air conditioning and marble bathrooms. A far cry from the flophouses, fleapits and theatrical digs of my childhood.

I woke up in the morning with the most sinister headache. The boys were sprawled fully dressed but fast asleep across their double bed, and through the thin filmy white curtains was a breath-taking view of an emerald sea sparkling beyond a pale gold beach surrounded by flowers, lawns and palm trees. Frankly I could hardly believe my eyes. After years of looking out at glowering mountains, rain clouds and muddy piles of firewood needing to be chopped, the whole paradise scenario took my breath away. I rolled over and groped for my bag desperately seeking painkillers, and the boys woke up.

They didn't have indigestion, tummy-ache or sinister hangovers. They weren't even tired. Jetlag has always been unknown to them. They still don't suffer from it and they're constantly on and off long-haul flights. Luckily they're just like my father.

Anyway, I was knackered, disorientated, over-heated and generally functioning on about one cylinder. Everyone else was insanely cheerful. There was swimming in a kidney-shaped pool, a nauseating buffet breakfast including an entire plastic lobster, several all too real roast hams, a lake of exotic fruit juice and a Cheshire Cat chef dishing up anaemic fried eggs on toast.

The whole thing was laid out in a room the size of a football pitch. The boys made determined efforts to clear the entire buffet whilst the Pirate drank several large Pernods and ordered vast quantities of melon ice cream, which he then didn't eat. ('No, take it off! They don-lie-kit!')

I swallowed more painkillers, stirred a muddy cup of tea and reminded myself to breathe in and out. The heat was intense, the light was blinding and the sight of so much food sitting on chafing dishes gently drying up reminded me of Nickie sitting at her kitchen table staring at a pile of wonky black carrots the day the banks went on strike and there was nothing left to eat and no gas to cook it on either.

Unlike me, Nickie had originally brought a man to France with her — not her husband, she'd already mislaid him somewhere — but the father of her kids. Trouble was, he pissed off to Hong Kong, ostensibly on a contract to sort out Toyota's computers but in reality to ram coke up his nose and shag a grisly selection of Oriental prostitutes.

He used to come back to France from time to time; broke, exhausted and bearing gifts in the shape of head lice or genital infections. Naturally his fantastic earnings never made it back to Europe. Or if they did, Nickie never saw them. And eventually he pissed off completely. There wasn't much she could do about it.

Like me, she didn't have the cash to go back to the UK even if she could have shoved her pride far enough down her gullet to do it. So she patched up the ceilings, painted abstracts, brought her kids up and talked to her dog, a black labrador called Max. Perhaps he was an Internet man substitute?

'Hey! Camille! Eat! Here, eat eggs!' The Pirate was making a spirited attempt to push a plate of fried eggs in front of me. I bared my teeth at him, smiled grimly and shook my throbbing head. Thank God, he desisted.

Perhaps he realised how fragile I was, because after breakfast the boys were taken outside to swim in the pool under the supervision of a cheery hotel play-leader while I slept in the blissful luxury of our air-conditioned room. The Pirate disappeared — presumably to blackmail someone into giving us a flight.

Because oh no. The journey wasn't over. This large island with its tarmac roads, its phones and hotels, its air conditioning, hot water, acres of green lawn . . . this wasn't our destination. Our immediate destination was an airstrip. Not the international airport of the night before, but a dusty airstrip staffed by one uniformed black hunk armed with a sub-machine gun, and inhabited by a collection of exhausted people in charge of vast amounts of shopping: a woman with a fridge in a crate, another with several suitcases containing rusty tins of Heinz soup (I know because Mr Uniform made her open the cases up) and a man in charge of a dodgy-looking teenager. There was a quantity of barbed wire, a small hut for shade, a tap that didn't work and a selection of posters announcing things like 'Ben Ja Shoe — We are caring always for your gentle feet — always!'

The Pirate left us there while he sat talking to a guy in a large black Ford, and then finally returned saying he'd cleared our visa problems, and could he have our passports. Visa problems? What visa problems? But we didn't need visas. Well, that was wrong. We did need visas, because we were going to fly down to a tiny island which was officially in another country and then we would get in his speedboat and whiz out to his Pirate's ship.

I handed over the passports.

I know, I know, Philippa. You'd have whipped a handy mobile out of your bag and called Muthar or Gus, or someone. Or run a quick credit card check, or called a taxi and high tailed it to the nearest champagne bar or nail salon. Or possibly to the nearest Embassy. Well, I didn't do any of that stuff. Frankly, I hardly thought twice. I just handed our passports over. How was I to know I'd never see them again?

All I thought was that the sooner we were on a plane, the sooner we'd be back in an air-conditioned environment. I was tired, and not just from the effects of a trans-Atlantic flight, I was tired from ten years of struggling alone; from the boredom and repetition of endlessly hauling ash, changing nappies, buttering soldiers, boiling eggs, counting centimes, working nights, attempting to cook over a wood-fuelled stove, having no running hot water, and making sure it all seemed like a laugh to the boys. I don't mean that exactly. I mean, living in France was a laugh but I was knackered. Exhausted to the pit of my stomach. All I wanted was air-conditioning, therefore I handed our passports over so that we could get in the plane. Because planes are air-conditioned.

How wrong can you get? The plane seated six, and must have been built in about 1935. There were two seats in the cockpit and four more faded yellow velvet seats facing each other in the back, with little ashtrays in the arm rests and rusty seat belts. You could have parked the whole thing inside a phone box and still have had room to throw a party. And as for air-conditioning, what do you need that for when the bloody plane isn't airtight in the first place and freezing cold air blows in from the cracks around the doors? Doors which don't close properly. Jesus Christ.

The pilot was pissed and the doors had to be fastened with a piece of wire twisted round the missing lock. The boys were wildly excited. We were all clearly doomed to die in this terrible old crate and, although death by falling out of an antique plane hadn't occurred to me before, I huddled back into the dull gold velvet and wondered whether it wouldn't be easier to bypass the gut-wrenching suspense and simply jump into the spinning propellers.

The Pirate sat up front beside the pilot and on the spare seat beside me sat a box, which I later found out contained most of the food we had failed to consume at breakfast. (The Pirate fed it to the tourists on one of his cruise boats the next day. Yes, of course with the exception of the melon ice cream. He's not a total nutter — oh God, what am I saying? He is.)

I know you're still wondering why I insist on calling him the Pirate — especially as his looks had nothing in common with one and he didn't have a parrot. (Although of course, he did send me one. But that was later. A lot later.) But no, he doesn't sail the seven seas with a flintlock in his belt, heaving to and attacking other ships. I don't think he's ever keelhauled anyone either, or made them walk the plank. And as for lashing people to the mast, well I have to admit, that turned out to be my speciality. But he is a Pirate. He just is!

It's his attitude, his approach to life. I mean, the only reason he doesn't board other ships is because he doesn't feel like it. But take that day, for example. I mean, he simply couldn't have bought tickets on the regular flight. In financial and practical terms he could have of course, but emotionally he absolutely could not have done it. That would have meant getting to an airport on time two days running, and that was simply inadmissible.

'Fuck the bastards. Why should I leave when they say on a paper I have to leave? I'll fucking leave when I wanna fucking leave. Anyway, this guy owes me a favour, so why should I go on the regular flight?'

I understood what he meant. Apart from anything else, I expect BA would have chucked his box of leftovers onto the runway.

And then there was his equally uncompromising approach to visas, taxes, licences, banks, governments, laws, officials, customs, conventions, socially accepted behaviour, women, dogs, meals, and business . . . but that wasn't all. He stole, he smuggled, he dealt with criminals and he kidnapped me. And if that doesn't make him a pirate, then what does?

Forget the First World. Forget police stations, phones, credit cards, consuls, embassies, letters, and all the rest of the paraphernalia of modern life over here in Western Europe. Forget zero tolerance, law and order, judicial systems and solicitors' advice. I didn't know it then, but when I got into that plane I stepped into another world.

I stepped into a world where personal contacts count for more than civil status, where locals leave Europeans alone for fear of reprisals, where the Pirate had more money and therefore more control than anyone else, and where the nearest lawyer was 80kms and a three-hour boat ride away. I stepped into a world where my pale skin would get me into any luxy bar I fancied, but would also mark me out as the Pirate's property and therefore unapproachable, untouchable. Certainly not someone you could befriend or help. Not that I knew it then. Perhaps just as well.

I concentrated on making the boys sit down, and on doing up their seat belts (probably the first time they'd been used since 1945). Then I concentrated on ignoring the incredible noise the plane made, the terrifying vibrations and the sight of the pilot swigging yet more beer from a bottle as he shouted jokes at the Pirate who was counting a large roll of American dollars.

The flight wasn't long, just over an hour, thank God, and our destination soon jiggled into sight over the edge of a large green mountain. We floundered over the ridges, swooped above a desiccated valley towards a golden beach, tottered across a series of corrugated iron shacks, wobbled down over a concrete bunker and flopped onto the landing strip only to accelerate towards a bed of sharp rocks tumbling into the sea. I closed my eyes.

'Mummy, we're here! Look, look! Mummy, open your eyes! We're safe! It's all right, Mummy!'

The pilot was already out of the plane and embracing a dusky lovely. The Pirate meantime was supervising the removal of his cardboard box and Nickie's suitcase. (He's way too fat to carry anything himself, and rarely even bothers to walk anywhere.) Sweat was rolling down his pulpy face as the twins followed him, nervously asking which of the ships they'd seen in the bay was his.

But they didn't bother him, actually. He's good with kids. He pointed his boat out and rolled off towards the concrete bunker with a boy hanging from each hand and me trailing along behind them feeling like a camel.

Oh, I don't know, Philippa! I just felt like a camel. You know: bad tempered, flat-footed, shaggy and smelly, with stinky breath, foul yellow teeth and a definite hump. Don't you ever feel . . . no. Oh well.

The island was small with only one main village huddled round the southern bay. It had a large quay at one end, various smaller jetties all along it and the airstrip where we landed was at the other end of the bay just below a point of land sticking out into the sea. Backing onto the bay were tangles of small rust-red shacks surrounding small cement houses with faded paint, large verandas and windows with no glass in them. The only area that looked at all built up was over towards the quay where there was a complex of low white buildings.

Thinking back on it, the Pirate was daunted. He was. I know he was, because he didn't shout or rant. He sorted the officials out, sent the luggage off to the boat and took us to a restaurant in the complex. It was run by an efficient Frenchwoman called Marie-Rose, and this time there was no hectoring, no bullying, no raving about child-care. I ordered what I wanted and dealt with the boys while he sat and watched. There were no demands for more ice cream, no dizzying orders of fried fish or vegetable stew.

We ate steaks with haricots verts and had fruit afterwards. He drank Pernod. I drank two glasses of red wine and took comfort in noticing that the bottle had come from our departement in France. A link with home, with sanity and normality.

Of course, I now know that this restraint on his part was a warning sign. But at the time I just thought that he was more relaxed on his home territory, assumed that he had a running tab at the restaurant and that his progress in speedboats was always inclined to be stately, because he was after all just an old guy. Ha!

Oh yes, you have to have a speedboat here. Well, some sort of little boat, anyway. The

Pirate has a large selection and drives them all at top speed. Always. Everywhere. Apart from that one night.

Cafés and restaurants shelter under the palm trees all along the seashore, and although a rough track winds along behind them, the easiest way to get around is by boat because most of the bars have little jetties where you can moor a speedboat or a dinghy.

So after supper we walked down the jetty, climbed into the Venus, and he headed out slowly across the bay towards his ship. A great creaking monster lurking in the moonlight with two large masts, a quantity of varnished decking, and ropes everywhere. As we drew alongside it, the Pirate cut the engine and stood up so that he could throw a rope onto the small landing stage and ladder that was lashed to the side of the ship.

Wobbling and squeaking with delicious fright, the boys climbed up the ladder croaking 'cool', with me behind them clucking 'don't fall in', and the Pirate biting his tongue. Normally that sort of maternal concern thing drives him totally spanner. You know, so rigid and silver-grey with fury that his mouth gapes open. But he behaved himself, merely showing us our cabins, and checking that Nickie's suitcase was already neatly stowed away and our belongings were stacked into lockers.

I was far too tired and shell-shocked to notice anything. I had no idea of the time, I just wanted some peace and quiet. So I put the boys to bed in their little cabin and amazingly they didn't complain. They didn't even grumble. They just went, and within minutes they were asleep in their berths.

The inside of the boat was all made of varnished wood. You came down the stairs into a small room — which I soon learnt to call a large galley — with wooden kitchen units built in down one side, a large table bolted to the floor in the centre with fixed benches either side of it and lockers forming a sofa opposite the kitchen units. Under the stairs was a pair of outsize American fridges, and opposite was a small door leading to our cabins and bathroom, tucked inside the prow of the boat. Behind the stairs was a second door, this one leading to a workshop, a shower and a large space where the Pirate lounged on his bed and watched porno-graphic videos.

Up on the deck there were curious moon shapes nailed to the deck to catch rainwater, and squares of canvas rigged up to provide shade for the teak table and chairs set out more or less above our cabins. I sat there and gazed at the celestial lightshow.

The Pirate sat and stared at me as I stared at the moon, and after a while I stared at him and he stared at the moon, and then we stared at each other, and then I said 'I'm going to bed' and he smiled at me, and I was about to try and tell him that he wasn't . . . that I wasn't . . . but I was too tired. So I just went, and he just let me go.

Which was truly bizarre, although I didn't think so then.

2

It was different in the morning. I was refreshed from sleeping round the clock, there was a breeze wafting through my cabin, and when I smelt coffee I suddenly realised my good luck. Out of the blue, undeserved, un-earned, unpaid for . . . I was on holiday. Oh, thank God!

Joy flooded my veins and I stretched luxuriously. Sunlight was flooding into the cabin through a porthole just above my double bunk. Directly above me was another single bunk. Beside me was a narrow space and a row of locker doors, one of which opened to reveal a small hand basin. I leapt out of bed. Well, no I didn't really. I did my usual early-morning imitation of a duck with stomach-ache and staggered to my feet quacking softly.

The cabin was tiny. Just about big enough for the small double bed I'd slept on, and the door to the twins' cabin. I pulled on a swimsuit and a pair of shorts, and went to see if the boys were still alive. I always have to check that they haven't died in their sleep. Mad, I know but I'd done it every night and every morning for ten years by then, and I still do it now. They were sleeping soundly.

Scratching my tousled hair and yawning, I went to investigate the smell of coffee. But it wasn't the Pirate rattling the pots and pans in the kitchen. It was a shiny-faced black girl with strong capable arms and a friendly smile.

'Hello there!' she beamed. 'Welcome to the Sun!'

I winced and managed some sort of grimace. 'Hi,' I croaked. 'Nice to meet you.'

Bettina was one of a band of young men and women the Pirate called 'pliroma' — crew. They weren't really sailors. I don't suppose any of them could actually handle a boat. They were just locals he employed to clean up, run errands and generally skivvy around the place. There wasn't much work for locals there, he paid better than most, and if he liked someone he would favour their family when looking for new crew, so the pliroma were hard nosed in their loyalty to him.

No, I'm not saying they'd put their lives on the line for him. Nothing so extreme. But unless you could fish out a better deal than the Pirate, they would do what he wanted them to do, and you could plead and beg, explain, cajole and blackmail to your heart's content. I know because in my time I've tried all those things and none of them worked. They still all obeyed the man they called The Boss.

Not that I knew that then. I just pulled up short at the sight of an unknown woman wiping the table. I found out later that the Pirate gets up with the dawn most days and spends a couple of hours in his office while it's still relatively cool. Don't ask me what he does there. I don't know. Beheads enemies, dodges officialdom, makes other pirates squirm, and shouts 'ahoy me hearties' down the phone, I expect.

Bettina poured coffee and put sugar and tinned milk out. Then she picked up the radio, set the call signal and started repeating, 'Sun Boat to Office, Sun Boat to Office.' Everyone uses short wave radio over there. It's cheap, it's reliable and it works. It's also incredibly public because even when you've moved off the call frequency, which you do the minute you've made contact with whoever you're calling, anyone can tune in and listen to you.

Anyway, she called the office while I sipped coffee and gathered from the conversation that she wasn't a stray wife, and then the twins emerged from their cabin demanding breakfast.

'It's coming, my lambs!' said Bettina. 'The Captain is sending Tommy over with bread for you. Do you want to come up and watch out for him?'

They scrambled upstairs at her heels and launched themselves happily at the railings to watch Tommy arrive, which he did in style, swooping out from the port in a speedboat which sent a wing of spray into our faces as he slewed the boat sideways and drifted in alongside the Sun.

Tommy leapt up the ladder with a plastic bag in one hand and the mooring rope in the other, tossed the bag to the twins, threw a kiss at Bettina and then slid off down the ladder into the throbbing speedboat.

'Oh, can't we go ashore?' I asked, and Tommy revved the engine like crazy and shot off towards the port.

'No. The Captain says you staying here, eating breakfast. He's coming soon. He's busy now.'

Well no, Philippa, I didn't think anything of it. It seemed utterly reasonable to me. Why on earth would anyone think 'Whoops, here we go, I'm being kidnapped'? I mean, it's not the sort of thing you think of. And no, I didn't remember my passport, I didn't check my bag, I didn't demand to see the British Ambassador. Give me a break. I was starving.

I went down to the galley to inspect the contents of the carrier bags.

There were pains au chocolat, croissants, French bread and two tubes of factor 100 sun cream. Bettina refused all help from me. 'No. The Captain says you relaxing,' she smiled, and bustled about capably producing hard boiled eggs, butter, jam, and juice from the fridge. It was already getting suffocatingly hot and sweaty in the galley, but she didn't seem to notice either the temperature or the humidity.

'You young men want to eat up on the deck?' she asked the twins, who were already stuffing themselves with pains au chocolat. Muffled yelps of 'cool', choking noises, and showers of crumbs made her laugh.

'You're like my boys. I got four. All eating like horses. Come on.'

We took everything up on deck and ate round the wooden table which was set out under the shade of a white canvas awning. I dipped bits of croissant into my coffee, Bettina drank juice and the boys scoffed the rest as we gazed at the shoreline. The sea was a patchwork of the most fantastic colours: turquoise, aqua-marine, azure, sparkling with pale emeralds, sapphires and diamonds and dotted with beautiful little sail boats. The beaches looked like golden frills, the buildings like bright embroidery squares, and the lush green inland hills like Never-never Land. The sky was absolutely clear and blue, and the air was soft and gentle on our skin.

Bettina finally out-cooked the boys by producing more boiled eggs than even they could eat, and then she called the Pirate on the radio and he came back and took us swimming at one of the beaches.

We went in his speedboat, the Venus, this time driving at his normal speed of full steam ahead, banging across the wavetops with our eyes full of spray. The beach was fine pale gold sand, scattered with shards of black palm leaves and lapped by little lacy waves as warm as bath water. I'd never been in such warm sea before. It was shallow and so transparent that I could see little fish nibbling at the chipped nail varnish on my toes. The boys were ecstatic, and the Pirate indulgently promised to buy them goggles so they could swim underwater.

Then we splashed back out to the speedboat and banged off to another island for lunch in a ritzy bar. And I do mean ritzy. The island we went to that day is privately owned and the whole place is one great big holiday resort. The sand there is combed twice a day so there are no sharp bits of palm tree in it, and the shells have all been polished

43

gleaming pink, and there are shaded wooden walkways along the beach so you don't burn your feet, and because the island is small and doesn't have mountains inland, you can stroll about the gardens admiring the bowers and arbours and shady seats. There are various beach bars too, all tastefully built to look native, but all actually equipped with electric lights, fridges, freezers, and ice-machines.

The restaurant was in the centre of the gardens, built on stilts so that it seemed like a tree house. There was a breathtaking view out over the sea and you could see all the neighbouring islands, including ours. The food was mainly Italian but there were also some French dishes on the menu and we ate like pigs. The Pirate obviously knew the place well and ordered by just nodding at the waiter. We had everything: pasta, pizza, fish, veal in cream sauce, sauté potatoes, salad, fruit, ice cream and real cappuccinos. We drank cocktails out of coconut shells, and the Pirate drank gallons of Pernod and massacred a boiled egg.

Then we wandered down through the gardens again and the Pirate took the boys into a shop on the beach, and bought them snorkels and goggles and flippers, and told me I was a stupid woman when I started whittering about not spoiling them.

'It's hardly worth it just for two weeks,' I said. 'They can share a set.'

'Shut up!' he snapped and glared at me furiously.

The twins stopped for a second then, their faces worried and their pleasure spoilt. The Pirate looked at them and sighed.

'Come on,' he said, in a softer voice. 'I jus-wan-ter buy them a present. Whas-wrong-wi-dat?'

'Nothing,' I said and smiled stiffly.

'You know,' he said confidentially to the boys, putting his arms round their shoulders, 'Your mother is a fine woman, but she don-understand men. This is a man thing. The sea is no fun without proper equipment, right?' And he pulled a mad face at us and made the twins laugh. I shook my head at him, but I smiled at the same time because I couldn't bear to spoil things for my boys. I'd just have to sort it out with the Pirate later, when they weren't listening.

So the twins got their snorkels and spent the afternoon splashing about in the sea while the Pirate and I sprawled on sun beds in the shade and I tried to talk sense to the man.

'Look, I haven't got the money to buy them stuff like this. I know you're only being kind, but if they get used to having anything they want, it's going to be a nightmare when we

45

get home. I mean, this isn't . . . '

'I never kind. I like to buy them tings. Nice boys. I got no boys. I only got girls. And they not stupid, they know I got money and you got nothing. Give them a break, Camille! Look at them, they happy now. So you be happy too. Relax! Here, throw that orange juice away, I get you a proper drink!'

I gave it up. I was full and hot and sleepy and I drifted into a kind of torpor where I could still hear the water splashing and feel the sun warm on my skin, but I was too far gone to speak or keep my eyes open. So in spite of myself, I relaxed. For the first time in nearly ten years, I simply let it all go. The boys were happy and safe, we had all eaten a massive lunch, and if anything went wrong with the house in France while we were away — if the roof blew off, or the windows started leaking again — I wouldn't know about it for another fortnight. I just lay there and let the sensation of total well-being flood through me.

He took the boys off for ice creams later on and I didn't protest, not even when they came back with huge polished conch shells and new T-shirts as well. I just smiled lazily and reminded them to say thank you. The Pirate beamed. That was all he wanted. Big smiles all round.

It was the start of the holiday of a lifetime. We slept, we ate, we swam, we drank, we slept again and sometimes we managed to swim and eat simultaneously — slipping into the clear turquoise water with a sandwich in one hand and a drink in the other. We saw the dolphins, fed the nursery sharks, visited islands, collected shells, ate at outdoor barbecue restaurants, walked along unimaginably beautiful beaches and had beads plaited into our hair. Well I did. The boys didn't, although their hair was long enough at that time, but they'd just got to the stage of being defensive about their nascent masculinity. Naturally the Pirate didn't have enough hair to make a plait possible. But he laughed at mine and said it was sexy.

'You know, you very sexy woman. You too thin, you too pale, you stiff like a board but I know what is inside, and I gonna let it out!'

Thinking about it later as I gazed at myself in the mirror, I wondered if he was right. I was nearly 40 and my eyes looked as faded as my hair. In spite of being a natural blonde, I've never been beautiful. My skin has always been too sensitive, too prone to break out in ugly red blotches, and although my eyes aren't small, they don't show up because they aren't a proper colour. They're just puddles of London rainwater.

But I used to be the sort of girl that people thought was pretty because she was always larking about, the sort of girl people called a madcap, and described as bouncy and full of personality. Years ago. Years ago when I regularly dyed my eyelashes and curled my hair and soothed the blotches out of my skin with expensive face creams. That girl had been buried for ten years under the weight of responsibility for two kids; the endless, useless attempts to do the right thing, to be a proper mother. I wondered if the Pirate was right, and that other younger me was still lurking inside, just biding her time to re-emerge.

He wallowed in the sea with us, shouting, 'I take holiday too! Hey, Bettina, when I last go swimming?'

'I dunno, Boss!' shouted Bettina from the beach where she was showing the boys how to bait fishing rods.

He was a surprisingly strong swimmer. In fact, he was surprisingly strong all round. You know, Philippa . . . more muscles than I'd thought, what with the sweaty shirt and all. He had skinny, wiry sticks of legs with tough stringy calf muscles bulging out of them, and a bloated belly, but he had this great barrel chest and huge powerful arms. No tattoos. Said they would mark him out, make him too easily identifiable. As if without them, he would fade into the crowd!

He disdained sun creams and simply got burnt. It didn't seem to bother him. Thick skinned. I watched as his skin turned furiously red and peeled off, revealing an even tan underneath. For myself I was doomed to swimming in T-shirts and hovering in the shade, endlessly applying sun cream. I plastered the boys with every skin product that came to hand and miraculously they developed smooth toasty suntans. But they didn't have my pale skin in the first place. And in the end even I got a decent tan. As you noticed, of course.

But anyway, the point is, the Pirate seemed to morph into something far less innocuous than a little old tubby-tot as that first week went on. The liver spots joined up as he tanned, the fat solidified and although no, he didn't miraculously grow a thick head of black hair, he did somehow gain in stature and I don't know . . . he just seemed less old and past it and more virile and er, well, up for it.

The truth is, of course, that with our arrival his habits changed. He spent more time outside, did more exercise, ate better meals and, although he seemed to be swigging Pernod down like water, according to

Marie-Rose he had drastically cut back on his drinking. So of course he began to look better. He would probably tell you that I started to look better too. He always said I looked ill when I arrived: thin, pale and harassed.

On his own turf he didn't bother with proper clothes. He wore black swimming shorts all the time, flinging a white linen shirt over them if he felt the need to dress up. He didn't look dirty any more because we swam all the time and, in the water at least, he was a nice little mover. In fact I think he must be genetically at least 50% shark. He swam like one anyway, and being in the water made his eyes gleam like one.

What can I say? It's boring, swimming and sleeping all day. Restaurants get boring too, especially when you go to the same two all the time, and we had to go to the same two all the time because all the others were closed out of season. Apart from them, there was a smattering of bars, a handful of shacks selling dusty watermelons and the small complex of low whitewashed concrete buildings which, apart from Marie-Rose's bar, housed a few little offices, a tourist centre, a yachting shop and the Pirate's office. This was one room which opened off a small courtyard to the side of Marie-Rose's bar. Running at right angles to the other buildings, the Pirate's lair had two windows which looked out through strong protective bars across the bay.

The bare walls inside were painted white, there were work surfaces and bar stools all along the window side of the room and a large heavy dark wooden desk near the door with an ancient teak swivel chair. Opposite the door was another smaller door, guarded by a heavy barred gate, opening onto a short path made of thick paving slabs set into the hard earth which led to a lavatory. Outside, but private nevertheless, protected by high walls.

Inside there was a computer, a fax machine, a photocopier, a series of telephones and tele-printers, a radio, even an old telex machine, and under the work surfaces were a set of heavy grey filing cabinets. A row of dark wooden cupboards had been built into the back wall and opposite the windows was a grey metal cupboard containing office supplies. The whole place was stacked with papers, and the lino floor was cluttered with cardboard boxes. He ran various businesses from that office: day cruises on the catamarans, yacht charters and some sort of T-shirt empire. You know all those tacky T-shirts you get in the Caribbean proclaiming 'No problem!' and 'Sex, sun, sand and

WEED — Enjoy!' — most of them are imported by the Pirate, and the ones that aren't have paid his taxes on their journeys.

And he flirted. I mean, you know . . . for God's sake! I'm not going to tell you all the gruesome details. Look, the boys were in paradise and that was the biggest relief of my life.

The thing is, Philippa, as a mother I was pretty crap, I admit it. I was totally unprepared, I had no experience of kids and asking Harriet wouldn't have done me any good. She and Daniel take my half-siblings on tour with a Russian nanny, for Christ's sake. A male one. (She's a percussionist, did I tell you that?)

As for Muma, well . . . she wasn't a musician but she toted me everywhere with Daniel, and although she wasn't creative, she wasn't practical either. I mean, to her mothering meant insisting, however crummy the hotel or the restaurant, that I should be supplied with live yoghurt. She thought it prevented infections, bless her. She made me eat barrels of the bloody stuff. So what do you expect?

I can speak loads of languages badly, I can manage train stations, artistic temperament and rehearsal rooms, but I can't cook to save my life, I'm hopeless at making forts out of washing up bottles, I can't change a plug let alone a nappy, and I hate football.

The only maternal instinct I had was worry, and I'd done so much of it that I'd turned myself into a nervous wreck, endlessly wanting the boys to stay inside with Maman. I could see what I was doing, but I didn't know how to stop. It was the only way I had of loving them. But after the first two days, the Pirate was having none of it.

'You good mother, but you worry too fuckin much,' he announced. 'You makem frightened. Leave em alone. Doe-skids is fine! Give em some freedom!'

I knew he was right. The boys had long outgrown my Beatrix Potter smother-love. They desperately needed to strike out on their own, have adventures, hang out with other boys, stand on their own two feet. Well, four feet. If you see what I mean . . . Anyway, the Pirate broke the nursery door down and they escaped into boy paradise.

They went fishing, swimming and sailing with Bettina's boys. They had unlimited ice cream, they messed about on the beach, they went for rides on an old scooter. I watched them growing in confidence and self-assurance daily, and had to admit that they didn't need me clucking at their heels. So after the first day or so, I let Bettina take

53

charge of them. Which left me with nothing to do. Except hang out with the Pirate.

And he looked after me. He took me places, bought me little gifts — beaded bracelets, a pair of jewelled flip flops, a gold heart on a chain . . . he smiled at my jokes, met my eye when I was amused, he understood exactly what I meant, noticed when I was tired, and let me sleep for hours without ever once bitching that I'd slept too long. He thought of little things like wanting a glass of water first thing in the morning, like not sitting with the sun in my eyes, like protecting my dry white skin.

He rubbed sun cream in slowly and gently. He handed me in and out of boats, looked me in the eye over every drink, he flattered, cajoled and complimented me at every turn, he showed me little things like turtle tracks and how to tie knots, demonstrating them round my arm.

'I like to tie you up and keep you here,' he said, tightening a reef knot round my wrist, and I laughed, pleased to be the object of so much attention. 'I wanna look after you. Make you happy,' he said, gazing into my eyes soulfully. Not original perhaps, but 100% effective.

In spite of myself, my heart hammered. But I'd heard it before from the boys' father, and look where that got me. Look where it got Nickie and Fiona. An endlessly unfolding drama of infidelity, pregnancy, passion, childbirth and poverty. We'd none of us had ever had any truck with furniture polish, Bizzy Lizzies and returning library books on time — we'd always been far too busy struggling to make meals out of half a tin of black olives and two mouldy onions . . .

Believing sweet nothings had simply got us into what Daniel called The B&P Club. B for barefoot. P for pregnant. (That was one of his jokes, cracked in a phone call from Sydney where he was supervising the digital re-mastering and re-release of his 1963 mega-hit 'Sax on the Sofa'. Apparently it had become a cult smash Down Under.)

Ten years down the road, I was determined not to fall into the same trap. So when my pulse raced because the Pirate smiled tenderly into my eyes, I reminded myself firmly that he just wanted to get me into bed. He just wants to get your knickers off, I warned myself.

It didn't take long. His experience was so much more than mine, in spite of my sophisticated globe-trotting upbringing, that it was inevitable I suppose. And to be honest I'd probably have fallen into his bed a lot sooner if he'd wanted me to. But he took his time, savouring my seduction in the same way that he savoured any of his take-over bids.

No, I didn't fancy him. No, he wasn't attractive. But he wasn't a rapist if that's what you're thinking. Just an expert seducer. An expert on women's bodies. He must have shagged everything under the sun to get the experience he's got. I've never been to bed with anything like it. There's no point in resisting. If you say 'don't touch me' he shrugs.

'I only putta crema. You burnin otherwise. Why so tense? Relax. I don-trape you.'

It was true, he was only rubbing my back. So I let him rub my shoulders, let him brush my hair, caress my cheek, and fell into a sort of blissful coma, like a cat. 'Hey, wass this? Tay-kit-off, I massage you . . . '

I let him take my top off. I didn't want him, I didn't fancy him, I told myself. But I wanted the sensation of hands on my back. So I let him take my top off. And he kept his hands on my back. No wandering. I was lulled, if you like.

Oh all right, since you ask. It was like shagging a bulldozer. No, I don't suppose you've ever . . . no. Well, imagine being in bed with a steam roller then. Massive, slow-moving and totally inevitable. And covered with liver spots. Yes, I went to bed with him.

What else can I say? I mean yes, he was short, fat and greying. Yes, his skin was red, peeling, coated in salt crystals and his hair was the texture of wire wool. Yes. All that. But he was also the most sensuous man I'd ever met.

Sitting on the deck, he was massaging my shoulders one night, when slowly and softly he bent his head and kissed my neck. His lips lingered there, and I could feel his breath on my skin. His hands tightened on mine and pins and needles ran down my spine. I couldn't move, I could hardly breathe for God's sake. I couldn't run away or push him off. I couldn't even speak, the whole thing was so erotic. The best I could do was just sit there attempting to pretend that nothing was happening.

Then his hands started wandering. (Such self-control, not to have done it before.) They wandered all over; he hauled me into his arms; kissed me dark and strong on the mouth. He dragged me to my feet and spell-bound I let him lead me down the stairway and kiss me again, holding my body hard against his own. Then he pulled me into his pit with the salty sheets, the oily bits of engine and the pornographic videos.

He didn't say he loved me or anything. He didn't promise me the moon or the stars. He just seduced me plain and simple, and I liked him the better for it. I'd never have believed him if he'd started on the old lurve-stuff, but I believed in random male lust. I could even admit to a bit of random female lust. So I let it all happen in the most passive way. Except one thing. When I felt sleep slipping into the soft, twisted sheets alongside us, seducing me with gentle caresses, I left him. I didn't want the boys asking awkward questions.

And that was it, really. I suppose I could have turned back, even then. But I didn't. I'd been too long on my own, spent too many nights curled up alone. So I closed my eyes. The days slid by: he claimed to have changed the dates of our tickets, and we went on with the pretence that him paying for everything was just a loan and that I would change my money in one go and pay him back just before I left. Two weeks turned into a month and I sent Nickie a postcard saying not to worry, that I was in heaven or something very close to it, that I'd be back soon and bring her some shells.

The Pirate was triumphant, taking me around everywhere, introducing me to everyone, always with his hands on my waist or my shoulder, or gripping my thigh or my upper arm with his podgy fists.

'Jealous? You fucking should be!' he would declare to other men. 'Have a drink!'

I laughed. I felt great. I looked great. My poor red skin was evenly tanned, my hair was streaked golden from the sun, my eyes were beginning to sparkle again. The tiredness was easing, and my sense of humour was returning. Looking in the mirror I told myself that it was amazing what a good bulldozering could do for a girl, and I could just imagine Fiona rolling her eyes: 'Told you so!'

The thought of Fiona made me laugh. She is so crazy, she even makes me look conventional. You know at one time she had this poetic tumble-down mazet, miles off the road, surrounded by acres of useless, overgrown land. The place was a mess, of course, undecorated, full of cardboard boxes and dirty clothes, but full of potential and possibilities. Fiona was living off the land. This meant scrubbing about with a camping gaz cooker and brackish water from her well until she got pissed off, when she would hitch a lift into town and raid her well-stocked bank account for enough cash to buy take-away pizza and beer for all the layabouts in the local bar.

Then the whole house burned down. I forget the details of it now, but I'm sure there was a party involved and rumour has it that the fire was started by a stray cigarette paper. Or was it a runaway candle? Anyway, the point is, the whole slummy edifice was razed to the ground. Fiona slept through the first stages of the fire, was dragged out into the fields by some alert hippies, went back for the goat, and then spent the night watching her house crackle and spit as the fire engines zigzagged to and fro some kilometres away, looking for the source of the flames that lit up the inky-black French night.

There were a few benefit concerts — world music and spliffs and even a house party run along the lines of a rent party, but the house wasn't insured and her parents must have buried their feet ten metres deep because the bank account dried up and her son disappeared to Scotland to stay with his grandparents for most of the year. Nickie says that they offered to rebuild the house, but only if she grew the green streaks out of her hair and got rid of the goat. Who knows the truth of it? Fiona didn't say much. She was deep into a local farmer at the time (well, vice versa actually) and she just shrugged. The caravan was a pay off when the farmer's wife threatened to castrate him with a ham knife.

I told you Fiona was mad, didn't I? But now I had embarked on an equally crazy adventure and I kept trying to remember delicious little details to tell her and Nickie when I got back to France. I knew I'd be going home with an endless stock of Pirate stories. Enough of them to last until the spring. We'd be laughing all winter.

In the afternoons the boys used to go fishing, and the Pirate used to retreat to his pit for a siesta. He had rigged a fan up over the bed and it was cooler there. At first I used to swelter on the deck, writing postcards and gazing at faded tourist information brochures, but once I'd given in on the bulldozing front, the Pirate was insatiable.

He didn't sleep in the afternoons any more and the brochures had long since blown overboard. He even made the pliroma change the sheets. I found it too hot, even with the fan. I couldn't move in the heat of the day. Couldn't even bear to be touched.

'Wha-dyou-mean, too hot? You know you fuckin-won-to!' he'd exclaim. He made me laugh. He used to look so totally flabbergasted at the idea that anyone might not fancy a seeing to, that I used to shrug and say, 'All right then, just so long as I don't have to move and you don't lie on me.'

That always infuriated him. 'I not gonna fuckin lie on you. I gonna take you to fuckin paradise!'

You see what I mean? The guy was a bulldozer. He was so determined to make the earth move, he'd have used explosives if he

61

had to. And then one afternoon, I was sprawling on his bed passively absorbing his sexual passion, when he seized my wrists and hauled me towards his chest.

'You stay here with me. I marry you tomorrow and you stay here with me, work in office. I pay you. How many dollars you want? I pay you two thousand a month. American dollar not Caribbean fuckers.'

I blinked in the gloom. The portholes were shaded with antique curtains and the place stunk, if I'm honest. Stunk of stale sweat, semen and diesel. The clean sheets were already greasy, the varnished woodwork sticky with salt. I gazed around me.

'You do what you like. You don-work, I still pay you. What you like. I don-cair. I marry you tomorrow.'

'But the twins . . . '

'No problem. You teach them here, you send them to school. I lie-skids. Boys is welcome here. They lie-kit here. Is paradise here for skids.'

His body hadn't stopped its earth-moving gyrations the whole time he was talking. He was bulldozing me into marrying him. If I hadn't agreed he'd have probably ploughed me to death right there and then.

'But . . . but it's mad!' I gasped.

'Yes!' he whispered, thrusting steadily.

'But I hardly know you.'

'Biblically you know me. Yes! Yes!' he said hoarsely, but without missing a beat.

I was trying to say no, but heard myself gasping, 'But! Arrrg! Ah! Ooof!'

'Yes! You lie-kit here. I treat you good, I fuck you good. Don' you feel it? You're mine.' As the hillside teetered on the brink of an avalanche, he slowed down.

'Say yes!' he ordered.

'I . . . er . . . arggh! Oooh! I can't . . . er, ha! Er . . . think about it . . . aegh! now, ah ah ha woof! Yes!' I cried, and he resumed his expert earth workings. I moaned and thrashed about in delirious pleasure, and he held me to my word.

As soon as his excavations were over he swept me off to the beach, gathered up the boys, told them he was going to marry me, and took us all over to another island for a big celebration meal. Dazed and hardly realising what we were doing, I smiled, ate and drank and admired the boys as they turned cartwheels on the manicured lawns. They were thrilled, that much was certain. They were totally over the moon that I'd finally found a husband, and the Pirate was hardly less jubilant.

'Yes, I gonna be your stepfather,' he told them, gesturing expansively. 'So if I say you gotta eat ice-cream, you gotta eat ice-cream! Here, have more chips!'

Oh Philippa! I know what you're going to say. How insane, how crazy, why did you do it? Shrug. What can I tell you? I was swept off my feet. I mean, I didn't even begin to work out what it would mean in practical terms. I just didn't want the dream to stop.

Also, looking back, I just don't think I could face another winter struggling to chop firewood and put food on the table. I didn't consciously think about that at the time though. I just thought how much it would make Nickie and Fiona laugh.

I knew they would be scuttled — utterly astounded. I mean, out of the three of us in France, I always thought Fiona would be the one to get married. Mainly because Nickie already had a worn-out husband in her closet. Also because Fiona was so scathing about marriage. And because as I said, I never expected to get married. It just didn't seem like something that would ever come my way.

I remember discussing it with Nickie one time. We were sitting on her terrace watching the three boys (my two weedy worms and her enormous loudspeaker) fighting in a leaky paddling pool when she suddenly slammed her tea down and said, 'Right. That's it. I don't care. What's the point? Just tell me that?

What's the point in hanging out for true love?'

'We are . . . ?'

But she had been, apparently. Having married a brainless sexmaniac straight out of art school, she'd decided that next time only true friendship would do. Soulmates, all that stuff. So she ran off with her best male mate and ended up with two kids, enough debt to sink the Titanic and naff all else — and since then had been hanging out for true love. Whatever that was.

'Well, bugger it. I'll marry the first nice chap I meet and sod true love. It'll make my parents very happy anyway,' she declared.

'Huh?'

'They've been itching to get their hands on my husband, but I just didn't want to admit that they were right and I was wrong. Well, I'll do it. They can gloat and fuss and enjoy themselves as much as they like, and then Daddy can get me a divorce.'

'Will he do that?'

'Oh yes. One of his biggest pals is a divorce lawyer, I'm sure they'll get him.'

'Like, er alimony? Like er . . . huge piles of cash?' My eyes lit up. In my imagination I could already picture Nickie eating meat, and having salad with no brown bits in it, and wine out of a bottle instead of that terrible petrol pump stuff in a plastic can. In my imagination she also had a huge fire crackling in the fireplace, built with bought pre-chopped wood, and a fridge full of supermarket puddings for the kids.

'No, no cash,' she said. 'Just a divorce. That's all I want.'

'What for?'

'So I can marry someone else.'

'Ah!' I grinned. 'I see! Come on, who is he?'

'The bloke in the tourist office. You must have seen him. Brown eyes and a mole. I'm sure I could seduce him,' said Nickie, fluffing her hair up. 'I mean, just think of it. He's young, he's cute, he's obviously 100% nice and best of all, he's a fonctionnaire — he's got a job for life!'

So she launched an all-out campaign against the tourist officer and meanwhile, the three of us went on struggling and giggling and laughing and wondering where it would all end. Fiona got a teaching job for a while, and I worked on the black as a cleaning lady and then that winter it snowed, and the road fell off the side of the mountain and suddenly we were totally cut off from the world. You could only get out of the village in a four wheel drive, and because of the strikes, power supply was sporadic and in any case the snow was piled up everywhere and whenever you shifted it, more of it arrived in the night. If it hadn't been for a charity organisation which came round doling out essential supplies, I suppose we'd have all just turned into little frozen corpses waiting to be discovered when the thaw came, huddled round the last packet of cigarettes, our skinny frozen fingers clutching empty glasses of wine.

As it was, Nickie, Max-the-dog and her kids moved into my house so we could pool firewood. We hadn't the faintest idea what Fiona was doing because the phone lines were down and the track up to her caravan was impossible, impassable and altogether out of the question.

(In the end of course, we heard from someone who had been up there that she was fine. Some Guy or other was up there with her and they were having the time of their lives. Hadn't been out of bed for nearly two weeks and still hadn't had more than ten minutes sleep at a time.)

Anyway, that winter went on a long time and we sat and endured it, and wondered how long we could go on before one of us went loopy-loo or developed cancer of the hair or some poxy thing. And we talked it all ways round and watched Max dreaming and twitching on the sofa as we huddled round the fire late at night while the kids were piled into our beds so at least they were warm and could sleep.

But the whispers didn't get us any further than string in the chin and stifled giggles and helpless sobs of laughter. And then eventually we'd fall asleep where we sat and wake up stiff and freezing because the fire had burned out and someone would have to brave the Arctic wind for more firewood and then all the kids would wake up and then we'd find that there wasn't any Nurofen left and that breakfast would have to be yesterday's bread dipped in chocolate milk er-gain and we would take turns to sleep in the big bed upstairs while the other one took the sprats outside for snowballs and finally it would be night again and the kids would have finally packed in their endless whining and giggling and we could start our own whining and giggling again.

So at the end of that winter, it was decided (as long as her parents could locate and divorce her husband, which seemed pretty likely to me) that Nickie was going to get married. Sadly not to either me or Fiona as none of us could quite get to grips with the lesbian sex thing, but she was going to find a husband . . . and Fiona . . . well, Fiona rubbished all this stuff. Men, she said were just extra children. She had no intention of getting married. She had her house, she had her goat, she had her son, her garden and her hippies, so what else could anyone want? Fiona would never have married the Pirate. Apart from anything else, he'd never have agreed to the goat.

But I married him. Even though I hadn't planned on it. I went full-steam straight-ahead into it. I married the Pirate. Of course I was more in love with him than I wanted to admit and, of course, he didn't leave me any time for second thoughts.

We got married just a few days after he asked me. He must have started putting the paperwork together months before because the papers stated that I'd been living there for six months and that the marriage had been announced three weeks earlier. I don't know how he did it. Don't ask me. I hauled in a few favours, paid off a few grudges, doled out huge quantities of backsheesh, who knows?

Strictly speaking we were married in France — in a registry office on one of the French Caribbean islands. We flew there on a regular scheduled flight and we wore clothes. Yes, the Pirate bought me a dress, a cream and pink halter-necked thing, and he made Bettina iron it. The boys wore new T-shirts and he produced a new pair of shorts and some clean espadrilles for himself.

Oh yes, it was legal all right. Tommy and Bettina came with us, and ran round carrying luggage and shouting for taxis to the registry office, where we held our hands up and listened to the list of French marriage legislation that the official read out to us, and agreed to everything, and signed the register and shook hands with everyone in sight.

It didn't take long, about half an hour, and then we took another taxi to a swanky air conditioned bar where the Pirate ordered champagne for everyone and we ate a vast lunch consisting of everything on the menu.

'I celebrating! Bring everything, everything you got! That-swot-we-wan-skids, innit?'

And then he insisted on taking us all to a vast air-conditioned shopping mall where he showered presents on the skids; telescopes and fishing rods and footballs, clothes and cds and dvds. Poor old Tommy and Bettina had to carry everything, and then he decided to buy them presents too and dived into a jeweller's shop for a pair of waterproof watches before dragging me into all the dress shops and pulling out all the most revolting things . . . I mean there's no way I can wear yellow or red or mauve, not with my pale custard colouring.

Anyway, he finally agreed about the colours

and we settled for a collection of printed cotton sundresses in white, blue and green with sandals to match. Then I'd had enough and wouldn't let him buy any more. So we all squashed into another taxi and went for afternoon tea. Yes, of course you can have afternoon tea in the Caribbean. All the posh hotels serve it. If you shout as loud as the Pirate does they do anyway.

The boys spent the evening at the cinema with Tommy and Bettina, watching a murderous detective film. We spent it in a vulgar wedding cake of a hotel watching a dreadful floorshow and drinking yet more champagne. I was in fits of laughter. Marrying the Pirate was the maddest thing I'd ever done in my life and I was revelling in it.

I remember thinking it was a shame he hadn't produced a white Elvis outfit for the wedding, and snorting with so much amusement that champagne went up the back of my nose. We were both drunk on insanity. The Pirate was absolutely wallowing in the craziness of it, and couldn't stop laughing. I even remember that his bulldozing activities were interspersed with fits of the giggles that night.

The next morning we all flew back to our island (on yet another regular flight — wonders will never cease) and the Pirate threw a party.

When we arrived back in the complex, two of the Pirate's catamarans had been lashed together and anchored to the jetty right by the office and Marie-Rose's bar. Music was blaring and the place was awash with food and alcohol. There was a poisonous rum punch, wine, spirits, orange juice, Coke . . . everything you could think of, and on the other tables, boiled eggs, hams, cream cakes, miraculously fresh bread, salads with feta cheese, tomatoes, cucumbers and rice, fish, aubergines, tinned red peppers, raw onions and more boiled eggs. The Pirate was potty for boiled eggs. Horrible things.

And he'd invited everyone. The catamarans were surrounded with little boats in all directions. People had come from our island, but also from all the surrounding ones. It clearly hadn't all been organised the day before. Not that I noticed, or would have cared even if I had noticed. I was enjoying myself hugely. I laughed and shook hands and answered questions and drank more champagne and ate bits of food and threw things overboard and cracked jokes and laughed again.

The Pirate was indulgent, genial and expansive. Dragging me to sit on his lap, he proposed toast after toast, ordered everyone to eat more, dance more, turn the music up, open more wine, have a good time. The moon rose, the stars shone, the music gradually calmed down so that the remaining couples could smooch on the decks of the catamarans, and just as I was falling asleep, the Pirate walked us down the jetty and Tommy drove us back to the boat so that he could collect Bettina, who had been baby-sitting for the boys.

And that, I think, was the only night I ever went straight to bed and straight to sleep with the Pirate. I was dead on my feet. Completely wiped out. I just curled up in his arms and the last thing I remember is smiling at him sleepily as he stroked the hair off my forehead.

The boys were exhausted too, after all the excitement. I mean, I'm sure you're asking how they reacted to Mummy getting married, and all I can say is they didn't. They have always been totally on the Pirate's side. They simply love him. He is an absolute God as far as they are concerned. He had scooters, boats, money and pliroma; he put the whole lot at their disposal, let them do whatever they wanted and best of all, never said annoying things like 'don't fall in' and 'be careful darling' and 'wait for me!' So they were over the moon.

And by the time they finally started to

wonder exactly what being his stepsons would mean in practical terms, the Pirate had all that organised too. He certainly didn't have any intention of moving to France, and he definitely wasn't letting us back to France without him. So he had decided to send the boys to boarding school in England.

The twins exchanged dubious glances. 'On south coast, by sea,' he continued. 'So you learn sail properly. Also riding. They have horses at the school. And you come back here every holidays.'

My heart sank but their eyes lit up like fireworks as he described it. Sailing, riding, games, larks in the dormies, massive quantities of pocket money, no uniforms, English sausages for breakfast every day . . . what more could two boys want?

It was all settled, although I clung on to them for a few more weeks, my little babies. But the Pirate had already chosen the school and the boys were hauling at their leashes, so there wasn't much I could do. After all, I hadn't totally hated boarding school myself, once I'd pulled myself together and stopped snivelling in corners.

There was another thing too. Having been to school in France, my skids were too far ahead to go to school with the locals, and I was incapable of teaching them myself. Those were the only two other options. I would miss them like crazy, but it was a heaven-sent opportunity for the boys.

And as I say they really wanted to go. They weren't torn sobbing from my bosom or anything like that. No, no, the twins were gagging to play rugby and tennis, they couldn't wait to sleep in a dormitory and have a matron to tease.

It was all extremely civilised. We flew to Heathrow and took a train down to the south coast to see the school that the Pirate had picked out from the Internet. Of course, he must have already enrolled them but we went through the rigmarole just as if there really had been any choice in the matter: the boys loved it, I agreed they should go there, the school offered them places, the Pirate flashed a credit card, and we launched into a week of frantic shopping for school clothes and equipment.

One day when the Pirate had proudly taken his stepsons down to the marina, I rang Nickie from the hotel with my news.

'Sounds like you've finally got the string out of your chin!' she said. 'Fiona's boy is loving his boarding school. Says the food is fantastic.'

'Well, he would say that, wouldn't he? After

a lifetime of eating Fiona's cooking!'

We both cackled with glee. There's nothing more fun than ripping your friends to shreds, and we loved Fiona really.

'So how are you doing?' I asked.

'Oooh well . . . I've got a new man too. Nothing as glamorous as yours, but at least he knows how to mend bicycle tyres.'

'The tourist officer?'

'No. He turned out to be gay.'

'Bad luck. What's this one like?' I asked. 'Do the skids like him?'

'Skids?'

'Oh, sorry.' (Christ, I was even starting to sound like the Pirate now.) 'Kids,' I said firmly. 'Kids. Do they like him?'

'Yep, they're already calling him papa . . . '

'Blimey. Is he living with you, then?'

'Not officially, but he keeps his toothbrush here.'

'Well done! And what does he do?'

'He's a geography teacher, but he wants to be a sailing instructor — you know teaching other people how to teach sailing. That's what he really wants to do. But I don't know if he'll find a job doing that around here.'

'And how about you?'

'Ooh, pretty much the same. The chimney collapsed last week and I've been trying to get someone to fix it before it starts getting cold.

There's a new arrival, living in that white villa near the river. Another Brit. Says her husband is joining her as soon as he's finished his contract. Apparently he works on an oil rig. They're going to open a crafts shop. I think she makes pots.'

'Oh Jesus, a potty potter. How many kids?'

'Three.'

'Poor cow. What's the betting hubby never quite manages to move to France?'

'Now, now . . . don't be cynical. You're blissfully married, I've got a new man and my divorce is on its way! Things are looking up.'

'And how's Fiona?'

'God help us all, she wants another baby.'

'Rather her than me.'

'Either that or she just fancies her gynie . . . you know that serious-looking one who works at the clinic on Thursdays.'

'Ugh! He's so revolting, how could she?'

'God knows. I don't. I think she's gone native. So she goes to see him practically every month just in case she's pregnant. I think if she saw him in the street she'd have her knicks off and her legs in the air before the poor man even managed to say hello.'

'Shouldn't think he'd say hello unless she did take her knickers off. Probably wouldn't actually recognise her face!'

We cackled with guilty laughter.

'So you think I'm doing the right thing then?' I asked, wiping my eyes. 'Sending the boys to boarding school?'

'For the twins? Who knows? Probably. As long as they're happy, it'll be fine. For you? Ditto. I just wish I could get the string out of my own chin so successfully.'

I grinned. It was true. There wasn't a sign of blue string anywhere and the boys seemed over the moon. I went down to meet them at the Marina and when I saw them I knew that however much I would miss them, I was doing the right thing.

Standing by the edge of the water, their light brown hair ruffled by the breeze, they looked different. They were no longer the skinny little Mummy's boys I'd taken to the Caribbean. They were confident, relaxed, happy and incredibly healthy. They were fit and tanned, with pink cheeks and glowing eyes, and I suddenly realised just how much they'd grown.

They were standing at the edge of the water pelting the Pirate with questions and he was laughing. He ruffled their hair and they caught at his hands excitedly, and they were literally hanging round him asking for more ice cream, when he caught sight of me.

'Hey, Camille!' he called. 'Look at these skids! They crazy about boats, you know that?'

'No, I don't think so,' I said. 'I think they're just crazy!'

The twins laughed and punched my arms and we went off for ice cream, and if anyone had been watching us that day, they'd probably have thought we were lovely. A lovely model family. To be honest, I thought so myself.

An illusion. An illusion which wouldn't last long. A few days later we flew back to the Caribbean leaving the boys to start their lives as termly boarders in a progressive, enlightened and friendly English boarding school.

And I still hadn't noticed that the Pirate had kept my passport. No, I hadn't noticed. I was totally preoccupied with getting the twins settled at school, and in any case, I was still blissing out on being cosseted and spoilt.

And then the Pirate took his gloves off.

3

Soon after we got back from England, there was a monsoon warning. No, we weren't about to be bombed by fashions, we were in for a free soaking. Storms blow up all the time in the summer which is why the main tourist season is in the winter — it's cooler and it doesn't rain. But it often rains in the summer and there are storm warnings all the time. Following them turns into a sort of hobby, like praying for fresh snow in ski resorts. Except you're not praying, you're crossing your fingers. All summer long people ask each other: 'Have you seen Erika on the move?' or, 'Did you see that Suzy veered off?' or, 'Saw Martyn on the telly last night, did you? He was coming on the news.'

But this particular storm warning was more personal than most; it was strong, it was female and it was blowing our way. Hurricane Julia was coming to get us. After a day or so of wondering if she would blow herself out or not, and gibbering about what to do if she really meant business, everyone realised that Julia was not only rolling her sleeves up, but was also heading our way armed with a rolling pin. Little groups gathered round the radio in Marie-Rose's bar to listen to the weather forecasts.

I veered constantly between being blasé and panicking like a turkey the week before Christmas. It seemed incredible that our small corner of the Caribbean could turn into a news item and yet, if Julia pulled out all the stops and put on a real show, I was petrified of being squashed by a flying palm tree.

Most of those who didn't actually live on the island hurriedly left, aiming to outrun the storm or at least get out of her immediate focus. The bay emptied rapidly, all the yachties up-anchoring and flitting away as fast as their little sails would take them until there were only the resident craft queasily riding the heaving sea. The locals pulled their fishing boats out of the water and dragged them up amongst the palm trees, the bar-owners nailed boards over their open windows, and the shack-keepers moved their stock to more secure premises. Julia was looking decidedly pre-menstrual.

By the time she got round to us, the island was almost deserted. The only people left were those who didn't have any choice, or those with something to protect. The tourists had fled, a lot of locals had decided to visit family and friends on other islands, and the rest were sitting tight inside their boarded up houses.

Along with Robert and a handful of other stalwarts, the Pirate was glued to the radio in Marie-Rose's bar when I joined him there after my afternoon swim. I still hadn't managed to get any sense out of him about money, although I had tried. More than once. But I had another go.

'Look, they're my kids, I'll pay for their school.'

'Have a drink!' he said blandly.

'I can rent the house in France,' I told him. 'It's pointless letting it sit there empty.'

'You wanna cocktail?'

'I just need to sort out transferring the money, so I can . . . '

'Peanuts?' he suggested, waving a bowl at me.

'Stop it!' I said. 'I'm serious. I want to get this sorted.'

'Okay, I listening. Go on . . . '

'So, did you mean it about giving me a job?'

The Pirate grinned. 'You can work in office if you wanna, and I'll pay you for it, but I pays for skids. They is my stepsons. I pay for school.'

'Look, I've just told you . . . '

'Okay, I think about it when you got

money,' he shrugged.

'And what about banking? I . . . '

'You don-need bank. I keep money safe. You work, you rent house out and then we see . . . '

'Yes, but . . . '

'You stupid woman!' he flashed. 'You making problems from nothing! I the man, you the wife! I got money, I pay! You relax, be happy, eat something!'

I might not be Jane, but he was determined to be Tarzan. I sighed and rolled my eyes at him. It obviously wasn't the right moment anyway, not with the storm clouds gathering.

'You better stay here,' said the Pirate. 'Don-go boat. Hey you, gimme a drink! What you havin', Camille?'

I ordered a cup of tea and sat at the bar untangling my damp hair with my fingers as the others obsessively flicked from station to station trying to get the latest forecasts. The tension mounted hour by hour as the sky darkened and the air weighed heavy on our shoulders.

Dismissing my fears of horizontal killer vegetation, I swung my legs on a bar stool and made some bad taste jokes. We used to get some fierce electric storms in France, really magnificent fireworky mountain things with deafening cracks of thunder and lightning so bright it was almost blinding. But this promised to be even more spectacular, and I had convinced myself that if we were in serious danger, the emergency services would have evacuated us hours ago. Insanely, I was looking forward to my first tropical storm.

'What do you get if you cross a thunder storm with a tea bag?' I asked. 'A typhoon in a teacup!'

The Pirate pulled a long face and spat on the ground. 'I take fleet to mangrove swamp,' he announced to the crowd around the radio. Snatching up a bunch of keys on the bar, he bowled over to his office door, kicked it shut and slammed the padlock into place. 'Tommy!' he yelled. 'Get everyone! I want all pliroma here, now!'

Shoving two stumpy fingers in his mouth he let out a piercing whistle and waved at a group of small boys on the beach. They came running and he sent them off with messages in all directions. 'Get pliroma pronto! Now! Capishe? Vite! Hurry the fuck up!' He bawled and slammed, and young men started arriving and buzzing around him. 'Get ready. You gonna do some real work!' he ordered. 'Lazy fuckers! Fill the gas on the Venus! You lot, get out to the catamarans!' Seeing him in action was like watching a volcano erupt. Very impressive. I shifted over to one of the tables for a better view.

He was obviously not that unhealthy or his heart would have exploded with all the shouting and yelling he was doing. In fact, watching him rolling about hurling directions at Tommy and grabbing others by their arms, I realised he must be quite fit. Grinning to myself I started to wonder just what he would be like if he ever decided to set sail in the Sun. A Catherine wheel, probably. He was stumping down towards the jetty, his pliroma tumbling around him like eager puppies, when he suddenly swooped down on me.

'And you! You shut up!' he yelled at me, and I hadn't even opened my mouth. 'You stay here. Stay!'

He hurtled back into the restaurant; more orders were hurled at the staff, money changed hands, keys were rattled and then they were all gone, crashing over the navy blue sea under a threatening, darkened sky. I sat there absolutely motionless, stunned. How dare the bastard speak to me like that? In front of everyone too. I hadn't done anything. The poxy storm wasn't my fault. In fact, for two pins, if I could have thought of somewhere to go, I'd have gone — right there and then — just to teach him a lesson. I mean, I was so furious, I'd even have gone to

Croydon. I'd have given anything for a black cab.

'Taxi! Take me to Timbuktu,' I muttered to myself. 'You bastard!'

Marie-Rose came over to my table with a salt-stained copy of French Vogue, sat down and lit a cigarette. She smoked casually for a bit and then she gave me a little smile.

'He doesn't mean it,' she said. She spoke in French and it was a relief to talk to someone who actually could speak the language properly. I was sick of endlessly trying to chat to people who were only just coping in pigeon English.

'It's not serious,' she added. 'Une bettise, c'est tout.'

I shrugged because I couldn't think what to say and at least shrugging gives you the chance to pout, which always looks stylish. Even if you are spitting fit to kill. I mean, was she trying to be on my side, or was she trying to do the Pirate a favour? Or was she just making it clear that she knew him better than I did? I hadn't a clue whether I was supposed to be jealous of her, suspicious, amused, or what? Was she trying to pal up? What a nightmare.

'Oh God,' I sighed under my breath, 'Ta-xi!'

Marie-Rose clicked her fingers at the

waiter. 'Have a drink. What would you like? Why don't you try a little brandy? Calm you down.'

There wasn't a taxi. There wasn't even so much as a child's scooter. There was nothing I could do but follow orders and wait, so what was the point of sniping at Marie-Rose?

'Thanks, that would be great,' I said.

Much as I'd have liked to teach him a lesson — steal a boat and shove off somewhere, or race after him, drag him out of his disgusting speedboat and make him walk the plank, or force him to parade through the office complex in nothing but heels and a Wonderbra — there wasn't a single thing I could do. I was wearing a bikini, flip flops and a T-shirt, and my bag contained a towel, a pair of dusty sunglasses, half a tube of sun cream and a squashed pack of Marlboros. No cash, no cards, no mobile phone, no address book, no keys, nothing. All that was in my cabin on board the Sun.

Not only that, but apart from Marie-Rose's, all the businesses on the island were closed, all the windows and doors were barricaded up, and what do you mean, public transport? I do hope you're not still thinking there was a handy metro station just the other

side of the shark enclosure. So I lit a cigarette, and flipped through last December's
Vogue as if I was seriously contemplating
spending £3000 on a chinchilla muff with
diamond trim.

The drinks arrived, and Marie-Rose tilted
her brandy at me. 'Santé?'

'A la tienne.' We clinked glasses and drank
together and surprisingly enough the brandy
did calm me down. Not enough to get me
seriously interested in Vogue's ideas for
winterwear, but sufficiently so that I felt less
like a camel. I smiled again, properly.
'Thanks, Marie-Rose. Yes, I'm okay. What's
he doing with the boats?'

'Protecting them from the storm. They're
taking them round to the other side of the
island to the mangrove swamps. They'll take
the boats right up into the trees and sink
them into the mud. That way they'll be
sheltered from the worst of the storm. In the
swamps they can't capsize or break loose and
get blown out to sea, and if a tree falls on
them the damage will be less than if he loses a
boat completely. He won't sink them much,
just enough to protect them from the wind.
This bay here won't be safe if the storm
continues its course.'

'Can't he just bring them in and anchor
them closer to the shore?'

'No, it's not deep enough and anyway the closer the boats are to each other the more they will bang into each other and be damaged. They are better anchored out there in the bay . . . but if this forecast is correct, then even the bay won't be safe, it's not a natural harbour or anything. The waves will sweep in right across it.'

I looked out at the ketch that had become my home, nosing uneasily into the wind, her backside shifting direction like the tail of a dog on the scent of a good dustbin. 'Is he going to move the Sun too, then?'

'Oh yes. He did last time. That's why he's taken all his pliroma with him. He'll move everything I expect.'

I didn't say anything. I just looked at my hands and noticed with vague surprise that my fingers were still twitching with anger. I took a deep breath and drank some more brandy.

Marie-Rose looked at my hands and shook her head. She blew smoke into the sky and then after a moment, she said, 'Don't take any notice of him. He shouts a lot. It doesn't mean anything.'

I looked at her and wondered just how come she knew the Pirate so well. She'd probably had an affair with him, I thought, in spite of being at least ten years older than me.

Not that she was revolting or anything. She wasn't, actually. She was pretty; dark eyes, wavy chestnut hair down to her shoulders and a neat figure — a bit flat chested, but loads of style, and she was nice, too. Lots of charm. Smiley eyes.

I bet he's shagged everything within a radius of about 500 kilometres, I thought. That's probably why he started looking for Internet women. Ran out of them in the Caribbean. The thought of him getting Marie-Rose into bed cheered me up immensely. The vision of Miss Paris-Model getting a bull-dozering in the grease-pit was so unlikely and yet, knowing him, so totally plausible.

The sky was darkening rapidly and the wind was picking up. I smiled, thinking how the boys would have enjoyed themselves. They would have been tremendously excited at the prospect of a tropical hurricane. Personally I just wanted to get home, have a shower and get back to normal life. Home. Not some bloody varnished floating wooden tub, but my own solid stone house nestled in the mountains. It was a shock to realise that I'd already been away for over two months, and I suddenly realised I was homesick.

True, my house in France was even more basic than most of the houses on the island, true it leaked like a sieve, true it rained far more in the Languedoc than anyone ever admits. I'd never stopped fighting the elements in France. If it wasn't the rain or the cold, it was the heat and the mosquitoes. If we weren't hungry we were thirsty, and if the kids weren't being kept awake by the heat in the summer, they were complaining of the bitter winter cold.

But it had been mine. It had been my struggle and my adventure, and at least I hadn't been in it alone. I'd had Nickie and Fiona to laugh with, and because we laughed at everything, even the worst days turned out all right because they just became food for more laughter. Perhaps that's why I was mad enough to miss a derelict house, an achingly empty bank account, a fridge that only worked intermittently and a lifestyle which meant that most of the time it didn't matter whether or not the fridge was working because there was nothing to put in it anyway.

I wondered what the others were doing. Wondered how Nickie was making out with her geography teacher, wondered if Fiona's goat was still sleeping in the caravan, wondered what was happening about Nickie's divorce. I really ought to get in touch, I told myself. Find out how they are. I decided to ring Nickie the minute the storm was over. I was also reluctantly aware that I owed Harriet and Daniel at least a postcard.

I ordered another drink and watched as a phalanx of little boats surrounded the Sun and the pliroma scrambled aboard. Sometime later the Venus arrived and within minutes the Sun, with the Pirate at the helm, slid serenely out of the bay, the speedboats bobbing along behind her and dozens of little figures standing on the decks. It was strange to see the gap where she was usually anchored. As if you came home tomorrow, Philippa, and found that your des-res had disappeared leaving a bare stretch of smooth green grass where it had been sitting only that morning.

It got dark. The storm came closer and I stayed ashore, sitting in the complex with everyone else, drinking and listening to the radio. The low concrete buildings were solidly-built with their backs hunched to the prevailing winds, designed to withstand storms. Large drops of rain began to splash down on the concrete slabs which served as furniture on the terrace, and within minutes the complex was awash. Soaked to our skins, we hastily gathered up our drinks and scuttled into the covered bar area to ride out the storm indoors.

Out of the lashing rain, we shook ourselves like dogs and found new places to sit. It was strange being inside a building with the doors and windows shut. Normally, even quite posh places on the island have open windows so as to catch whatever breeze is blowing, but wooden boards had been nailed up across the side windows of the bar to protect against the wind leaving only the recessed seaward windows open, and even they had been covered with thick perspex sheets.

Having always sat on the terrace, I'd never really noticed the interior of Marie-Rose's bar before. The walls were painted white and hung with little pictures of France. There was a faded Eiffel Tower, a herd of mad Alpine cows, a field of Provençale lavender and a view of the Promenade des Anglais.

The bottles behind the bar were decorated with seafaring junk and bits of fish — a shark's tooth, the tip of a whaling spear, several aggressive fish skulls and a selection of grisly hooks and floats. On top of all that, someone, presumably Marie-Rose, had added a graphic depiction of a bleeding heart surrounded by a writhing mass of faded plastic flowers and fairy lights.

The atmosphere was almost tranquil as we watched the rain lash sideways across the bay. The wind had whipped the sea into a frenzy and lightning flashed across the whole scene like a disco strobe. The bar relied on its own generator for electricity so the power stayed on, but climatic interference made the weather reports incomprehensible. Still, the radio continued crackling and buzzing behind the bar. Just in case reception improved.

But we didn't need weather bulletins. We could see perfectly well what the weather was doing. It was going bananas out there. Bananas, coconuts, pineapples and mangoes, too. The sea spray was blowing right up to the office, the palm trees were sweeping the sand with their leaves, waves were crashing down on the jetty, rain was washing over the terrace outside and in spite of the lights from the bar we couldn't see more than a few yards of the beach. The noise was colossal, not just howling wind and banging thunder, but the crashes of things outside breaking.

Inside the bar, the old hands feigned nonchalance. Obviously it wasn't cool to be running to the door every two minutes wringing your hands and moaning, 'Oh my poor boat!' So they sat at the barstools with their backs to the windows and indulged in whisky and wishful thinking. They swapped stories of monsoons they'd known, women won and lost, fortunes made and wasted, dogs kicked, enemies vanquished, cards played, cunning moves, come-backs, come-off-its, come-ons . . . all the usual old male bullshit.

'You know, she was sitting there with her tits out, just begging for it, and I told her, I said I'm world class with a scrambled egg, I am. I mean, you know, she already knew I was the fastest racing driver this side of Silverstone and I think the reason she wanted to fuck me in the first place was because of me being a boxing champion, but she hadn't reckoned on my having trained with the world's top chefs in Paris as well. So I slapped the curry powder into the eggs and whipped them up. Very important to whip them thoroughly you know . . . tha's the secret. Whip your eggs. So then I added the cream and just a small handful of raisins before throwing the whole lot into smoking hot butter. I mean, there she was just gazing at me with sex-crazed eyes as I showed her how eggs should be cooked and I'm standing there scrambling eggs, stark bollock naked with an erection the size of the Titanic and tha's wha did it, you see. She couldn't eat the curried eggs, she just kept grinning at me and her mouth was dribbling so in the end, I just gave her what she was begging for . . . but then she was surprised again cos she hadn't reckoned on me keeping it up for six hours straight. Wey hey . . . come on Marie-Rose, over here! Fill em up, wha's yours?'

I abandoned *Vogue* and played with a bowl of sugar lumps. I was bored. I'd sat through hundreds of storms in France but there it had been completely different — a panicky struggle to bail out the attic before the whole house was flooded. Here, the roof was completely watertight and there was nothing to do but wait. I told a few parrot jokes as a mild revenge on the Pirate, but even got bored with that. Frankly, I'd sooner have been out battling the elements with the pliroma than staying home in the dry waiting for the results of the battle on the front line to be broadcast on the radio.

In the end I knelt up and gazed out of the window leaning my head on my hand and finally the wind eased off leaving just the rain sloshing down in silence. Even the wishful thinkers piped down, staring into space and wondering what other exploits they might have enjoyed if they really had been born world-class boxers, racing-drivers and chefs. Marie-Rose produced some cold fish and bread and after that everyone drank and dozed for an hour or so until around midnight the door burst open and a panic-stricken face peered in.

'Robert! Where's Robert? I think me

brother's broken his head!'

Robert was a tall Scot who was married to a Portuguese woman. They'd been living on the island for ten or eleven years in a purple and orange house just around the point. They painted hideous sunsets and sold them to tourists, but apparently before he ran away to sea Robert used to work in a chemist's shop in Glasgow. Or perhaps he actually did train as a pharmacist, I forget the details now, if I ever knew them in the first place. Anyway, he was the nearest thing we had to trained medical aid on the island so he'd become the first port of call for any injury or sickness and always used to wait out bad storms at Marie-Rose's so that people could find him without battling out to the point, which was impossible during a storm because the winds whip along there too fast.

'Aye,' he said, unfolding his limbs. 'I'm here, what is it?'

'It's Teffi. It's my brother. One of the shutters broke lose and me brother went out to tie it down and it slammed on him. I think he's broken his head. I give him a beer and he drank everything but there's blood every-where!'

'Definite case of string in the chin,' I muttered.

Robert pulled a face and picked up his

cigarettes. 'Okay, I'm coming now. I'll send someone down if we need to radio to the clinic,' he said to Marie-Rose. 'Ciao!'

After he'd gone, we all went back to waiting the storm out. Listening to the short-wave radio when it finally burped into life again, we realised we'd been lucky — the centre of the storm had veered away and we'd been spared the worst. But the news was bad: roofs blown off, shipping capsized, power lines down, communications cut, trees all over the place, sea water halfway up what passed for a main street on the island, and a couple of cars blown into the bay. (Although the general consensus about it was that if their idiot owners had moved them inland like everyone told them to, they could have spared everyone the bother of dragging two wrecks out of the water to clear the quayside.)

Robert came back with his shirt covered in blood, and announced that Teffi was suffering from alcohol poisoning more than anything else. But at least the beer had numbed his thick skull enough for Robert to stitch him up without wasting expensive anaesthetic.

Then Tommy stumbled into the bar, soaking wet but still extraordinarily cheerful.

'Tommy! God, you're drenched. What's happening?'

'Boats is fine, Missis! No damage!'

'Hang on, Tommy. Marie-Rose, have you got a towel?'

Tommy wiped his face and shook his head, sending raindrops flying in all directions. He looked like a lawn sprinkler. 'No worries. I gotta go in a minute.'

'Well at least have a drink,' said Marie-Rose.

'Okay, I have a coffee,' he said, and she brought one over for him.

'I gotta message for you, Missis. The Captain says you stay here, he come in the morning. Oh, and he says you gotta eat. You too thin.'

I rolled my eyes at Marie-Rose. 'It's three in the morning and he wants me to eat? He's not just off his trolley, he's a totally trolley-free zone.'

'He just doesn't want you to be hungry,' she said apologetically. 'Do you want something? A sandwich or some fruit?'

'No, I'll be fine,' I said. 'Do you want something, Tommy?'

Busy pouring coffee down his throat, Tommy nodded enthusiastically so Marie-Rose went and got him an enormous doorstep of bread and cheese. Then he hurled himself back out into the rain.

I stuck to the fags and brandy diet. It felt good, and what's the point of spoiling a good thing while it lasts? And anyway everyone knows that phase two of the F&B diet ain't sandwiches and fruit, but C&A: coffee and aspirin.

Naturally the Pirate stayed all night with the fleet. Apart from the Sun and the speedboats, he had taken half a dozen smaller craft that he hired out to tourists and a couple of catamarans which he used for taking tourists out on day-cruises, fishing, swimming and rum-swilling.

The rest of the boats were mainly involved in smuggling scams disguised as a T-shirt business involving regular trips to Venezuela and I suppose they were round at the mangrove swamps too, but I don't really know. I hadn't the faintest clue why he was staying with the boats. I mean, if the storm was going to scuttle them or damage them there wouldn't be much he could do about it, so why stay to watch the carnage?

But of course, he wasn't there to protect his property from the elements. He was there to protect it from the locals. He explained it to me some days later, when the storm was history and we were eating supper by candlelight at the other restaurant. He was stuffing grilled fish down his throat like a boa constrictor, and I was picking through a dodgy paella.

'Look, I keep all fleet in the bay. So all peoples sees everything. An they know I watchin from the office. In swamps, any little fuckhead can climb aboard . . . '

'Would they do that?'

He looked pityingly at me. 'Stupid. They think I got money on board. Cash.'

'And have you?'

'No.'

'Then why do they think you have?'

'Fuck! What do I care? Any fucker messes with me and I'll kill them.'

Drawing his lips back he bared his teeth at me. The top row were all perfectly white and even, the bottom row were irregular, chipped and stained. 'See this?' he demanded. 'See this?'

The top teeth were all false because his own had been knocked out one night by someone who came onto his boat looking for money.

'I heard something . . . maybe in those days I was stupid too, but I take a metal bar and I go out to see what is happening and they jump me. Locals. I don't know how many. Three? Four? Anyway, they knock me down, they sit on me, they push a gun in my mouth. You ever had a gun in your mouth?'

'Er, no . . . that's not something . . . '

'That's where my teeth went. They push

them down my fuckin throat with a gun. Fuckers.'

'So what happened? I mean what did you do?'

'Nothing. I look like an old fuck, so I shake, I shiver, I give them the money and they fuck off.'

'But I thought you didn't have any on the boat.'

'Forgeries. Fakes. The bastards got picked up in Martinique first day they tried to spend it.'

'Forged notes?'

'Fuckers. I know them, I'll get even. Next time I see them again . . . '

'You had forged bank notes on the boat?'

'Yeah, of course I did. Why the fuck not? Do I look stupid? Here, eat fish!'

'What, you mean you had them there especially in case someone tried to rob you?'

'You don-lie-kfish? What-you-wan?'

'Weren't you scared?'

'Wha-tyou mean, scared? You mean, did I wan-ter cry for Momma?'

'Well, didn't you?' I asked, curiously. 'Weren't you scared? Not at all?'

'Course I was,' he said seriously. 'But thas no good, is it?' He waved his fork in my face. 'Fear is la petite morte. Fear is for babies that spend all their lives trying to live safe. You can't live safe in this world. It ain't a safe fucking world.'

'But what if they come back?'

'I shoot the fuckers.'

'You mean, you've got a gun on the boat?'

'Course I have.'

'Good grief! Where?'

He tapped the side of his nose and rolled his eyes.

'Come on, tell me. Where is it?'

'You bloody woman, you know that? Eat prawn and shut up.'

Rigid with fury, I stared at him. I mean, my childhood was awash with temperament but the Pirate wasn't being temperamental. He was habitually foul-mouthed and crude, but this was deliberately insulting. I felt rage boiling up in my stomach and wondered how he'd like a taste of his own medicine.

'Don't tell me to shut up!' I snapped.

'I tell you what I like. Eat!'

'I don't have to stay here and take crap from you!'

'No?'

'No! I'm not some tart you picked up in a Guadeloupe cathouse. I don't need you. I can leave any time I damn well like!'

'How?'

'What do you mean, how?'

'How you gonna leave?'

'I don't know! Plane, boat, roller skates, whatever!'

'An you think I let you leave? You think I simply say okay, you leave, here is your passport, you want I book you ticket?'

I stared at him. He was grinning as he forked grilled fish into his mouth, and little bits of it showered all around him. He looked at me and raised his Pernod in a toast. 'I'm not stupid. You my wife. You think I let go? You think I let you run away? No. You stay here, like it or not!'

He was smiling at me and I hadn't the faintest clue how to react to him. Was he joking? Or was he a nutter? I met his eye and read a challenge in it. More than that, a declaration of war. My pulse began to race. What on earth was I to do? He was a human steam-roller. If I let him he'd flatten me. For life.

Suddenly, out of the blue a loud rebellious voice in my brain said 'Bollocks to it!' and excitement flooded my body. No more crying for Muma, no more worry-scurrying. I would take him on. In fact I was itching to take him on — insanely eager to beat the Pirate at his own game. Whatever game that was. Yeah, bollocks to it. I returned his smile and raised my glass.

'You sushi-mouthed, sponge-brained piece

of pond scum,' I whispered. 'You're going to regret you said that.'

'Dum spiro spero!' he grinned. 'Here, eat bread. You too thin!'

'Dum spiro spero?'

'While I breathe, I hope,' he said, and laughed out loud.

4

The arrogance of the man took my breath away. Did he seriously think he could keep me on the island against my will? What planet was he on? The whole thing was totally insane. I only had to make a phone call, to a consul at the British Embassy for example, and the police would come and get me out — passport or not, marriage or not.

'What are you going to do, then?' I laughed at him. 'Keep me tied up on the boat?'

He wiped his mouth on the back of his hand and carefully brushed all the bits of fish and rice off the table, showering the cats waiting for scraps at our feet. Then he raised his eyebrows at me.

'Not a bad idea. I never fuck a woman tied up,' he said, draining his Pernod. 'I never havta tie em up . . . usually havta lock em out.'

He wasn't backing down, he really meant it. My spine tingled and it took a moment to realise that it was exhilaration. Oh yes, if he wanted a fight, he'd get it. I'd play him at his own game and I'd damn well win. Without resorting to officialdom. I mentally rolled up my sleeves and slicked on my scarlet lippy. Into battle. First things first: allay his suspicions.

'Don try anything,' he said seriously. 'I warn you. I not patient man.'

There was no point in arguing about what he would and wouldn't do. My game plan wouldn't involve head-on conflict. I smiled at him sweetly.

'Isn't this a bit silly? I don't want to leave anyway — you know that. I love it here. Can I have some water melon?'

We finished dinner and went back to the boat where we sat on the deck and drank Perrier water, eyeing each other up like a pair of mouldy crocodiles. I'd always refused to move my belongings into his cabin, telling him that there wasn't enough space. So every night there was this tussle. Would I sleep with him or not? It was just a game, a routine seduction, a power play — although I have to admit that it was fuelled by the repellent muckheap that the Pirate called our bedroom. But he was having none of it that night. When we finished the Perrier he simply ordered me to get downstairs. I got. I know it sounds peculiar, but the truth was I could hardly wait anyway. The challenge to battle hung in the air between us, bringing us closer together. Perhaps even then I subconsciously recognised that we were two of a kind, very evenly matched.

In any case, I had no intention of trying to beat him on his winning suit. Defiance and outright conflict wouldn't get me anywhere. I was going to beat him with cunning and brain-power. And cheating too, of course.

'This way!' he said, turning my shoulders towards the workshop. 'Now, stand still! I undress you!'

You can't argue with an earth-mover. And anyway, I didn't want to. So I smiled and er . . . went with the flow, so to speak. He stripped my clothes off in seconds; I obediently lay down and he raked and sieved and sowed. Predictably, the ground began to shudder, boulders smashed around our ears, cliffs cracked wide open, buildings tumbled, trees crashed over. We were overtaken by an enormous earthquake.

Breathless and sweaty, we lay tangled together, our hearts thudding loudly as we gasped and laughed. Propped up on one elbow, he gazed at me with a smile playing round his lips, and I gazed back and smiled.

'So now can I have my passport back, please?' I whispered.

The little lines round his eyes creased as his smile broadened into a wide grin, and he shook his head.

'You are mine,' he said. 'I don't let you go.'

'But I don't want to go!' I exclaimed. 'I just want my passport!'

'Wha-for?'

I couldn't explain it. I couldn't even explain it to myself. I lay awake gazing out of the porthole at the clouds scudding across the moon, waiting for him to fall asleep. He had my passport. He'd had it ever since we'd arrived. What else had he taken? I wanted to check my bag. But he never went to sleep first. Never. And that night was no different. He lay awake watching me until I finally fell asleep.

So it was the next morning before I went through my bag, and that was when I found out that everything was missing. I should have known. Bastard.

My purse contained a selection of old supermarket receipts, some French stamps, a few loyalty cards, an old shopping list and some small change. My bank cards were gone. My French identity card was gone. I went through the rest of my things slowly. Everything was gone. My address book, my driving licence, my cheque book, everything. There was other stuff: scent, sun tan lotion, and a new bikini he'd given me the day we got married. But he'd even taken the wedding ring off my finger while I slept.

I couldn't believe it at first. I got on the radio and yelled at him, 'Sun Boat to office — answer me you bastard!'

But he didn't respond and when I looked at the stupid thing, I realised he'd switched it off or immobilised it somehow. Anyway it wasn't working anymore. Shit. And as he well knew, I hadn't the faintest clue how to get off the boat unless someone came out to get me.

So I had to wait for him, and he really made me wait. No-one came near the Sun all day. Not even Tommy with bread for breakfast. I sat on the deck in the shade of the canvas awnings and waited for Bettina to show up, but she didn't come either. By noon I was pacing up and down the deck, starving and swearing under my breath. But still no-one came, and finally I went back downstairs into the galley. It was like a sauna in there. The air was thick and sticky, and wrenching open cupboard doors and raking through the contents, I felt as if I was covered in stale honey.

I don't like kitchens at the best of times, but this one was woeful. The utensils were old and dirty, most of them were broken, the china was covered in salt, the glasses opaque with grease, and as for supplies, it was pathetic. Well, I admit I'm not exactly a bustling housewife, but I do at least keep a few tins and supplies in my store cupboard. This kitchen seemed to have nothing in it except dozens of jars of white pepper. All of them slightly open and slightly used, all of them decorated with faded writing and greasy fingerprints. Yuk. Apart from that there was some instant coffee, a few packs of herbs and spices, oil and salt, and that was it.

The fridges were full of bottled water, champagne, white wine, bitter cucumbers, rotting tomatoes and the most foul-smelling rancid feta I'd ever seen in my life. There were also several open tins of sour condensed milk and a damp box of eggs. Revolting. How could he live like this? So disgusting.

I boiled the eggs, just hoping that they weren't so rotten that they would explode all over the galley. No, Philippa, of course I haven't the faintest idea whether rotten eggs do explode when you boil them — but if they do, I bet there'd be green slime everywhere.

The heat and steam from the gas cooker turned the galley into a torture chamber but I went on until the eggs boiled dry. Just in case there were bugs in them. Which there weren't — I don't think there were, anyway. I mean, when I peeled them on the deck they seemed perfectly normal apart from the nasty blue line between the yolks and the whites reminiscent of school breakfasts.

Anyway, I ate them and drank some champagne and slept for a bit and when I woke up it was cooler, although the sky was still unforgivingly bright blue. I sat down and did some logical thinking.

Calling in the authorities remained an option, but I didn't want to have to explain my whole life to some civvie-street slug in a suit. And also . . . also what if the local police thought it was right and proper for my husband to keep all my papers? No, I decided, I would only call the cavalry as a last resort.

I laughed to myself. I wasn't scared. I didn't even care about going without a meal or two. Hunger and me are old friends, and in any case I knew the Pirate wouldn't actually starve me to death. He wouldn't do anything to the twins either. He loved kids and he was particularly fuzzy about my two. So I wasn't frightened of him in that way. I was irritated more like. Furiously irritated that I'd let someone get the better of me. Particularly a man.

So no, it wasn't a medieval torture tournament. It was the Pirate being intolerably bossy and me wanting to turn the tables on him.

So far he'd won every round — but I was determined to show him that I wasn't just some brainless little bimbo. I would play him at his own game and win. I wouldn't just take him down a peg or two, I'd grind him under my heel until he begged for mercy.

Tapping my fingernails against my teeth, I started to plan. He held all the aces. He had the cash, the staff, the infrastructure. I had nothing but my wits. To win, I had to stack the deck in my favour. For a start off I told myself, this hanging about waiting for lifts on and off the boat would have to stop. I needed my own transport.

I stared across the sea at the buildings cuddled round the bay and at the sandy beaches spreading out like wings either side of the village, and wondered if I could swim ashore. It didn't look that far and it wasn't very deep. I mean there were coral reefs and stuff.

No, I couldn't have actually walked ashore, it wasn't that shallow, but at least it didn't look deep enough to be harbouring sharks or whales or monstrous women-killing squid with fifty metre long tentacles to wind round your feet so that they could drag you down into the briny sea and eat you alive — very slowly. No, it wasn't deep enough for that sort of thing. I'd have to learn to swim.

Oh, of course I could already splash about in the shallows but I couldn't actually properly swim, like breast stroke or anything. All else apart, I wasn't fit enough.

You'll have to start training, I told myself, if you're going to swim in the sea. Especially long distances. Like from here to the shore.

I laughed out loud. Once I could swim off the boat, I'd never be trapped on it again. I immediately got up and took my T-shirt off. I already had a swimsuit on underneath . . . And then the thought crossed my mind that the Pirate might be standing in his office watching me through his telescope.

I dismissed it. Bollocks to him! If he sees me going down the ladder and getting into the sea, he'll just assume I'm hot and want to cool off. I kicked my flip-flops off and climbed down the boarding ladder.

Once in the sea, I doggy paddled round the prow of the Sun with my chest heaving and a sour taste in my mouth but I'd only managed a few metres before I was totally blown and had to tread water. Bloody hopeless. I paddled slowly back to the ladder again. This was going to take time. Luckily for me the sea was as warm as a baby's armpit with not a wave in sight.

Come on, I told myself and pushed off with my feet again, trying to remember any other swimming strokes and wondering what I could use as a float.

I swam on and off for the rest of the afternoon, only stopping when the sun began to set. I had a shower then and washed my hair, but once I was dressed I had nothing else to do. I was absolutely exhausted anyway, so I took some champagne up onto the deck. I sat there and drank it and my head spun round and then suddenly I was sober again. You know how that happens sometimes? You drink and get sober? No, you probably . . .

Anyway, I sat there with every muscle aching and my stomach rumbling after all that exercise, drinking and getting increasingly sober as I fantasised about roast pork and parsnips, bacon sarnies, chicken curry and beans on toast, until finally late that evening when the sky was black and the moon had risen, the Pirate returned to his lair.

I heard his speedboat and was waiting for him at the head of the ladder when he clambered aboard. In spite of my resolution to play it cool, my heart was racing with fury and I had to fold my arms to stop my hands shaking. I probably wasn't as sober as I'd thought.

He looked amused. 'Waz-the matter with you?'

'Where are my papers?'

'I have them. Don-worry.'

'What do you mean, you have them? You mean you've stolen them. I want them back. Now!'

'Wha-for? Where you going this time of midnight?'

Well there wasn't any point in saying I was going anywhere. We both knew perfectly well that there were only two ways off the island — boat and plane — and that neither would operate until the next morning at the very earliest.

'I'm not going anywhere. I just want my papers back.' So childish. I already knew they weren't mine just for the asking. I haven't a clue why I took such a boring tack.

'Okay, I give them to you tomorrow,' he said dismissively. 'Now we eat.' He had a carrier bag in his hand and he dumped it on the table as he spoke. 'You already had a drink I see.'

'Any objections?'

He shrugged and shook his head. The smell of chicken wafted out of the bag on the table and I was so desperate for food I could have torn a live chicken limb from limb and eaten it raw let alone a roast one swimming in butter and garlic. But I was damned if I was going to admit I was hungry. I sat down, put my feet up, and filled my glass. It would be a small victory, but a certain one. I'd just remembered that he was far more likely to feed me to death than vice-versa.

He chuckled and bowled off down to the galley, reappearing in a few minutes with another bottle and a second glass. He sat down opposite me and eased the cork out. My stomach was groaning and moaning with hunger as he filled our glasses and then he started unpacking his carrier bag. There was also bread and fruit. He spread his feast out on the table and looked at me enquiringly. I stuck my nose up in the air.

'Come on, forget it. Pace, mange!' he said. 'Eat.' He tore off a leg and held it out to me. I ignored him, and sat there stubbornly gazing at the moon.

'Don give me angry eyes. What you wan, anyway? You wanna go back and starve in France with your lezbie girlfriends? Fuck it. You're here, I'm here. You've escaped, carthimou. Enjoy, eat!'

I shrugged.

'Eat!' he ordered.

I shrugged again.

'Come on, carthimou, eat,' he said coaxingly. 'Please?'

'Why?' I demanded, turning round and leaning over the table, gazing into his eyes. 'Just because you want me to?'

His eyes met mine and I could almost see

his brain ticking. I had him. I could hold out longer than he could, because he didn't want me to go hungry but I don't care about eating. Suddenly he broke into laughter.

'Okay, you win! Wha-tyou want? I gotta beg you?'

I grinned and raised my eyebrows at him. I was about to chalk up my first win. He stood up, smiling broadly, and came round to stand before me. In spite of myself I grinned back at him. Then he acknowledged my tiny bullseye with a deep bow. I bit my lip to stop myself laughing out loud, and stared down my nose at the deck. He creaked down onto one knee and put his hand over his heart.

'My baby-sweet,' he said formally, 'I beg you to eat. Please eat and make me happy.'

One to me! At that moment my stomach rumbled like thunder and we both laughed. I took a chicken thigh and bit into it ravenously, leaving him to haul himself back into his chair.

We ate and drank companionably while he talked about Venezuela ('frontier country, lodoff bandits') and I listened to him and wondered what Nickie was up to, and then we went to bed. It would have been childish to go on arguing, idiotic to complain that I'd been alone, fasting all day because the ship's fridges were full of compost instead of edible food. So once I'd finished eating, I burped a bit and went to bed with him.

No, there was never any question of refusing to sleep with him, Philippa! It just wasn't in the rules. In any case, why would I shoot myself in the foot? I would never have let him know it, but I wanted him. He'd learned the map of my body by heart; he knew precisely what to caress and when, and anyway you can't resist a man who can turn you on with the merest touch — even when you are determined to be cold and frigid and unforgiving. Especially not when you're half in love with him.

He could have me any time he wanted and he knew it. He didn't give a shit that I struggled to pretend I didn't fancy him, that I really didn't find him aesthetically pleasing. In fact he enjoyed being able to seduce me in spite of myself. It made him laugh. He often laughed in bed. At me. Attempting to deny that my body was, once again, enthusiastically begging for more.

When we got ashore the next day, he said he'd left the keys to the office safe on the boat, but that I could have the papers later, and the day after that he had the keys to the safe but didn't want to open it because there were too many people about.

I wasn't surprised. I knew he was just going

through the motions until the bell rang for the next round. He wouldn't ever give my papers back. Not just for the asking. If I wanted them, I'd have to steal them. So I stopped pestering him, shrugged and agreed that they probably were better off in his safe.

Instead, I asked him to teach me how to drive a speedboat. I was sick to death of swimming round the Sun, although I could just about manage it by that time.

'Wha-for?'

'Well, so I can get about without Tommy having to come and fetch me. Since you won't give me a job, I've got nothing to do all day . . . I can't just sit here all the time. I mean, what if I want to go er . . . shopping while you're in the office?'

'Tommy got nothing else to do.'

'Yes, but I don't want to rely on someone else.'

'It's not safe. You know fuck all about boats. How you gonna manage a speedboat?'

'I could learn.'

'Too dangerous for you.'

'Please?'

'No.'

And that was the end of that conversation. He refused to speak about it again and there was no point in nagging. If I so much as mentioned boats, he clammed up. So a few days later, I tried it on with Tommy.

'Can I try and start the motor, Tommy?'

'What for?'

'Oh, just for fun.'

'Maybe the Captain don't like it.'

'It's a surprise for him, Tommy. I want to surprise him, show him that I can drive a boat. So he sees I'm not such an idiot after all.'

He chewed it over for a minute and then nodded. 'Okay, so you gotta turn the fuel on, you prime the engine like this, and then you pull the starter handle like this . . . nice and gentle. Yes, that's right, but you didn't pull long enough. Try again.'

The first time the motor roared into life, I staggered backwards, tripped on a petrol can and fell into the sea. Tommy fished me out, spluttering and choking, and I had to go back aboard the Sun for a dry T-shirt.

But the second time I managed it better, and then Tommy let me steer the thing along a wonky line across the bay. I was thrilled with myself but it didn't last long. The Pirate was waiting for us on the jetty of the office complex, rigid with fury.

'Wha-the-fuck!'

'She's only learning, Boss.'

'Get out, you!' he ordered, stabbing a finger at poor hapless Tommy. 'Not you,' he stabbed at me. 'You stay there.'

Tommy shot out of the boat, ran along the jetty, leapt onto the beach and disappeared. The Pirate heaved his bulk into the boat and I didn't wait to be told. I moved over, he stuffed himself behind the outboard motor and took off at top speed for the Sun. Once on board, he shoved me towards the galley and followed me down the stairs. 'You! You nothing but fucking trouble!'

'Why don't you let me go, then?'

'I tell you to stay!' he yelled. 'You do what I tell you, and you don't play games with the fucking pliroma! You hear?'

'I'm not a dog, you mealy-mouthed pot-bellied tub of lard! You can't order me about!'

'Oh no?'

I was so furious, I didn't think twice. I stormed up the ladder onto the deck with him trying to catch at my heels. 'Where you fucking going, now?' he shouted.

'I'll show you! I'll show you if I have to stay or not! You think I'm so bloody useless, but I'll show you!' I screamed back, tugging my shorts and T-shirt off so that I was just wearing a swimsuit.

'Now wha-tyou doing?'

'I'll show you . . . ' I muttered savagely and kicked my flip-flops off. By this time the

Pirate was half way down the boarding ladder. I scrambled after him, but he was faster than me and by the time I reached the little landing stage, he'd untied Tommy's boat and pushed off. I didn't care. I didn't have my sights set on Tommy's boat anyway.

I shoved my hands into the air and launched myself into an untidy dive, landing in the water with a huge splash. I surfaced, gasped for breath and dragged the hair out of my eyes. I could see palm trees in the distance, so I struck out for them in my best doggy paddle. I'd show him.

He followed in the little dinghy, yelling like a maniac and slapping his thighs with frustration.

'Wha-tyou-fuckin doin? You gonna fuckin drown, you crazy woman!'

I didn't stop. I just kept kicking my feet and paddling along. It was a nightmare, of course. I was panting within minutes, every muscle in my body complaining as I swam. Swimming in the sea is hard, and I've never been sporty. Not even at school. So in spite of all my practising, I'd probably have drowned if I hadn't been so angry.

When I was out of breath I stopped swimming and pretended I was just having another bout of fury. Hanging on to the side of Tommy's boat I abused the Pirate like a fishwife . . . well, like a drowned rat actually.

I bet you've never seen a drowning rat, have you, Philippa? I found one in a bucket of rainwater once. Outside the back door. It was swimming in circles scrabbling at the slippery edges of the bucket, hissing and spitting and panting for breath with its yellow teeth bared and its eyes full of hatred and survival. I bet you'd say I should have killed it, but I couldn't. Apart from anything else, I didn't want to. Poor thing. I just tipped the bucket over with a long-handled yard broom and it scarpered. And no, it didn't come back at Christmas to show me its babies. Give me a break. It was a poxy rat. It would have bitten me if it could.

Where was I? Oh yes, so there I was in the sea, hanging onto the edge of the boat exactly like a drowning rat, scrabbling at the paint and snarling at the Pirate, calling him earthworm, scumbag and pot-scrubber, anything I could think of while I got my breath back . . . and the minute I could I let go of the boat and started doggy paddling again.

'Fuck! Wha'ja doing?' he yelled, as I started swimming again. But I wouldn't give up, I just kept batting along and in the end I didn't drown, and the Pirate even stopped yelling. That's the advantage youth has over age — stamina.

After what seemed like hours I made it all the way and staggered up the shore leaving him to belly flop over the side of Tommy's boat and drag it up through the shallows onto the beach. I used the last of my strength to stay on my feet, and stood under a palm tree with my hands on my thighs, my flanks heaving like Rover's, watching him barrel across the golden sand towards me.

'All right, all right. You win. I give you boat!' he panted, coming up level with me. 'You fucking mad woman, you know that?'

Round Two to me! He enveloped me in a huge hug and kissed me and I was so pleased that I hugged him back and kissed him with real passion. He groaned.

'Mine,' he muttered in a thick voice. 'Whata woman!'

I was still out of breath, and my legs were already like jelly. I collapsed under the weight of him and he fell on top of me. We lay on the hot sand, panting and laughing in between kisses and getting all covered with sand. Leaving our legs all tangled up together, he shifted onto his side and propped his head up on his elbow so that he could look at me as I lay on my back beside him, grinning at him triumphantly.

'Carthimou,' he whispered and then added something in Greek and I didn't catch it.

'What?' I said and my voice was suddenly hoarse because he looked so serious and the way he was stroking my hair so tenderly made my heart thump painfully in my chest. For a split second I was terrified that he was going to go sloppy on me and start spouting about lerve under the moon in June with a spoon and then I'd have to say something back and . . . I mean quelle nightmare, frankly. I was really starting to panic. But he just sat up and all he said was, 'You bloody woman, you know tha?'

And I pushed him over because I was so relieved and I didn't know what to say, and he smiled at me and I smiled back at him and then we both lay down together again, and gazed companionably up at the palm tree until we got our breath back.

Finally we staggered down the beach together, dragged Tommy's dinghy into the sea, and climbed into it. Good job he didn't make me swim back though, because for all my bravado, I couldn't have done it.

The next day the Pirate gave me a dinghy for my own. It was blue with a yellow stripe round it, little red seats, a plastic watertight compartment, and a temperamental oily outboard motor. It was called Little Star.

I was pretty pleased with myself until I realised that it was equipped with about the smallest fuel tank you ever saw and that if I tried going anywhere much further than just round the bay I'd be out of gas and in serious trouble. And then there was Tommy. The Pirate deputised him to look after me, so everywhere I went, Tommy went too. Not as a gaoler actually. Tommy is way too good-natured for that.

'I jest coming to look after you, Missis. Where we going first?'

'I'll be fine on my own, Tommy.'

'Captain says I look after you. I gotta do it, Missis.'

En plus, he had strict ideas on what I should and shouldn't do for my own safety and hey, wouldn't you know, they just about chimed with the Pirate's ideas in every detail.

For example, shopping was fine. I could buy anything I liked anywhere on the island: at any market stall, and in any of the little shacks which passed for shops. Tommy just sent whatever I'd bought to the Pirate's office and he paid for it when it was delivered to him.

(Or never, or whatever was the arrangement he had. I don't know. Did he give them vouchers they could use to get let off walking the plank? Or was it just savings stamps for a free parrot? I don't bloody know.)

Anyway, officially it was organised that way

so I didn't have to carry anything in the heat. Why would I want to carry anything? Drinks, snacks and food were just paid for later or perhaps never paid for, perhaps it was just Pirate tax. God knows.

And people. Tommy didn't like me talking to locals: 'Bad man' he'd say, or 'dirty girl' — but I wasn't allowed to talk to strange Europeans either: 'We go now, we go eat. Come.' It was pointless trying to shake him off. If I misbehaved, he'd send a message and either the Pirate would turn up and take me back to the boat, or someone else would spring into action.

Like once, I met a couple of really nice cheery Australian girls who were working their way round the world and they asked me if there was any chance of getting work on the island, and we got chatting and I said I wasn't sure but I could ask around, and I told Tommy that he could relax because we were going to have lunch and he wandered off (well I thought he did) so I sat down with them.

They wrote their phone numbers down on paper table napkins and I really hoped that they'd stay on the island for a while, because they were funny and interesting. But when I went to the loo, I got accidentally locked in, accidentally on purpose of course, and by the time I was liberated, the girls had left the island and the napkins had been blown away in the wind. There was no way Tommy was going to risk his job for me again.

Another time I bumped into a Canadian family who had hired a Jeep to drive round the island and they invited me along, but they mysteriously ran out of petrol before we'd even got 100 metres up the hill, and oh, quelle surprise, Robert just happened by at that moment. He would give the Canadians some diesel but my husband was looking for me, so I'd better come back to the village with him.

Another time, when I was talking to a sweet French couple they got an urgent message to phone home and by the time it was established that the message wasn't in fact for them at all, the Pirate had joined us and within minutes arranged to get them a lift on a catamaran to another island where they could go shark fishing. I never saw them again either.

So it was pointless trying to make friends. And if I did manage to strike up any sort of acquaintance, the Pirate would shift base, and we'd be anchored off some even more remote island for a week or so until the coast was clear again. He did it two or three times, always saying that I looked tired and needed a rest.

Naturally I could only 'rest' on the smallest and most remote of islands, especially those privately owned ones where there were no tourists and he could borrow someone's house. Needless to say, by the time I was 'better' my acquaintance had drifted on and I was once again as isolated as the last dodo on earth.

I finally wrote to Daniel, a long-overdue letter informing him that I was married and giving him addresses for both me and the twins. Not that I expected him to write of course. He never does. I didn't even know where he was, so I sent it via Aunt Lottie. She's his sister. My aunt. I used to spend my school holidays with her years ago but I hadn't seen her for ages either and didn't quite know what to write to her, so in the end I just sent a picture postcard with lots of kisses on the back. She's always very busy anyway, surrounded by dancers and opera singers.

I suppose I could have written to Nickie too, but I wasn't even sure my letter to Daniel had been posted, and anyway there didn't seem much point in writing a letter that would almost certainly be censored by the Pirate. So I kicked around on my own most of the time.

I was allowed to talk to Marie-Rose and

she made various friendly overtures, but I was suspicious of her. What did she want with me? Why was a chic Parisienne hanging out in Port Grotsville? What was her connection with the Pirate? I couldn't work her out and as a result wasn't ready to take her into my confidence, so I steered clear.

As for the Pirate's other friends, that was fine. I was allowed to talk to them all right and anyone he introduced to me, because they were mostly fellow crooks, people who wouldn't even dream of embroiling themselves in the marital affairs of a man who had a cutlass embedded in every pie across the Caribbean.

'You beautiful woman' he would say, 'You thin-kime stupid? I look after my belong-kings, and you are my Treasure.'

I learned to play the game. I realised that he wouldn't let me wear my wedding ring in case I sold it or used it as a bribe. So I told him that it was shameful, that he was shameful, that to have a wife without a wedding ring showed that he was poor, that I wasn't really his wife, that I didn't really belong to him.

Narrowing his eyes and staring at me, he laughed. 'I know your game! You . . . you . . . woman!'

But two days later he took my hand as we

sat in a restaurant and slipped two handsome rings onto my wedding finger: a large diamond set in a cluster of smaller diamond chips with my plain gold wedding band to act as a keeper. A third tiny victory.

The next morning when I looked, around the inside of each ring was engraved 'Treasure of The Captain'. No-one in the Caribbean would have touched those rings, not even as a bribe.

'My wife, my Treasure,' he said softly as he admired the rings glittering on my finger. 'Be happy.'

To hell with it. I smiled and kissed his fingers. 'Thank you, minou.'

I was happy; and not only because of him. I mean, if you just ignore the kidnapping aspect of the thing, who wouldn't have been happy?

There I was, living in Bounty paradise, skipping along the silver sands of life light-headed with relief because, although I still missed them, for the first time since they were born I didn't have to worry about the twins. They were flourishing and I could relax.

The boys sent postcards from school describing the teachers as random and the other kids as decent, and on Sunday afternoons they phoned me in the Pirate's office and I listened to them jostling each other and joking as they asked for paints, pocket-knives, more sports gear, tinned cakes (where on earth was I supposed to get a tinned cake from?) and cash.

The cash was never a problem. The Pirate used to send it to them between two postcards crammed into a thin little envelope. I just wished I could send them some money of my own.

He was proud of the twins, dead chuffed to be their stepfather. Almost to the point where I wondered if that was the attraction. Had he married me in order to move in on my sons? Nah. If he had, why would he ship them off to England within weeks of marrying me? No, I think he just loved them. Still does, actually.

They are fantastic boys, I have to admit. Sturdy and tousle-headed, clear-eyed and snub-nosed, nowadays they look exactly how I always thought boys should look. But then I would say that, wouldn't I? My beautiful, gorgeous, precious sons.

So life went on and I admit it — part of me, the lazy part of me, was just revelling in being looked after. I'd never been the object of so much attention before and of course I enjoyed it.

I never had so much as an envelope of my

own of course. The Pirate swore that he hadn't read my letter to Daniel, that he had just posted it . . . but I knew that was a lie. He read every letter I wrote. I'd finally written to Nickie, but hadn't heard anything back. I'd have emailed her, but the Pirate wouldn't let me near his computer.

With nothing else to do, I slept and swam and trailed around with Tommy, and looked forward to the twins coming home for Christmas while the Pirate screamed down the phone in the office complex, supervised the re-painting of his fleet ready for the season, and attempted to type up publicity handouts in five languages.

Being polyglot, he always thought he could write in any language, but the truth is he wouldn't recognise a grammar rule if it sprouted out of his left nostril — and because no-one ever dared to point out that his translations were atrocious, all his boats were splattered with notices written in pidgin English, pidgin French, etc . . .

Sitting in his sweltering hot office one day, watching him grumbling and stabbing away at the keyboard, I just rolled my eyes.

'Wha?'

'Nothing . . . '

'Fuckin wha?'

'All right. There's no point in typing that

stuff out. I don't know about the Greek but the rest of those translations are rubbish. Completely senseless gibberish. Since you ask.'

'Fuckin rubbish!' he yelled. 'You fuckin do them, then. You sit there doing nothing and critique me! You bloody woman! Tommy!'

'Oh just give them to me, for God's sake and stop making such a noise.'

He was surprised and pleased. 'You do them? Really? No tricks?'

'No tricks. Just hand them over.'

'Why? Why you do them?'

'Well, if you must know, I'm bored so I might as well do this.'

He was pleased. 'Carissima! I pay you!'

I shrugged. If he did pay me it would be in currency I couldn't use, or into a bank account I couldn't access. 'Forget it.'

The Pirate turned on his heel and left. Tommy raised his eyebrows at me. 'What?' I demanded. 'So what?'

He just looked at me.

Tommy was right of course. As far as he could see it, the Pirate was ready to give me everything and I wasn't giving much back.

How could Tommy understand that I couldn't bear being a prisoner? It itched and rankled every minute of every day. I couldn't bear the Pirate not realising that I'd stay with him even if he gave me my papers back. No, of course I didn't tell him ... He wouldn't have believed me anyway. And I couldn't explain it all to Tommy. In any case all he would have said was, 'The boss is the boss.'

Whatever. I started working in the office and enjoyed it. I also quickly saw the practical advantages. So much so that I was amazed that I hadn't thought of it before. But then I thought that if I seemed too keen the Pirate might get suspicious.

I bit my tongue, kept my eyes down and started waiting until I was alone when I could gradually start going through the files. Not that there were many. You don't think Pirates keep accounts do you? No. Exactly. But there were papers; bills, insurance claims, sheaves of documents in Greek, old passenger lists, junk mail and other useless rubbish.

It was a waste of time. I learned nothing. The only useful stuff I found was a stack of dictionaries in the bottom of a filing cabinet. They helped me with the translations, but they were hardly flying carpets. They weren't going to get me out of there.

Of course, now that I was working in the office I was allowed to use the computer but it was a dial-up connection and I didn't have the password to get online, and I still couldn't phone anyone because the fixed line only worked for local calls on the island. The Pirate kept his mobiles locked into a drawer in his desk.

There was a photocopier and a fax machine which would have been useful except that I didn't know anyone else with one and even if I had, I didn't know any numbers. My address book was locked up with my other papers.

I knew the safe was set into the storm-proof cement of the back wall behind a small wooden door because Tommy told me about it one day. But I never saw it opened. I never even saw the cupboard door unlocked and I couldn't find any keys in the office. Not a single one. Not at the back of any drawers, not fallen down behind the desk or the filing cabinet. Nowhere. No keys. It drove me bonkers, knowing I was so near to my papers and yet so far.

I just couldn't figure out where he kept the keys. He didn't carry them on him, that was for sure. He hardly ever carried anything. So I started spying on him, trying to watch where he went and who he went with, but it was impossible. He disappeared on his incredibly noisy little scooter, the machine bowed like a banana under his weight, and how could I tell where he'd gone or who he was talking to?

Then I thought maybe he's got them

hidden on the boat? So I started searching the Sun, carefully and methodically, whenever both he and Bettina were ashore. I started with the obvious stuff: went through more papers, read letters, flicked through books looking for papers, rifled through his clothes, inspected the contents of boxes and lockers. Nothing.

So I went a step further. I appropriated some tools from the Pirate's workshop, cleaned the black grease off them to avoid telltale smudges, and started unscrewing things.

At first I just unscrewed things at random — toilet roll holders and door handles and hooks — but I quickly got more methodical. I learned to hit rusty screws on the head with a hammer to loosen them, and to clean out the grooves on their heads with the bread knife so that the screwdriver wouldn't slip. I also discovered that a potato peeler shifts those disgusting little screws with the hot cross bun tops.

I started methodically unscrewing panels, hatch-covers and bits of planking. Bit by bit, whenever I was alone on the boat, I dismantled all the lockers and unscrewed every single screw I could find until finally I realised that I'd been through every nook and cranny and still found Sweet Fanny Adams.

Not so much as a whisper of a key, let alone any guns or forged banknotes. I scratched my mosquito bites and stamped around banging things. I must have overlooked something.

So I started again. Turned out all the kitchen cupboards, delved into engine compartments, went through the Pirate's terrible stinky pit with a peg on my nose, and still found nothing more interesting than a blunt razor and two perished condoms.

Until one day I went through the bookshelves again, this time not bothering to leaf through the books themselves, but concentrating on the wooden boards behind them. Not that he had many books — a few raunchy reads, a collection of Captain Hornblower tales and a series of mechanical manuals in Italian. He isn't much of a reader, the Pirate.

Then I decided to check behind his videos. I closed the hatch in case anyone came aboard and, working as quickly as I could, raked them out half a dozen at a time and stacked them in order on the seating units running round the walls of the galley. Once all the shelves were empty, it was easy.

I could see a square panel behind them held in place by four nice clean brass screws. I lifted out the centre shelf and got busy with the potato peeler. I was shaking with excitement, because if anyone came aboard I'd have to get the panel and the shelf back in place quick enough to say I was just dusting . . . or find some other plausible excuse . . . God knows what.

My fingers were trembling as I lifted the panel out and revealed a nice neat cupboard containing two shoe boxes. I took the lid off the first one. Were the keys in there? I blinked. It was stuffed with large denomination American dollar bills. I put the lid back on and shook it slightly but there was nothing else in there. No keys.

For a split second I held the box — but I was sure the notes must be fakes. Looking back on it perhaps they weren't which would be ironic, but anyway, at the time I assumed they were fakes and put the box back in its place.

I opened the second one in a hurry. I wasn't looking for keys any more, I was just consumed by simple curiosity. A heavy waterproof bag tumbled out of the box onto my lap, and I unwound it. Inside was an irregular lump wrapped up in a towel. I held one corner of the fabric, shook it gently and out fell a small black revolver.

It lay there heavy and cold on my knees and for a moment I just gawped at it. He really did have a gun. OmiGod! I picked it up gingerly, wondering if it was loaded or not. I'd never even seen a gun before let alone held one, and I hadn't the faintest clue how to check whether it had bullets in it or not.

Pointing it carefully away from me, I fiddled with it, but couldn't get anything to budge. I held it in my hand and wondered. Was it loaded? Did it work? If it wasn't loaded, how did you load it? Would I be able to fire it? The base of my spine twitching with excitement, I held it out with two hands and closed one eye. How did you aim a gun? Would this thing kill someone? And then with shaking hands I dropped it on the seating cushions. Jesus. Where did the word kill come from? What was I thinking of? What if he caught me with it? What if he noticed I'd found it?

I used the hem of my skirt to rub it over, carefully avoiding any bits that might be a trigger, and put it back in its hiding place. Then, working very hurriedly, I replaced the girlie vids hoping I'd got them all back in the right order.

I looked round the cabin. Everything was back to normal. I brushed my skirt down, opened the hatch and went on deck.

What should I do? Learn to use it? No, what was the point? I could simply shove it in his direction and tell him to open the safe. I laughed out loud at the idea. Lordy-Lord! I'd got it sorted. He didn't know it, but I'd evened the field. I was now pulling level with the Pirate.

Perhaps even inching ahead.

5

As the autumn wore on, more tourists began to arrive and the atmosphere on the island changed. People woke up; buildings that I'd taken to be derelict blossomed overnight and became beach bars, restaurants, fast food joints; market stalls lined the roads selling tourist trash and postcards; suddenly all sorts of places I'd assumed were abandoned revealed themselves to be night-clubs and lounges and funbars. A hitherto closed hotel parked a row of golf buggies on the quayside, and chalk boards everywhere announced happy hour prices, no problem, enjoy, and eat at Jack's. Or Betty's, or at the Shark's Hut or the Sailor's Cabin or at any one of a dozen nameless little barbecue shacks lining the rough tracks round the port.

The residents got busy, Europeans and locals alike. It was time to stop fishing, drinking, and sleeping in the sun and time to make a year's worth of money in four short months. They went at it. Concrete was painted with bright colours, the beaches were raked, rubbish hauled out of the port area, ice machines coaxed into action, bottles lined up on bars, and foodstuffs imported from larger islands. Pots of flowers made their appearance outside the more ambitious enterprises. Everyone was gearing up for the tourist season and we were no exception.

'Day-cruises. Very legit,' said the Pirate, looking at the booking sheets with satisfaction. 'Bene, molto bene.'

Rich Europeans started to arrive, jostling with not-so-rich Americans and the usual yachtie flotsam and jetsam. There were also wannabe drop-outs in hired schooners, idiots in brand new craft they couldn't have piloted round a fishpond, and genuine millionaires in expensive cruisers with hired professional crew.

I worked in the office and really got into it. I even forgot about searching for the keys to the safe, I was so busy sorting out the day trips. A good thing too really, as Tommy was too busy with the catering side to look after me. If I hadn't mucked in and worked like all the others, I'd have ended up sitting on the Sun by myself.

So I slogged it out in the heat. We all did, and it was fun. We were a good team. I soon took over the timetabling of the day cruises — who had booked, what time they had to leave, what time they were due back, who was to crew which catamaran, checking that

Tommy had loaded the right food and drinks onto each boat. It was interesting and getting it right meant that the tourists were happy and tipped the pliroma, which meant they slapped me on the back and called me Treasure.

The twins came for Christmas, looking taller and fatter, ate everything in sight, went fishing, swam every day, got marvellously brown, ran around with Bettina's four boys, learned how to tie knots, drank gallons of Coca Cola, hugged me whenever they thought of it and went back to school rapturously clutching a $50 note each.

'Fine boys,' said the Pirate smiling at me fondly. 'I have beautiful stepsons.'

I gave him a glowing look. People generally love kids on the island, but they did especially love my boys. I don't think it was only the Pirate's influence. Marie-Rose spoiled them rotten, letting them run tame in her kitchen, giving them ice creams at all hours of the day and night and letting them invent revolting cocktails by piling ice cream, yoghurt, cola and fruit into her blender.

The Pirate found them at it one day when he bowled into the bar for a Pernod. 'Wha-tyou doin' skids? Cookin? Molto bene! Here, I buy a cocktail. Ten dollars each, here y'are. Okay, go with Tommy. He take you diving for coral now. Fine skids, fine skids . . . here, Marie-Rose, throw this off, gimme a Pernod!'

She told me about it later when I went across for some lunch.

'Whatever else, he really loves those boys of yours, Camille. He's crazy about them.'

'Hasn't he got some kids somewhere?' I asked casually, pushing salad around my plate. 'I thought he had some.'

Marie-Rose raised her eyebrows and for a second I wondered if she was going to tell me it was none of my business. But then she recovered and smiled. 'Yes, I think he's got various kids, I know there was a daughter, years ago in Greece . . . and then I think he's got a couple more girls over in Venezuela and perhaps another one in Florida but as far as I know, they're all daughters. I don't think he ever had any sons.'

It didn't worry me, I mean once you're over 25 practically everyone you meet has some ex-wives and skids clunking about in their past. In fact, I was rather amused to think that the Pirate was so conventional. I mean, when I married him I became the only one in our family to actually make it up the aisle — and even that was more or less accidental.

'Oh,' I said. 'Well, I knew he'd been

married before . . . '

'Twice. Once in Greece but it didn't last long. Then there was the Venezuelan connection. He didn't marry her but they had two daughters. Then he got married again in Martinique, to a Frenchwoman. But that didn't last long either, and then there was the American girlfriend a couple of years ago.'

'Was it you?'

'What?'

'You? Were you the woman he married in Martinique?'

She laughed suddenly. 'Oh no! Once is enough for me and anyway, as far as he's concerned . . . '

She stopped and shook her head.

'What?' I demanded. She had obviously bitten something back, and my curiosity was aroused. 'What? What were you going to say?'

'Nothing. But believe me, I never would have married him, and I never will.'

'Are you saying I shouldn't have married him?'

She smiled again then. 'Oh no. Not at all. In fact, I think you might be the making of him.'

But just then a whole bunch of Yanks came into the bar demanding mimosas and eggs over easy, so that was the end of that conversation and somehow I couldn't ever get

Marie-Rose back on the subject so I never did find out what she meant.

She couldn't possibly have known that I was vaguely planning to force him to open the safe at gunpoint. If only I could find some bullets for the damn thing. And find out how to use it, of course.

The Pirate worked all the time. He crashed about on his little scooter, raising clouds of dust behind him, swearing loudly at stray chickens and cats that got in his way and mainly driving on the pavements. He would roll into the office, check the passenger lists, puff and pant, mop his forehead and roll off again, the scooter moaning and complaining as he thrashed it uphill to the airstrip to collect frozen chickens, or bribe officials to let his customers through the gate. Then you'd see him sweating at the bar opposite the complex, knocking back Pernod like it was water and eyeing up teenage Americans in string bikinis.

Minutes later he'd appear in the office, bearing a plastic bag of prawns or a tin of olives. 'Hey you! What you doin? Fucker! Sit there and check the boats off. Eh you, Treasure, c'mere! Eat!'

I'd raise my eyebrows and he'd roll his eyes. 'Yeah, all right. Please, Treasure, eat!'

And he'd take me to the bar, heave his

grotesque pot belly onto a barstool and order drinks. Fruit juices, water, anything long and cold just to quench our thirst, and champagne as a reward for sorting out the office.

We'd sit there together laughing and gossiping in the shade, making plans for the day trips and bitching about the tourists like a real married couple. You'd never have guessed that I was virtually a slave. Well, all right. Not a slave. But a prisoner. You know what I mean.

Ah, but he made me laugh, Philippa. I wasn't lonely when I was with him. He was funny and smart, he's . . . but he'd nicked my passport.

Sometimes he went away. Disappeared for two, three days at a time. I never knew when he was going, where he went or what he did. I would just wake up and he would be gone. Then Bettina would come, clean up the boat, change the sheets, bring me food, and ask softly: 'You lonely, Missis, without de Captain?'

Yes, I missed him like hell when he wasn't there. Not that I would admit it then. Not even to myself, let alone to Bettina. On the other hand I could hardly tell her to get out because I wanted to search the place for bullets. So I used to drink coffee with her, and give her bacon out of the fridge.

I was still on the warpath. Like a little terrier, I just couldn't let go. I wouldn't rest until I got my papers back. So I had to find some bullets because having thought about it, I'd realised that forcing the Pirate to open the safe at gunpoint would only work if he was convinced that the gun was loaded, and that I would use it on him.

So obviously I had to get hold of some bullets, and I could hardly add them to the weekly shopping list. Especially as I think bullets are like bras and come in different sizes. I'm sure you can't just buy little-black-hand-gun bullets. In fact, I bet they're like hoover bags and you have to know some code number or something to buy the right bags to fit the gun. Bullets to fit the hoover. Well, you know what I mean, Philippa.

Anyway I was obsessed by the conviction that the bullets must be somewhere around the place if only I could find them. So I'd misappropriated the potato peeler again and was putting it to improper uses (but with no result at all) when I suddenly did a double-take at the fridges.

They were monstrous things; old cream-coloured American Kelvinator types with built-in ice-makers, must have been made of cast iron. I mean they were so heavy they weren't even bolted to the deck.

I got a torch and tried to look underneath them, but couldn't see a thing. So I got a crowbar from the workshop and used it to lever one of them away from the bulkhead so that I could see behind it. It just looked like the back of a fridge. But when I tried the same trick on the other one, it rattled and the torch showed up the edge of a small cardboard box.

I levered the fridge out as far as I dared, reached into the gap behind it, grazing my forearm against the rusty metal, and inched the box towards me. The cardboard was soft with age, but I was sure it contained bullets and when I picked the top up with my nails, I saw that I was right. A full box of only slightly corroded bullets. Looked pretty much like a box of tampons, if the truth be told.

I couldn't get the box out completely because I didn't want to move the fridge out too far. What would happen if I couldn't move it back into position? So one by one, I extracted half a dozen bullets from the box and laid them on the floor beside me. Would that be enough? Guns in westerns all only take six bullets, everyone knows that. Was my gun from a western? How many bullets did it take? I wasn't sure. And anyway, how many bullets would I need? What if I had to reload the thing and start again? I pulled another handful of bullets out of the box and then, gathering them all together in my skirt, scurried off to my cabin wondering where to hide them.

I really didn't have time to mess about, but I couldn't think of anywhere foolproof off-hand. So in the end, I just tipped them into a pile under my pillow. Then I went back into the galley to get the fridges back in place, but of course I couldn't shift them an inch. Without the bulkhead to use as a brace, the crowbar wasn't any use at all.

The Pirate would definitely notice they'd been moved. Particularly as he must know about the hidden bullets; he'd be on the look-out for any fridge-fiddling. I wrenched the doors open and started snatching bottles out and stacking them on the table. Without the weight of all that glass, they might be light enough to move back into position. But it was no use. I couldn't budge them. So I took all the tinned milk out, and then I could hear the Venus approaching so I just swept everything out of the second fridge (the one with the bullets behind it) and heaved with all my strength. By some miracle, it suddenly jerked backwards and settled into its original position. I could hear banging as the Pirate tied his speedboat up and mounted the ladder.

Breaking into a cold sweat, I grabbed a bucket and filled it with water. By the time the Pirate's feet appeared at the top of the galley stairs, I was kneeling on the floor in front of the empty fridges swabbing them out.

'Wa's this?' he demanded. 'Wha-tyou doin?'

'What does it look like?' I said, my heart thumping with excitement. 'I'm not doing my nails, am I?'

Then he noticed the crowbar, and instantly realised that I'd moved one of the fridges out. I thought he was going to blow a blood vessel, his face went so purple.

'Wha-tyou moving the fridges for? Wha-tyou lookin for?'

'Mushrooms,' I said flapping about with a filthy wet cloth and getting soaked in the process. 'You've got enough of them in here to supply the whole of mainland Europe.'

'You fucking lying to me! You was searchin for somethin!' he yelled, brandishing the crowbar like a rapier.

I scrambled to my feet, wondering how I could distract him. I had to convince him that I was seriously cleaning out the fridges, and yet I'd never cleaned one out in my entire life. He grabbed my arm furiously but I shook him off and grabbed a whole cardboard tray of mouldy cucumbers off the table.

'Look at this!' I yelled at him. 'Bloody disgusting.' I brandished it in his face and he whacked at it viciously with the crowbar, but it was so old that it didn't crack in half. It just made a dull thudding noise and bent in the middle. We both looked at it, and suddenly we both burst into laughter.

But then I remembered the fridges. I badly needed a distraction. So still laughing I charged up the stairs with the bendy crate, tripping as I went, and staggered onto the deck with it. I heard the crowbar clang onto the floor in the galley and thumping noises as the Pirate crashed up the stairs behind me.

'Wha-tyou fucking doin?' he demanded, as I hurled the whole tray of cucumbers overboard. I didn't answer. I'd forgotten the bullets to be honest. I just couldn't stand to share boat-space with a single mouldy cucumber for a second longer. With the Pirate on my heels I plunged back down to the galley, grabbed another cardboard box and started hurling rotten vegetables into it pell-mell.

All those horrible soft tomatoes, and all that disgusting sour feta went in, along with the revolting half-used tins of yellow milk and all those stomach-churning damp boxes of stale eggs. The whole stack and stagger. Not even the Pirate could stop me chucking the whole bloody lot overboard.

'Don-tyou even think about it!' he threatened, but I shoved the bulging box into his belly with all my strength and thundered up the stairs again, leaving him reeling back against the table. But the bottom of the box was wet, and it broke, showering us both with rotten tomatoes. I didn't care. I just laughed and, hugging the remaining loot to my chest, continued my headlong rush to the railings with the Pirate pelting my back with tomatoes as I went.

He caught me up just as I reached the deck and grabbed my ankle sending me sprawling across the wooden planks. The flattened box skidded off towards the railings, spilling antique food in all directions. I dragged myself after it with the Pirate hanging on like a ball and chain, reached the first stray box of eggs, seized it and kicking and twisting, lobbed it into the Caribbean.

'Here, eat that!' I shouted at the crabs and the 20-ton monster squids. 'Bon bloody apetit!'

The Pirate went totally ballistic: 'You fucking woman, what you done? Don-you-do-tha! My fucking eggs!'

With a final twist, I got free of him, scrambled to my feet and heaved the rest of the box load over the edge and into the squid's kitchen.

'How dare you?' I yelled back, thoroughly enjoying myself. 'That fridge is a disgrace! Call yourself a bloody Captain? Captain Salmonella, that's the only Captain you are! This place is disgusting! How can you live like this?'

'Because I got a slut wife, thas why!' he yelled with equal zest. His eyes were gleaming and his mouth was twitching with amusement. I scuttled down the stairs wondering what else I could throw overboard, and then turned to face him as he rolled down them after me.

'My fuckin' eggs!' he screamed.

'You worm, you slug, you slimey-bottomed prat, you . . .'

He laughed.

'You Standard Issue Class A Bastard!'

He stopped then, and his eyes froze for just a split second. I gasped and started towards him . . . but he turned on his heel, climbed up the stairs, banged the hatch shut and left the boat. Hearing the Venus roar into life, I felt tears stinging my eyes and slammed my fist on the table.

'Shit!'

I was furious with myself. But what could I do? I almost went after him but water was slopping all over the floor, there were squashed tomatoes everywhere and the generators were working double time to keep up with the open fridge doors.

I slammed them shut and went into my cabin to find the best hiding place for those wretched bullets. Nothing too cunning, nothing too complicated. Somewhere easy, but somewhere he would never look. Bettina would find them if I left them in my bed, and ditto in the lockers with my clothes. I picked things up at random, wondering where I could hide a handful of little metal kisses.

Tampax box? What if Bettina needed one? Nope. I picked up my sponge bag and wondered about that. There was a side pocket with a zip . . . nope. They'd rattle. And then I picked up a half-empty box of cough sweets. Perfect. I already knew Bettina didn't like them, and no-one else would touch them. The Pirate would never admit to being ill, let alone actually go searching for cough sweets. I tipped the bullets into the packet, folded the cardboard top over and replaced the box in my sponge bag. Then I put that away again, stripped my filthy clothes off, shoved them out of the port-hole, slung on a clean swim-suit and went back into the galley to put the crowbar away and clear up the mess I'd made.

Half an hour later, I'd just about mopped all the tomato puree up and got the drinks back into the fridges when Tommy came over from the island.

'Missis?' he called, climbing up the ladder nervously. 'Missis? It's me, Tommy.'

I went up to meet him. 'Hi,' I said. 'How're you doing?'

'I fine, thank you. The boss sent you this,' he said holding out a carrier bag. 'I'm sorry you so sick.'

'Sick?'

'Yes,' he said, looking at his feet. 'The Boss says you really tired and need to rest.'

'Come on, Tommy. You know what he's like . . . '

'He's the Boss, Treasure. I got brothers and sisters. I got a family to feed.'

'Yes, I know, but I'll tell him . . . '

'Sorry, Missis, but he's the Boss.'

'Why? What? What's he told you to do?'

'You need rest. I taking boarding ladder so no-one disturb you. The Boss says boarding ladder is an invitation to trouble.'

'Where is he? Is he in the office? You stay right there. I'm going to get him on the radio . . . '

'He's not there, Missis. He's gone.'

'Gone? Gone where?'

Tommy shrugged. 'Gone off in the Venus. I come to get boarding ladder.'

'Tommy!'

'He's the one that pays me. He's the Boss,' repeated Tommy putting the carrier bag down on the deck.

'What's that?' I asked.

'Shopping. Some cheese, some fruit, bread. They didn't have any left in the shop, so Marie-Rose send you some stuff from the café. I bring you more tomorrow.'

He was backing away as he spoke. I let him go. I certainly wasn't going to fight Tommy for it — he was far too strong — and I wasn't going to argue or beg. I doubted that I could enlist him on my side anyway, and I felt guilty. I mean, it's one thing to steal bullets from someone but there's no need to hurt their feelings, is there?

Tommy went down the first few steps of the boarding ladder and then turned back. 'You cross?'

I smiled at him. 'No, Tommy. The Boss is right. I'm just tired. I'll be fine after a little rest.'

He smiled back at me. 'Is good thing. You been workin' too hard. Boss going to service motor for you, too.'

'What?'

'I take Little Star and we service outboard motor.'

I should have known. Pirate gone, boarding ladder gone, dinghy gone. I wondered how long he'd leave me alone for this time. I watched Tommy unlash the boarding ladder, and wrestle it into his own boat. Then he untied Little Star and with a final sheepish wave, he let the throttle out and roared away back to the office with my dinghy bouncing along behind him.

Without the ladder, I could have dived off the boat I suppose but it would have been impossible to get back on board and I'd have looked pretty stupid stranded on the island, especially as the Pirate had told everyone I was ill. I could have gone on arguing with Tommy over the radio but it would have been pointless. So I smiled, waved and resigned myself to an extended siesta.

And another period of fasting, I supposed. Not that it mattered much. I've never been especially food-orientated, and being a fully paid-up member of the B&P Club, I got so used to being hungry that it had become second nature.

We were all thin in France. All of us. I can tell you, we were like sticks, the amount of running about we did, sorting our kids, chopping firewood, digging our gardens, mending our houses and all the while struggling to find jobs and arguing with the authorities to get residence permits and health insurance and driving licences.

That was the worst. Changing your driving licence. What a carry on. I never did it, frankly. I simply used to lie when I was stopped by the police, swearing blind that I'd only been in France for a few months. But the others did it and it took forever and involved them in the sort of conversations you can only have when dealing with French bureaucracy.

'I see this is an English birth certificate?'
'Oui, Monsieur.'
'But you were born in Paris?'
'Oui, Monsieur.'
'And your parents were British?'
'Oui, Monsieur.'
'So you are English?'
'Oui, Monsieur.'
'From London?'
'Yes.'
'I have a cousin living in London. In En-donne. Do you know him?'

At this point you have to wrack your brains. Do you know any Frogs from Hendon? Because if you do, you're in. You're made. You're practically part of the family and all formality will be abandoned.

'Er . . . is he called Jean-Pierre?'

A shrug.

'Michel? Gerard? Bernard? Andre? Jean-Marie? Jean-Michel? Jean-Louis? Jean . . . er

161

. . . Jean? Er . . . Pierre?'

'Non, non, Madam. He is Spanish.'

And off you go again: 'Er Juan-Carlos? Er
. . . Juan? Er . . . Carlos? Er . . . Picasso?'

'Non, non, Madam. His mother was
German. He is called Gerhardt.'

'Oh . . . Gerhardt. I see. In Hendon. Well,
let me see . . . '

'No. I do not think you know him. You are
here since six years, and he only went there
last week.'

Back to the application to change your
driving licence. This time with disfavour on
the official side.

'So, you have learned to drive in
Angleterre?'

'Oui, Monsieur.'

'On the left?'

'Er . . . oui, Monsieur.'

'Not on the right?'

'Non, Monsieur. Except on one-way streets.'

'I beg your pardon?'

'One-way streets. Sens unique. Then we
drive on both sides of the road.'

'So you can drive on the right?'

'Oui, Monsieur.'

'And tell me something, Mademoiselle.
Why do the English insist on driving on the
wrong side of the road? And why do they eat
jam with their meals?'

'Jam with their meals?'

'Yes. Jam. My cousin — '

'Gerhardt?'

'No, not Gerhardt. Another one. And no, Mademoiselle, I do not think you know him. He was in York-shire and for his souper was given an omelette au fromage with strawberry jam and mon cousin, I can tell you, is neither a liar nor a fool. So why do you eat this?'

'Er, well . . . I don't know.'

The eyebrows go up and there's nothing for it but to launch into fulsome Franco-philia: 'That's one of the things I love about France, Monsieur. The French savoir-faire when it comes to the arts of the table, their elan, their panache, their complete éclat, their . . . '

'But you do not drive on the right?'

'Oui, Monsieur. In France everyone drives on the right.'

'Hmmm. And have you a certified copy of your Driving Test Report, along with an official translation of your birth certificate, a letter of Good Conduct from the UK authorities, postage stamps to the exact value of 7 euros et 31 centimes, a stamped addressed envelope, an official approval of your application and a recipe for le pooding? My wife would be grateful.'

So you retreat, defeated, to the kitchen

table where you forge documents, get drunk and repeat all this ridiculous rigmarole over the phone to your mates. And then the next week — because these offices are only open for a few hours per week — you go back and the whole spindle starts again. Anyway when Nickie did it, she reported back that the fonctionnaire had asked when she was getting her steering wheel changed over to the other side. Blimey. So French.

The Pirate came back two days later towing Teffi and two of his brothers in his wake — all of them staggering under the weight of cleaning products and groceries.

Having spent two days in solitary confinement, regretting the loss of my dinghy and blaming the Pirate for locking me up, I was furious. So I supervised the unloading and storing of the Pirate's shopping without looking at him. All right, all right, I'd been at fault. I shouldn't have called him a Standard Issue Class A Bastard. But he was at fault too. He shouldn't have provoked me, he shouldn't have called me a slut, he shouldn't have taken my papers. It was all his fault. Who insisted I come to the Caribbean in the first place? Crab-faced old toad. Verminous pond scum. How dare he make me into the baddie. Me? I'm nice. I'm the nice one. He's the fucking outlaw.

I'd had time to clean the rust off my bullets because I'm pretty sure firing rusty bullets can be dangerous. But more to the point, I'd had time to work out exactly how to load them into the gun. I'd even fired one into the sea during a storm the night before.

To hell with getting my passport back at gunpoint. If I wanted my life back, if I wanted the freedom to earn my own dosh and spend it how I liked, if I wanted to see my kids whenever I liked . . . There was only one thing to do with the Pirate.

Shoot him.

6

I didn't really mean it of course. I was just furious because he was so high-handed, and tooth-grindingly irritating. And in spite of everything he'd done to me, I had this horrible guilty itchy feeling of having been wrong-footed. Which made me even crosser, of course.

Worse, he didn't take me seriously. He just laughed and shrugged. Why couldn't he apologise? After all, he was the man. Of course it was all his fault — even if it wasn't. Which it was.

Over the next few days I became even more determined to settle the Pirate's hash. I even started seeing superstitious signs all over the island; all of them pointing the same direction. Signs like Stevie saying he couldn't work Sunday or his wife'd kill him, and Robert claiming his wife would have his guts if he went home drunk.

And when Suzie re-did my braids (two fine plaits either side of my face finished with very small gold beads) and I asked what she'd do if her man stole her money, she just laughed and said, 'Girl, he wouldn't survive to spend it!'

Then one of Marie-Rose's magazines had an article in it about shooting mad dogs and as for Bettina, well, she chuckled in her throat and said 'A man's place is in the wrong. Everyone knows that, Missis!'

All in all, I got the distinct feeling that various people would be more than happy to see me beat the Pirate at his own game — so I chugged about sulkily in Little Star, muttering to the mermaids and laying my plans, oblivious to the hangman's noose I was tying for myself.

Yes, I'd got my boat back — by dint of threatening to stay in bed and leave the Pirate to deal with the day trips himself. Not that he couldn't have coped with them of course. But he liked me doing it. One, it kept me in the office, and two, it left him free to roam at will.

So I was back into my routine: up at day break and flying off to the office in my dinghy. Well, not flying actually, because if the outboard motor had been serviced, which was doubtful, it certainly hadn't made any difference to its performance and my maritime progress still consisted of juddering up one side of a wave and sliding down the other rather than banging gaily across the surf-tops like everyone else.

Still, I didn't care. I told myself that it gave me time to get organised. I mean, you can't just shoot someone in between feeding the cat and filing your nails; you have to make a proper plan. Otherwise you might scare the cat or smudge your nail varnish. Not that I had a cat, of course. Or wore nail varnish, but I . . . oh well. You know what I mean, Philippa. Don't you?

Puttering up to the jetty near the office complex, I reminded myself that I didn't just want to shoot the Pirate. I wanted to escape. Otherwise it would have been straightforward — merely pull the trigger and send him down to Davey Jones's locker. Let him kidnap a squid.

So I needed a decent plan. I had to get hold of my papers and some money — cash or plastic, but preferably cash. By that time, I'd picked up the Pirate's distrust of banks and all large organisations. Cash is safer. You know where you are with cash and it is harder to trace.

I slid the dinghy into a gap at the jetty, got out and tied the mooring rope round the post in an especially large, especially difficult knot. I yanked it tight, feeling efficient and ready to kill.

'Organised!' I muttered to myself. 'Get organised!' Straightening up, I dropped the end of the rope untidily on the decking and threw my shoulders back.

Of course, I could still take the easy option and throw myself on the mercy of an Ambassador, but I was married to a corruption expert with long tentacles. As I strolled up the jetty I could almost feel them winding round my waist and dragging me into the deep blue briny. Bribing his way into an Embassy would be child's play for the Pirate. He'd easily kidnap me again — and the next day the papers would feature photos of wide-eyed innocent Embassy apparatchiks saying they hadn't seen a thing.

Ho hum. I bet the papers would use a hideous photo of me, too. Some incredibly old grainy snap featuring acne, dental braces, wrinkles and strange shadows under my eyes. I strolled into the office absent-mindedly forgetting to say hello to Marie-Rose on my way through the bar.

No, I wasn't ready to call the cavalry, but I was still determined to teach the Pirate a lesson, get even with him, show him single-handed that I could play hard ball as well as him, if not better. Yes, and I would get my money too, and my papers. All by myself.

Feeling tremendously Famous Five-ish, I smiled like a crocodile, flicked the lights on in the office and settled myself on one of the tall stools. Do we have a passenger list for today? Ah yes, here it is — reasonable numbers too. The season really was starting to pick up. I scanned the list perfunctorily.

I'd have to get into the safe and steal my papers. But where could I hide them? If the Pirate realised I'd stolen them back, wouldn't he merely find them and remove them again? And second time round, there was no saying where he might hide them. Or cripes, what if he decided to destroy them?

I shook my head to get rid of the mental picture of the Pirate cackling with glee as he keel-hauled my passport, buried the shredded pages of my address book on a desert island, slivered my bank cards with a cutlass and bounced my cheque books down the plank. Nightmare. I'd have to do some major Famous Fiving to prevent any of that sort of thing. Timmy the dog would have to bark at him. Then we could have lashings of ginger beer for tea.

But this wasn't an Enid Blyton adventure. I dragged my attention back to the office and made a note: get pliroma to check catamarans for drinking water. Now that visitor numbers were increasing we'd need more supplies. I wondered if anyone had ordered the rum punch mix. A party of factory workers from Wales had practically wiped out all our stocks last time I'd looked. Ah yes, there was a stack of boxes on the floor. I'd have to get one of the boys to make it up.

But I wasn't making anything up with the Pirate. I was still on the warpath. He wouldn't destroy my papers, I reassured myself. That was just me being silly. I'd leave them where they were for the time being. There was no point in arousing his suspicions. As long as he had my papers he would be confident that I couldn't leave the island. I would still have to break into the safe though, to check a) that my papers really were in it and b) that I could actually crack the safe whenever I felt the urge.

What was the time? I craned my neck to see the clock in Marie-Rose's. Not even 7am. Good, I had time for coffee before the first day-cruise passengers arrived. I called through the window to Mike to get me a coffee and a couple of croissants, and went back to checking the lists and sucking a biro.

The cash question was more straightforward. I mean frankly, why shouldn't I take a cut? I was working, wasn't I? Why shouldn't I get paid?

At that point, I felt like I'd covered all the angles. I gazed out of the office window across the bay. The sun was just coming up over the horizon, its rays looking for all the world like a child's drawing of a sun. So beautiful.

'Here you are, Missis,' said Mike, obligingly carrying a tray into the office for me.

'Thanks.'

'Lots of people today?'

'Not bad,' I said, 'What's happening about the rum punch?'

'Teffi's dealing with it, Missis. But we're out of orange juice.'

'No, I don't think so. There just wasn't room in the office for it. Have a look out the back. Here, you'll need the keys to the door.'

Mike found the orange juice and went off cheerfully to tell the others. They hated running out of drinks because then the passengers didn't tip them.

Feeling thoroughly organised and pleased with myself, I had my breakfast and strolled out to watch the pliroma bringing the catamarans round from refuelling, all ready for loading and boarding. The sun was higher now, and already burning off the early morning mist. The sea was sparkling and there wasn't a cloud in the sky. It was going to be another fantastic day.

By the next morning, I had devised a systematic book-cooking operation. By jigging the figures around, I could put more passengers on the day cruises than actually appeared on the booking lists and pocket the extra ticket money. The Pirate never counted passengers on or off the catamarans. In fact, he always destroyed the real lists and re-wrote them to show fewer passengers on paper than in reality. I just did the same.

It worked like a dream. No-one was looking over my shoulder and there were enough of Rabbit's friends and relations going on freebie trips each day to make accurate figures impossible in any case. I started lifting the money for one or two tickets, knowing that I'd gradually be able to steal more.

But after only a few days I had a problem. I didn't know where to hide my ill-gotten gains. The first day was easy because you can hide one or two banknotes anywhere, and I simply shoved them down my bikini top; it was fine, they didn't fall out or make crackling noises or anything. I just had to remember not to go swimming. I could hardly ask Bettina to iron a bra-full of wet greenbacks for me. She didn't launder cash.

The second day I stuffed them into a packet of cigarettes, and that was fine too because I don't smoke that much. But my stack of banknotes was increasing daily, and they were mostly small denominations, so before long I had a fairly major problem on my hands. I needed a secure hiding place. Either in the office or on the boat, because there wasn't anywhere else. I mean, you can hardly walk into a stranger's house and ask if you can secrete several hundred dollars behind their sofa, can you? And I couldn't ask Marie-Rose to look after it for me.

I did think about doing the gangster movie thing — wrapping the cash up in plastic bags and hiding them in the lavatory tank of a back-street bar. Too mad. Just imagine me wandering around all over the island whipping in and out of all the loos in all the bars . . . Apart from getting my hands wet, I'd be bound to break the damn stopcocks or something, and then every single loo on the island would be out of order. Which would mean someone would have to go round mending them and then they'd find my cash and pocket it quick smart. Hopeless. So I could hide my loot either in the office or on the boat. But both were dodgy.

There was precious little privacy in either place, and the Pirate was quite capable of carrying out a detailed search just on a whim. But there was nothing I could do about that. I had to rely on him being too wrapped up in the season to bother playing games for the time being.

So I got the potato peeler out again and sniffed round the Sun looking for likely hidey-holes. I didn't find anything clever because in the end I realised that using a cunning cash-cache would make urgent retrieval tricky.

So in the end I hid rolls of soft under the wooden bunk boards in my cabin, behind a large framed photo of the twins and in the galley cupboards. I slipped the cash between the pages of old newspapers and, folding them up, just shoved them to the back behind the saucepans, the buckets, the papers and the un-used everlasting tins of milk. No-one ever cooked more than boiled eggs on the Sun, so why would anyone ever even look in the cupboards?

I had another set of hidey-holes in the office. One under the lino, another round the back near the lavatory and yet another one behind the middle drawer in the Pirate's desk. Even if he found one cache, he'd never find them all.

Then I started a serious filching pro-gramme. Nothing was safe. I lifted cash any which way I could. In my new role of proud housewife I took to folding up the Pirate's shorts instead of kicking them out of the way, and I systematically took the second smallest bill out of his pockets. In bars, I filched notes out of the top pocket of his shirt under cover of sitting on his lap. I whipped cash off the top of transactions, and eventually my motto was any time, any place, any where . . . Whatever I saw I nicked and stuffed into my bikini top. Dollars of course. American ones. I wasn't interested in Caribbean dollars. (No use in Europe.)

And I still wasn't scared, although I should have been. But I didn't suspect the presence of submerged rocks, I just took the game at face value. Although I'm beginning to wonder now, Philippa, if the whole thing wasn't just an enormous double-bluff distraction move. I mean if he'd come on hot and strong with the lovey-dovey icky-stick, I'd have been overboard quicker than a politician bails out of a sex-scandal. As it was, I stayed in the game . . . God, must stop it, all this think and double-think makes your hair go kinky, and it's too late to change anything now.

Where was I? Yes, anyway, I turned my attention to the safe. I just couldn't figure it out. Where did he keep the bloody key?

One evening, after all the boats had come in, I started searching the office again. It had to be somewhere. I tapped on the wooden cupboard door which hid the safe. If only I could open it, I'd be able to see exactly what the safe looked like and figure it out. Would I need a key, or did you have to find a combination like in westerns where the bank robbers have to click and listen? If it was a dial thing, would I be able to hear it clicking? I ran my fingers round the edge of the wooden door, tugging and testing. It didn't seem that thick. I wondered whether I'd be able to prise it open or whether I'd have to smash the lock with a hammer.

'Wha-tyou-doin?' The Pirate had rolled into the office and was standing in the doorway with a large box of frozen prawns under his arm. There was no point in lying, so I brazened it out.

'Seeing if I could break into the safe,' I said rolling my eyes at him. 'What does it look like?'

'Wha-tyou looking for?' He raised his eyebrows and wiped the sweat off his forehead with a handkerchief. 'You not still wantin your passport?'

'It's mine,' I said crossly. 'Why shouldn't I have it? I could force you to give it to me tomorrow. All I'd have to do is contact the Consul or the Embassy . . . '

'You won-do that.'

'Don't be too sure of yourself!' I snapped. 'You don't know what I might do!'

He grinned back at me. 'You got guts!' he said admiringly. 'But the keys ain't here.'

'You mean, the keys to the safe?'

'No, I don-keep them in the office.'

Bugger! I flushed red with annoyance. Where were the bloody keys then, if not in the office? Surely not on the boat?

Like a mind reader, he grinned and shook his head. 'You won-find them! C'mere, Treasure. Have a prawn!'

Tucking the cardboard box under one arm, he reached out, pulled me close and kissed me. 'Be nice, baby,' he said, pulling my dress up. 'Come on . . . '

'Don't! Someone might come in . . . '

Laughing out loud, he kicked the door shut, grabbed my arms and pinning them together with one hand, swiftly pulled my dress up and snatched at my bikini bottom. Furious, I trod on his feet, kicked at his legs and, twisting away from him, grabbed the box of prawns and swung them at him. I missed, only making a passing connection with his shoulder. But it was enough to split the box open and he was showered with rock-hard, bright-pink, ice-cold, prickly pink prawns.

He stared at me in shock. He'd got so used to thinking he could grab me anywhere, anytime, it hadn't occurred to him that I might object to being hurly-burlied over the office desk. For a split second we just stared at each other and then we both started yelling. Me because I was furious about not finding the keys, and him because yelling was his second best hobby after sex.

'You bloody woman! You vache! You my wife, you my property, I fuck you whenever I want . . . '

'Don't you touch me! Who are you calling a cow? Have you seen yourself, you short-arsed, fat-bellied pig!'

The office door burst open and Tommy eagerly dashed in. 'Yes, Boss?'

'Get out!' We both screamed in unison. Behind him, the excited, curious faces of Marie-Rose and all her customers gaped at us as if frozen.

'Get out!' we chorused again.

Tommy beat it double quick and the Pirate lunged at me and grabbed a fistful of my dress, just at the hem. I tugged at it uselessly but he just laughed again and started reeling me in. I grabbed a pair of scissors and stabbed at his hands with them and he swore at me. I missed his hands and tore a jagged hole in the printed cotton and then I swore at him. He started laughing so much he let go, and I took my chance. I ripped the lid off the box of frozen prawns and flung the remaining contents at him.

'What the fuck?' he exclaimed, fending them off.

I didn't wait for anything else. I rolled backwards over the desk scattering papers and pens everywhere and stumbled towards the door.

'Come back here! I not finished with you yet!' he yelled and I looked back at him in fury, intending to yell something hurtful at him. Anything. You know, just hurt him, because he'd nicked my passport and wouldn't give it back to me. Just because I was frustrated and angry and hated him laughing. I must have inherited more of my father's temperament than I thought.

He stood there snorting like a bull. But stuck in his hair, just above his left ear, was a prawn. It looked like an earring. I couldn't help it. I just burst out laughing and he lunged forwards, yelling ferociously in Greek.

As I wrenched the door open, I heaved the desk towards me to stop him following me out of the door. Then I quick-stepped smartly out of the office and slammed the door shut behind me. Across the arcade, Marie-Rose put her hands on her hips and stared at me.

'And what are you going to do now?' she enquired. I crossed my eyes at her and laughed. I hadn't the faintest clue. Actually, I was pretty hungry. I'd been working all day and hadn't eaten since breakfast. I mean, I really like prawns. That was why he had brought a box of them into the office, of course. A peace offering.

For a split second I was tempted to call a truce. If he could only understand that I didn't want to leave, I just wanted my passport back . . . if only we could wind the whole film back and re-shoot the scenes differently . . .

But I could hear the noise of the office desk being shoved aside. In a second he would be after me out through the door, probably with his prawn earring still swinging. Cripes, I'd have to find some mayonnaise . . .

I spun round, and saw the padlock swinging open on its keeper. My heart beating like a steam train, I shoved the metal plate over the loop, slammed the lock through the loop and clicked it shut just as furious hammering broke out on the door.

Marie-Rose raised her eyebrows. 'You want a drink?' she drawled.

'No, too hot for me here,' I said, attempting to drawl back. The truth was of course, I didn't fancy being in the front row when the Pirate got out of the office. He was unlikely to be in his most melting mood. 'See you later.'

I knew they were all watching me, but I didn't give a damn. I was so disappointed at not being able to get into that sodding safe (let alone having been caught) that I was ready to scream and scream.

I stomped down the jetty looking for Little Star, but it had been blocked in. The Pirate had moored his fancy fucking speedboat onto my . . . I looked again. He had left the keys in the ignition. I could see the glittering keyring swaying to and fro as the Venus rocked up and down on the water.

I didn't think twice. I'd been longing to drive that boat. I knew exactly how; I'd watched everyone else driving speed-boats around for months, and with electric ignition, getting the motor started was hardly going to be a challenge. How typical of him, I thought scornfully, to double park it and leave the keys in the ignition.

No, Philippa, the keys weren't in it in case someone wanted to move the bloody thing. You can move a small boat any time you want to, keys or not. He'd left the keys in the ignition because he knew for a fact that no-one on the island would even think about touching his precious boat.

And he parked it wherever he wanted to because he was oblivious of the inconvenience he was causing to Ordinary Mortals who got around in Small Wooden Dinghies with Minuscule Fuel Tanks and Temperamental Outboard Motors. And of course, he didn't give a damn if he was forcing Ordinary

Mortals to spend hours fiddling about getting their Small Wooden Dinghies unparked because they wouldn't dare to take their husband's Flash Speedboat and leave him to fart-arse about with a Small frigging Wooden frigging Dinghy.

The hammering noises behind me had stopped. He was yelling his head off instead. 'Get me outa here! You bloody woman, I kill you! Get me outa here right now!'

I undid the mooring rope and stepped down off the wooden decking onto the nearest boat. Then I carefully walked over the other boats, pushed off with my foot and sat down in the seat of the Venus. As it drifted backwards out from the jetty, I simultaneously turned the wheel and the key in the electric ignition. Nothing happened.

The Pirate was still roaring like Vesuvius behind the flimsy wooden door and my heart thumped in my chest. Start, you margarine tub! Then I realised I'd forgotten the fuel switch. Oops! I turned the fuel on, rammed the key round again and thumped the dashboard for good measure. Finally, the monster sprang into life and I gave a shout of joy. I felt like Toad. Power! Speed! Freedom!

As I accelerated away from the jetty, I heard more furious yells and saw the Pirate standing on Marie-Rose's covered terrace shaking his fists at me. Christ, he looked fit for murder too. I gave him a cheery wave, opened the throttle up and bounced away over the tops of the waves.

But at the entrance to the port, heading for the Sun, I changed my mind. Why should I go back to the boat? That's exactly where he would come looking for me. I had the distinct feeling that making myself scarce would be the best option for the time being. In any case, it wasn't late, just about apèro time. Definitely time for a drink, in fact.

I turned out to the open sea. Perhaps I'd go over to one of the other islands. There were some decent bars there and I'd never been there on my own so it would probably take some time before he figured out where I'd gone and came to find me. But a glance at the fuel gauge told me that there wasn't enough gas to go that far. Thinking about it now, I probably should have checked the lockers. I'm sure he must have had a stash of extra fuel on board. I could have easily filled up the tank if I'd thought of it.

But anyway I changed course and headed for the most expensive hotel on the island, The Shells. Situated right up on the point, it boasted real grass lawns, golf buggies, flowers, rattan sofas with cushions, a grand piano and twinkling lights in the palm trees.

It was soothing, civilised and calm. Just what I needed after a hard day at the office.

Once out of sight of the complex buildings, I slowed down. If the keys weren't in the office, where were they? On the Sun? Or somewhere else? With someone else. With an old flame? An ex-lover? A lover? I rattled my fingers across the dashboard, thinking hard. Marie-Rose? Maybe she had the keys. The Pirate always swore she was just an old friend, and she certainly didn't treat him as if she was in love with him or anything like that. But you never know. Maybe the connection between them ran deeper than it seemed?

My thumb hit something under the dashboard and I swore. Sucking it, I bent down to see what it was and found a peculiar, flat box shape soldered to the underside of the dashboard. It wasn't well made either. In fact it looked decidedly homemade. The sides were rough and there wasn't a single right angle in sight.

Suddenly my heart turned over with excitement. Could this be . . . ? I felt around it with my fingers, and sure enough there was a space at the back . . . just big enough . . . I reached a bit further. Just big enough for a small bunch of keys, perhaps? I pushed my fingers into the gap, feeling all around and then touched something that moved. Eureka!

A small bunch of keys.

I pulled them out and grinned. No wonder the Pirate was livid. I'd finally got the keys to the safe. But then my face fell. I'd got them, but he knew I'd got them and he'd take evasive action: change the locks, hide the documents somewhere else, make sure I couldn't leave the Sun for a couple of days . . . ?

He was totally capable of locking me in a cabin or tying me to a bunk or something. But if I left them in their hiding place and went on nagging for them, perhaps he'd think I hadn't found them after all and he wouldn't find a new hiding place for them. That way, at least I'd know where they were. But if I left them there, how could I use them? I mean, apart from anything else, I had to check that they really were the keys to the safe.

Soap, I thought. Make imprints in a bar of soap. I'd have a drink, nick some soap (fingers crossed they hadn't installed a liquid soap dispenser) and then take some prints of the keys when I got back to the speedboat.

What I was actually going to do with the imprinted soap, I hadn't the faintest clue. Use a nail file to make a new key out of a suspender clip? Find someone else who knew how to make a key out of a soap imprint? Ring up a friendly bank robber for advice?

Well, I'd have to remember not to drop the soap in the sea, anyway.

I had rounded the headland by then and could see the lights of The Shells dancing and winking as the sun sank behind the island setting the sea aflame with its gold and pink rays. I shoved the keys back into their hiding place and cut the engine. No point in making a show of arriving in someone else's speedboat.

My hair was covered in sea spray, my dress was torn and apart from that I was only wearing a bikini and some old flip flops. Not exactly Vogue's ideal ensemble for drinks at The Shells. But my tan was even, I'd put on enough weight to regain my cleavage and I was still a natural blonde. I was also married to the Pirate. I threw my shoulders back. What did I care? I could do what I damn well liked.

I moored the speedboat between two larger ones at the end of the jetty, strolled up the raked sand path and sauntered through the garden looking for a table. I knew I'd be safe from a scene here. It wasn't the setting for a stand-up scream-fest. It was way too classy.

There was soft jazz playing, subtle floodlighting and coloured lights strung between the palm trees. Underfoot, the garden sand had been raked into intricate patterns and swirls. There were small groups of people sitting at the tables, ice clinking in their glasses. There was muted laughter and relaxed conversation.

I walked up the shallow steps onto the terrace, wondering if I could bag one of the sofas, but they were all occupied and I wasn't in the mood to share with a stranger, so I went and sat at the bar. I knew Mannie, the barman, anyway.

'Hello, Treasure, how you going?'

'Fine, and you?'

'Very fine, and what can I get you?'

'I don't know.' I shrugged and smiled. 'I just don't know. What's a really happy drink? A celebration drink?'

'Champagne?'

'Hmm . . . '

'Champagne cocktail?'

I grinned and nodded. 'You're a genius! The very thing!' Crossing my legs and wriggling my shoulders with pleasure, I twisted round so I could see who else was in the bar. No-one I knew. Just tourists.

'Hi there, are you waiting for somebody?' drawled a lazy voice from behind me. I straightened up and looked at him. Mr Dishy, definitely. Dark eyes, waving hair, full lips . . . tall, nice broad shoulders . . . in short, a Handsome Hunk.

If the Pirate saw me drinking with him, he'd go absolutely stark raving spanner. Sushi, even. Yes, sushi, Philippa: pale and gritty, wrapped up in black slime and firing raw fish germs. Excellent. That would show him.

I had to have someone to celebrate with anyway and with a bit of luck it would take the Pirate a couple of hours to find out where I'd gone.

'Mmm . . . no, I'm not waiting for anyone,' I husked, 'just feeling happy, that's all!'

Mannie, mixing my drink with his back to us, caught my eye through the mirrored back of the bar and raised his eyebrows. I stuck my tongue out at him. He grinned but still kept on shaking his head at me. I didn't give a toss. When he came back from answering the phone, I made him mix another cocktail for the Hunk, and we went and sat down at a table on the terrace.

We clinked glasses and I asked him where he was from. 'New Jersey,' he said, a nice American suburb. He was on holiday with two co-workers, telecoms engineers, and he was meeting them later for dinner. 'Would you care to join us, Ma'am?'

To be honest, he was about as fun as an old egg and cress sandwich. All he could say about the Caribbean was that it was a lot different from home, and he must have noticed my wedding rings, because he kept on calling me 'Ma'am' every second word. But he was seriously easy on the eye and if Mannie would only turn the music up, he might ask me to dance and that would be pretty nice, I thought to myself.

No, Philippa, of course the Pirate didn't dance! I told you, the only physical movement he ever undertook voluntarily was bulldozing. In fact, perhaps that's why he refused to move at any other time? Saving himself. Bloody hell.

I shoved the Pirate out of my mind and concentrated on Mr Dishy-But-Dim. I wouldn't mind leaning against him. The words washboard and six-pack inevitably sprang to mind as I inspected his body. It would be nice to dance again, and even nicer to dance with someone taller than myself, and covered with hard, young, well-brought-up, milk-fed, American flesh. Love? What's love got to do with it? Mr Dishy was destined to be a mere tool in my hands.

Dinner with him and his two colleagues? Yes, absolutely! I smiled at him. Eating dinner with three nice polite young men all on my own — very nice indeed-y. Might even get to dance with them all. I tucked my chair more firmly under the table and licked my lips. I should have locked the Pirate in the office months ago.

Oh don't be so shocked, Philippa. I wasn't planning on anything more than a little light flirtation. I was just buzzing from the thrill of rebellion. Same sort of lift you get from skiving off work to go to the hairdresser . . . Oops, sorry. Forgot you're the boss.

Anyway, what was I saying? Oh yes. I can't remember what we ordered, because we never got round to eating it. I can't even remember what the friends were like, or what we talked about, because just after we'd ordered, the Pirate strolled in through the gardens with Marie-Rose, Tommy and a large collection of his cronies and their womenfolk.

Mannie started flapping around calling for more waiters, tables were pushed together and suddenly the three of us quietly eating dinner together were sidelined by a long cheerful table of merrymakers scoffing lobster. At the head of the table sat the Pirate, gazing around the garden, hailing friends, inviting them to join him and simultaneously ordering dishes, proposing toasts, bullying everyone to eat more and introducing people to each other. He looked like a man with not a care in the world.

He also looked straight through me. Furious, I pretended to ignore him, pulling my chair round to show him my back and tossing my hair at Mr Dishy and pals.

'Do you know these guys?' asked one of them, gesturing at the Pirate's table.

'Which guys? Oh, you mean them?' I trilled. 'Over there?' I shook my head gaily. 'No, haven't the faintest clue . . . probably just package tourists on a day trip!'

My words fell into a gap in the music and echoed round the garden. I could feel the Pirate's eyes drilling into my spine. In the silence I heard a chair pushed back, and my three companions watched over my shoulder as he approached the table.

'Treasure!' said the Pirate, standing right behind my chair and caressing the nape of my neck possessively. 'My Treasure! There you are!' He smiled genially round the table. 'Thank you for entertaining my wife. I was er . . . locked in the office this afternoon, as you might say . . . '

The Americans laughed uneasily.

'But now I am free,' he added silkily.

'Absolutely, Sir!'

'Gosh, Ma'am, is this your husband?'

'I say, Sir, I hope you don't . . . '

The three boys were looking confused, but the Pirate smiled blindingly at them.

'Join us! I insist! You my guests! Come, Camille.'

His eyes bored into mine as I sat looking up at him. Everyone was watching us. If I refused, I'd look ridiculous. Out of the corner of my eye I saw some woman whispering to Marie-Rose and snickering. The men round the long table were smirking openly.

'Come!' said the Pirate, and Mr Dishy stood up obediently, along with his work colleagues from nice New Jersey. They were all ready to join the top table. The Pirate held his hand out and smiled as he met my eye. 'It is okay, Camille,' he said outrageously, 'You can come too. Promise. I take you to bed later!'

Everyone was watching. He had me beat and I knew it, so I smiled, tossed my hair back and stood up.

'Good girl,' he murmured, his eyes glinting in amusement. I pulled a murderous face at him but he was imperturbable. He took my elbow and we walked over to his table together with the three boys trailing behind us as the gang started barracking the Pirate about the size of his anchor. The Pirate laughed genially and threw himself back into his chair at the head of the table.

'Yes, she's a real woman!' he announced, pulling me down to sit on his knee. 'Caprices, moods, changing her mind all the day. Dirty girl, bad woman, needs a strong man, needs a real man!'

And when they stopped laughing over that one, he pulled me close to him in a vice-like grip. 'This my Treasure,' he said. 'Any fucker touch her, I kill him!'

There was a smattering of applause from the men and some banging on the table, and a shouted obscenity in Greek.

'Even if he is American!' added the Pirate, and guffaws of laughter exploded up and down the table. 'Hey you, get some chairs for my wife's friends!'

Of course, that finished Mr Dishy off. He and his mates left the restaurant rapido and I never saw any of them again. Not that I minded, I just felt sorry for them. The Pirate must have scared them stupid. Still, I suppose it gave them a good story to take back to their co-workers in nice New Jersey.

I shrugged and smiled as if I was in on the joke. But the Pirate hadn't finished staking out his territory by a long chalk. The feast was only just beginning and he insisted that I stayed on his knee, ate from his fork, drank from his glass and showed everyone my wedding rings. His hands ran possessively up and down my limbs, sometimes slipping inside my frock — and he played with my hair, tangling it down my spine and twisting it round his fat, powerful fingers.

To be honest I didn't mind. In a weird way I even understood him. If the other guys thought he was even slightly complacent, they would be perfectly capable of moving in behind his back despite the fact that I was knocking on middle-age and rapidly becoming as bad tempered and insane as the Pirate himself.

I smiled, leaned against him, ate lobster, drank wine and let him play his games. Then Marie-Rose told a joke about a priest and I remembered another one and leaned forward eagerly.

'Oh, I know one . . . '

'Hey you,' yelled the Pirate at Tommy, cutting right across me. Everyone fell silent, looking at us.

'This is a great joke, about a priest in a plane . . . ' I continued, but the Pirate cut straight across me again.

'Take my wife back to boat now,' he ordered flatly. He pushed me off his knee so I had to stand up, but kept an iron grip on my wrist, and from the other side of the terrace, Mannie shrugged and mouthed 'you asked for it'. I stuck my nose in the air and hummed loudly.

'You hear me, Tommy?'

Tommy flushed red and dropped his eyes

to the table. 'Yes, Boss,' he muttered.

I tried to snatch my arm out of the Pirate's rock hard fist and failed.

'Let go, you're hurting me!' I said furiously. 'You fucker . . . '

'If you two lovebirds don't stop squabbling we'll have to throw you both in the sea,' said Marie-Rose. 'Pass the salad, Robert, and the potatoes too if you can reach them. Sit down, Camille. And as for you . . . ' she raised her eyebrows comically at the Pirate. 'Behave yourself!'

Various people laughed nervously, and the Pirate looked at me. I raised my eyebrows.

'You wan me to take you?' demanded the Pirate and the light of battle was in his eye. He'd seen off the Americans, he'd made it quite clear to all his cohorts that I was his exclusive property and now he wanted capitulation from me, in public. If I refused, he was capable of forcing me. I had no clear idea how, but I was uneasily aware that he wouldn't accept defiance — not right now, not in front of all his cronies. There was way too much riding on it.

I smiled at him brilliantly. I had the gun, I had the bullets and what's more I'd polished them all up nice and shiny. I knew where the keys were too, so the safe was as good as open. He didn't know it yet, but the deck was completely stacked my way. What was the point in defying him?

'You know I do,' I purred outrageously. 'I always want you to take me!'

The table exploded into loud guffaws of laughter and giggling and someone shouted 'But not here!'

'Not on the table!' yelled Robert.

'Let me finish my dinner first!' called someone else.

The Pirate went on staring at me for a long minute. I shrugged and raised my eyebrows and then finally he shook his head and laughed out loud.

'Come, sit down, eat! What a fucking woman!'

'Santé!' said Marie-Rose.

7

The lobster party continued with no more dramas, and after the last of the champagne was finished, the other guests had gone and we were all beginning to yawn, the Pirate held his hand out and I took it and we smiled at each other. His face softened and for a split second I thought he was going to say . . .

But he just shook his head. What a relief. We walked slowly through the moonlit gardens arm in arm. I was too tired to argue with him and anyway I didn't feel like it any more. I was glad he was there to help me into the boat, drive it home and help me climb into bed. I'd had quite enough rebellion for one day.

I yawned and leaned against him as he manoeuvred the Venus out from the jetty. He looked down at me, smiled and slipped his arm around my shoulders as he accelerated over the moonlit water back to the Sun. On board he steered me off to his pit without another word, and the subject was never mentioned again. By either of us.

I never asked how he escaped from the office. When I got there the next morning, there were no signs of him having broken the door down. The bars over the windows were still intact and the lock was still in place. Inside, all the papers had been picked up, the desk was back against the wall and the prawns had gone. Swept up and binned? Or swept up and fed to the tourists? Probably the latter. Anyway it all looked the same as usual. Perhaps a tad cleaner. I suppose the prawns must have melted and left little pools of fish juice on the floor; one of the pliroma must have had to swab the decks.

The only difference was that he never again left the office padlock hanging on the door. Apart from that, nothing changed.

What can I say, Philippa? It was the height of the season. Life went on. I worked in the office, the Pirate bowled about swearing and sweating, the pliroma toiled away on the catamarans feeding and watering an everlasting stream of tourists, and I didn't have a chance to check if the keys were still in their hiding place or not. To be honest, even if I'd had the chance, I wouldn't have had the time, we were all so bloody busy.

Twice I found the office filled up with wooden crates which I was told contained T-shirts. Bloody heavy, bloody clanky, metallic-sounding T-shirts, I said to myself. But I didn't even have the time to investigate them. I kept my mouth shut, my nose clean, and my fingers out of everything except the till.

But I was uneasily aware that my hidden loot could be discovered any minute and confiscated. And if that happened the Pirate would have the drains well and truly up. So under cover of all the extra correspondence flooding through the office, I started posting cash to bank accounts in France and England. I simply folded it into letters asking them to pay it into my account.

I bet you're shuddering, aren't you? The employee with her fingers in the till. But I didn't count it as stealing. I was working just as hard as anyone else and I never saw a penny in wages. Not a sniff. The Pirate swore he was paying it into an account for me but since he refused to give me any account details I was sure my salary was a load of old baloney and felt completely justified in helping myself because whenever I asked him, it was the same thing.

'Can I have some cash?'

'Wha-for?'

'Oh, I don't know. Just in case. I mean, I might want to buy a postcard, or a stamp, or a packet of cigarettes.'

'You don-need cash for that.'

'But what if I want to play the juke box or something?'

'What jo-box? There snot jo-box here.'

'No, I know, but if there was . . . '

'Well there ain't.'

'Well, what about your birthday?'

'Whabou-tit?'

'Well, what if I want to buy you a birthday present?'

He smiled at me then. 'You wanna gimme present?'

'Well I might want to,' I said pulling a stupid face. 'You never know.'

'Mon oeil! You wanna murder me. I know you!' he said. 'But I think abou-tit,' he murmured, pulling me close. 'You bad woman, gimme a kiss.'

What can you do with a man who knows you want to murder him and still keeps on asking for kisses? Okay, okay you'd have called Interpol, or Interflora or Inter-the-breach, or some such sensible thing. I didn't. I just laughed as his arms went round me again and kissed him back.

If only he'd given me my passport then! We'd have been saved such mountains of trouble. It really was the only fly in the ointment. Well, not a fly, more like a dinosaur. I just couldn't stand being held prisoner. I mean, given the choice I might even have stayed. As it was, my missing passport itched and scratched at the back of my mind so that

I was ripe for anything. Even murder.

Looking back, I put it down to tiredness. We were all getting tired, God knows, as the season progressed. It was relentless; getting up with the dawn, working through the heat of the day and not getting to sleep until nearly midnight, seven days a week. No wonder we were all beginning to droop. Not the Pirate of course. He's never drooped in his life. He doesn't know what the word means!

In spite of his vast girth and outrageous Pernod consumption, he seemed to be everywhere at once, directing and yelling orders, snatching up booking sheets and beguiling tourists into going on day cruises, pinching taut teenage buttocks and supervising the loading and unloading of endless crates from the fleet. He seemed to have unlimited energy.

He ran most of his empire from Marie-Rose's bar, where he could keep an eye on me in the office, the fleet in the bay, and the tourists on the beach. But he turned up all over the islands, buzzing about in his speedboat and panting into the least likely places just at the very moment when he wasn't wanted. The pliroma knew this habit of his and kept strictly to their itineraries, but new people were often taken by surprise. On the island, he was just as omnipresent, arriving on his scooter just when people thought he was safely taking a siesta on the Sun.

'I keep the fuckers guessing,' he said with relish. 'So they don-cheat me.'

'Really?' I asked, my bikini top stuffed with swag. 'What makes you so sure?'

'Don-worry. I know everything that goes on here. I even know what you sendin in those letters.'

'What letters?'

'Pos-toffice tol me. You sendin lot of letters to Europe thee-stays.'

'So?' My spine was crawling; all the little hairs were standing up. 'I write to the boys. What's wrong with that?'

We were waiting for the day cruises to come back, sitting on the wall of the shark enclosure eating melting ice cream and gazing out to sea. He wiped his mouth on the back of his hand and gave me a patient look.

'Don-lie. You sendin them money. I know you.'

I shrugged and licked at the dripping strawberry swirl. 'Just a bit. Not much. Just some pocket money now and again.'

He finished off his melon sorbet and tossed the soggy cone to the sharks. 'I know you clepsi-clepsi,' he said beginning to massage my shoulders lazily. 'Thas why you ask me for cash. For your skids. Well, I don-cair. You takes a bit. No problem. But I watchin you!'

I chucked the rest of my ice cream after his and twisted round to look at him.

'Why don't we stop all this?' I asked him suddenly. 'You give me my papers back, pay me properly like you pay the others, and I'll stop spending my time trying to get into the safe and nicking ten dollar bills to send to England. Why can't we just call it quits?'

Putting his hand up to shade his eyes from the sun he looked at me, and caressed the side of my face. 'You beautiful woman,' he said softly. 'You my wife. My Treasure.'

'Quits?' I held my right hand out but he didn't take it.

He laughed then and shook his head. 'No, you think I'm crazy? You stay here with me.'

Just then Mike came panting over from the office. 'Mars is coming in, Boss. And I think I see Uranus just behind.'

'Okay, Mike. You go down to jetty. We coming.'

The moment was gone. He liked to keep his finger on the pulse and his foot up the backside of his multifarious business interests. He liked to see everyone slogging it out.

But just as everyone was wondering how long they could keep it up, the tidal waves of tourists began to abate, and at the same time, letters began to arrive from Europe. The hottest news was Nickie's. Her divorce had come through and she'd married the geography teacher. Sailing teacher. Anyway the man with the magical gift for mending bicycle tyres.

A far cry from her first wedding, she wrote. That time, she'd dragged her prize back to her parents' house and done the whole white wedding whoosh in a C of E church. Halternecked meringue, bridesmaids, flowers, photographer, be-ribboned Cadillac, Leaning Tower of Pisa cake, speeches, and a huge reception in a tent all paid for by Muthar in a blancmange hat and Farthar at the bottom of a vat of whisky.

This time, she and Fiona had raided a theatrical costumiers for feather boas and after a brief ceremony at the Mairie, Fiona had coerced the hippies into organising salads and nut bread while Nickie and her new husband had eaten vast quantities of chocolate gloop out of an antique china po. Apparently to acknowledge that being married means eating a lot of shite.

Nickie also wrote a long screed saying that she'd had hell's own job of re-homing her neighbour's cats. Yes, the white villa woman had given up waiting for her husband and had run off with the local pizza chef taking her kids but leaving the felines behind on the grounds that they wouldn't like living in a Paris slum. She herself could face this horror with equanimity because she was in love for the first time in her life, reported Nickie, po-faced.

Nickie couldn't take the cats in herself as she was already having problems with Maxie-dog. Sick to the back teeth of wearing rags and reeking of cheap red wine, she and the teacher wanted to head back to the UK, but only if she could take Max. She'd read somewhere that the law had changed.

'But I don't care, Milly,' she wrote. 'If I can't do it legally, I'll smuggle him back. I'm not leaving him behind. I couldn't bear it.'

'Fuck em,' said the Pirate when I told him about it. 'I'll get Rudi on the job.'

'Rudi?'

'Animal fing. What you wan, he get it. Lion? Tiger? Talking monkey? Rudolph snows how to geddit. Anywhere in the world. No problem.'

'So this Rudolph the Red Nosed Animal Wrangler could smuggle Max into the UK for Nickie?'

'Smuggle a whole herd of fuckin elephants into the UK if you wannim to.'

That was the Pirate. If you wanted to buy a black market diamond, or smuggle a tap-dancing tortoise into China, or sell a batch of only slightly faulty condoms or trade your revolver up, he was your man. And if he couldn't oblige you himself, he always had a mate that would. A cousin, a brother, or a pal from the army. He made me laugh.

'Rudi'll get your lezzie friend's dog outa France. Where's he gotta go?'

He looked quite disappointed when I said it didn't matter.

Shortly after that, I got a letter from Harriet. 'Sax on the Sofa' hadn't sold as well as Daniel had hoped, and Harriet had been asked to lead a series of percussion workshops in Berlin, so they were heading back to Europe. One of the littles (I think she has three kids, but it could easily be four by now) — one of the littles had won a talent contest and was to appear on television. The Russian nanny's passport had been stolen resulting in what she said Daniel described as 'major amounts of dragsville', and Daniel's old pal Rexie Kent was putting a neat little combo together to tour the Netherlands with a Jazz Age nostalgia show.

Harriet thought he would enjoy it tremendously and that it would do him good to play live again for a while. Oh and by the way,

Aunt Lottie was looking for new lodgers because the Italian dancers had gone back to Milan. Did I know anyone? Massive hugs, Harrie.

Putting the letter down and gazing out at the emerald sea, I guessed it wouldn't be long before she was asking how I was getting on with my piano and when I was going to join them in Prague or Vienna or Lyons or Brussels. Harriet had completely ignored my marriage to the Pirate. Even the twins didn't get a mench.

Typical. I tore the letter into tiny squares and chucked them overboard. I decided to get in touch with Aunt Lottie though. It had been ages since I'd last seen her and I felt a bit guilty, so I sent her an arty postcard apologising for not keeping in touch and promising to write properly soon.

I got a scrawled note from Fiona. She was working la vendange again — grape picking. Back-breaking, skin-searing work. A bloody nightmare involving six o'clock starts, masochistic overseers, sun-dried sandwiches for lunch and getting home not a second earlier than nine o'clock at night. I felt for her. I really did. Incredibly hard work. Those long lunches in a shady courtyard with groaning tables and gallons of bonhomie don't exist outside telly adverts. In my experience you take your own baguettes, dump them at dawn and crunch them at noon. Still, the pay wasn't bad and at least the vendange doesn't last long. Just a few weeks.

Then Nickie wrote to say she had solved the Max problem. Fiona was going to keep him while he got all his vaccinations, and then bring him over to the UK in the summer. They were having a major leaving bash in the village, with a barbecued sheep and a sozzled accordion player. Her kids were happy she said, and liked their new dad.

But she covered several pages describing the bureaucratic nightmares involved and the general awfulness of leaving France — and what could I say? What else could she do? You can't go on struggling forever, and her parents were going to bail them out. If they moved home.

Lucky Nickie. Her nice solid Telegraph-reader parents were standing by with the Elastoplasts. I hadn't heard from my father since a scribbled postcard six months back in reply to my letter telling him I'd got married: 'Congratulations darling. Hope to fit in visit after Sydney biz — sometime in autumn. Keep your Joanna up. Love, D.' D for Daniel, not for Daddy.

Nickie said she was jealous of me. To her my life was one long round of luxury — all turquoise sea, soft white sand and cocktails. But to all extents and purposes I was still a prisoner and the chains irked me, even if they were fashioned out of conch shells, ice cream cones and sun lotion.

I tried to explain it to her once but by that time she'd moved back to the UK, and she just replied that all women were prisoners and at least I didn't have to slog through the rush hour at 7.30 every morning.

The chains were weighing me down, but she was right. I mean, I was living on Easy Street. Why would I miss Skid Row? I hadn't driven a car since I'd left France. There were only a few cars on the island anyway, and what did I need with one? I hardly ever went anywhere inland and it was easier and quicker to whizz round the coast in my dinghy than bothering with the heat, dust and inconvenience of the roads. As for slogging through the rush hour, buzzing across the bay in a dinghy at 6am when the sky was pale, the air clear and the sea fresh and sparkling around me . . . that hardly compared to sitting in tail-backs listening to some moron detailing the morning's traffic jams, did it?

So I did nothing. I said nothing. I even agreed when Nickie asked if Fiona could set up a pottery shop in my house in France. Why the hell not? Fiona might as well use the place and she swore blind she would insure it this time. Not that it mattered. I couldn't see myself living there again, even if I did manage to escape from the Pirate.

Anyway Nickie had moved back to England where she had ended up on the south coast so that her teacher-man could drool over the sailing boats. Admittedly she wasn't thrilled to be doing the school run, but she was enjoying her temporary job with an architect and after years of scrimping, was really thrilled by being able to browse the special offers in Tesco. Even if the central heating boiler did have to be repaired every single public holiday.

But communications were strained. The odd letters and postcards I managed to send were pretty meaningless and took weeks to reach Europe. And I received very few replies. Writing letters is such a drag. But then came an overdue revolution. One of the bars installed a computer for their customers and before long various others followed suit.

It would be going too far to say that we actually had an internet café, but suddenly I could get on-line and sod the Pirate's computer. I got myself a hotmail address and bingo, I could finally reach the outside world without the Pirate sticking his oar in. I was back in touch with Nickie on a daily basis because she had email at work.

The first time I sat down at one of the computers in the café, Tommy didn't do anything. He just went on twisting two straws together and looking out to sea. But he must have made a full report back at base, because later on when we were eating lunch, the Pirate suddenly stabbed at me with his fork.

'What you doing with computers in Jack's?'

'Surfing the web, reading the news, looking at the weather forecast,' I shrugged. 'Why?'

He stuffed a great forkful of feta cheese into his mouth and disembowelled a bread roll while he was calculating his next attack.

'Why you wannnews?' he demanded.

'Why not? Why shouldn't I read the news?'

He shouted for more Pernod and squeezed lemon onto my fish. 'Is all porn, on Internet. You shouldn't be reading it,' complained the Pirate.

I just laughed. 'Jesus, talk about the pot calling the kettle black! Pornography! What about you? Your bloody boat is practically sinking under the weight of the porn vids and magazines you've got stacked away in there, and you accuse me of surfing the web looking for the stuff? Give me a break!'

He changed tack. 'You know nothing! I am lonely man. I live alone, I stay alone many years with no-one, with nothing. Okay, I have

212

some pictures, pretty girls, nice titties, but . . . '

'I think I'm going to be sick. You've never stayed alone in your life. You're a one-man fucking machine. You wouldn't know what celibacy meant if it jumped up and bit you in the balls!'

He abandoned that cast completely then, and gave me his most pathetic look. 'You trying to leave me.'

'I just want my passport back.'

'No.'

I shrugged, he shrugged, and we finished lunch together. It was bizarre. By that time we'd reached the point where we could have these arguments without even really getting angry with each other. I suppose he didn't have to get angry because he thought he had the whip hand and I didn't get angry because I secretly knew I could leave any time I wanted.

'If you try and stop me using the computers,' I said thoughtfully as we finished our wine, 'I will cry. A lot. All the time. Everywhere. In the office, in all the bars, in all the restaurants. I will cry in the market, in the shops and in the street. I will cry and cry, and I will never smile again.'

That stumped him. I couldn't have done it of course. I'm not naturally lachrymose and I can't imagine ever crying for more than about two minutes. But I was gambling on him classing feminine vapours in with scorpion bites, under the heading of Avoid At All Costs. He eyed me up and down and I gazed at him limpidly, attempting to look like a woman only holding back floods of tears by a sheer miracle.

'I only want to read the news,' I gasped, trying to hold back my laughter and hoping he would think I was holding back the entire Atlantic Sea.

'Okay, okay. You read news!' he snapped. 'But don-try anything. No dating sites!'

I smiled at him. 'Okay, I promise. No dating sites.'

'Bloody woman!' he muttered, and stumped off to check on a bread delivery.

So that was that. I still didn't have the password for the office computer, but at least I was back on-line.

Nickie's kids were old enough to be able to look after themselves a bit more now and their lives were pretty well straightened out. She and her new husband had settled in fine and he had fallen on his feet, very quickly finding a job training people to teach sailing. Within months (and with Muthar and Farthar's help) they'd bought a house, and although the mortgage was heavy, both of them were working. She'd started off working for a translation agency and soon been taken on directly by one of their clients, which meant more money and paid holidays, and now she was moving up the corporate ladder.

Her life sounded exotic to me. Imagine wearing shoes and socks, having winter clothes, staying clean and tidy all day long. Imagine not having to get into a boat and be splashed with sticky seawater on your way to work. I liked the idea of a house with closed windows, a house with no dust blowing in constantly because it was too hot to keep the windows closed.

She got up every morning, had a shower, did her hair, put on things like shoes and tights and jackets, sorted breakfast, let the cat out, and then drove her car on tarmac streets, with traffic lights and white lines and shiny street signs. She went to work in an office with clean carpets and coffee machines and everyone freshly washed and dressed in clothes which had been ironed.

She went to the gym, and the cinema, and the theatre, and these places weren't just shacks built out of corrugated iron and conch shells, they were real solid brick buildings with doors and shiny floors. Proper places with mains electricity, car parks and lifts. I was sick to death of sand creeping in everywhere, of wearing salty clothes and having to tie my hair up because it was impossible to keep it clean for more than five minutes.

I envied Nickie her sane and normal life. Think about it, Philippa! That's what I was trying to explain to you. I started off with do-lally Daniel and Muma, moved on to potty Aunt Lottie and then to Fiona and Nickie in France, and ended up getting kidnapped by the Pirate. Of course Nickie's life sounded exotic to me. I mean, even at the record company I never used to start work until at least midday. I've never had a normal life, and I wanted one like Nickie's. Like yours! Wouldn't anyone?

I wanted to sit in the rush hour listening to the radio too. I wanted a sofa, I wanted English television, I wanted to be able to go round the corner for a curry. I was sick to the back teeth of eating bad food; locally caught fish and limp salad and badly prepared vegetables. I wanted to spend three hours picking my way through the millions of cheerful tins and packets in a Western hypermarket; I wanted to go up and not down stairs to bed. I started to fantasise about traffic jams, cold rain and cosy firesides. I wanted Guy Fawkes and roasted chestnuts and Christmas shopping in the snow.

I'd had enough of living in cramped spaces, of never being able to get properly cool and clean, of swimming instead of having a bath. I was sick of wearing flip-flops and having insect bites on my legs. I wanted a fresh green garden with a muddy lawn and a herbaceous bed. I wanted order above all.

People think living on a Caribbean island is paradise, but it isn't by a long chalk. You can buy drinks and bikinis, of course. Yes, there are lots of tourist activities during the season, but what if you don't like sailing or fishing? And what if you can't sunbathe because of having pale, sun-sensitive skin? And what if you spend too much time alone, waiting for someone who doesn't tell you where he's going or when he'll be back?

Being in contact with Nickie made me realise that I was lonely. The island was crawling with people but I didn't have anyone to talk to.

There were the locals of course but I only knew the pliroma and they all thought I was lucky: a rich and glamorous European woman who didn't have to work for her living. Which I was, if you ignored the fact that I was being kept prisoner and I was actually working full time for no pay at all.

The resident Europeans included a handful of couples who had dropped out and were bringing up grubby children on tatty, unseaworthy yachts on about fourpence a day, and saying dreamily that it was better than living in Croydon, or Milan or Ghent or wherever they'd come from. I suppose I could have made friends with them, but they reminded me too much of Muma and Daniel. The whole impracticality of it, the dreams, the travelling. What would happen if one of them died?

There was also of course a selection of dodgy men: illiterates, emotional cripples, runaways, criminals, rich kids escaping the pressures of life in the fast lane, men in love with the sea, rejects, drop-outs and drunks, drug addicts, dreamers, and losers; all sorts of flotsam and jetsam had washed up on the rocks here. But there was no way the Pirate was letting me near any of them. And frankly, why would I want to get near them? I already had a dodgy man. Why would I want another one?

Then there were the business people. First-worlders who had seen an opportunity to invest and make it big. They were the ones who arrived with financial backing, built the smart hotels and ran them efficiently, making a nice profit and spending two or three months back in Civilization every summer. They sent their children to boarding schools, lived in air-conditioned flats and rode around in covered, air-conditioned boats so they always looked clean and well presented.

They fascinated me. How did they do it? How on earth did they organise their lives so well? Half of me wanted to be like them, and yet I knew that I wasn't cut out to wear a pencil skirt. Also, the Pirate was right — I just didn't care about money. It's never been a motivating factor in my life. So these incredibly high-income, low-sweat people obviously wouldn't appreciate me or my faded flip-flops. They certainly wouldn't find mutiny an amusing career-option.

And in between were the self-contained ones who had simply arrived, liked the life and stayed. There was a couple out by the mangrove swamps who ran a tortoise hospital, there was Robert and his wife selling lurid sunset paintings, and a gay couple who lived the other side of the airstrip and apparently wrote novels together. All of them were incredibly quiet and I didn't really know any of them to talk to — not to talk to properly I mean.

So I didn't have any friends on the island. Not close ones like Nickie. The only person I ever really talked to was the Pirate, but the passport business was hanging over us like a cloud by then and we always ended up stalking off in different directions.

Marie-Rose watched us, and in return I watched her and wondered. She didn't look like a dropout or a refugee from the real world. No, she was way too stylish and effective for that. She had arrived with her husband, clung to the rocks when he left and built the bar up gradually, starting off with a roadside shack. Rumour had it that she was connected with the Pirate in more ways than one, and I wondered about that but I could never see it myself. She was way smarter than me. In every way. Far too smart to tie herself up with a pirate.

It was strange about Marie-Rose. I couldn't help liking her but I didn't trust her further than I could have thrown the Titanic. She definitely knew more than she was letting on and I wasn't sure where her loyalty lay. If I told her what I was planning, would she tell the Pirate? Probably. So I steered clear of her.

Out of season, the island was almost deserted because we weren't near enough to an international airport to attract the cheap package holiday companies. In season we got invaded by sailing enthusiasts: people who loved messing about in boats and wanted to do it on a millpond so that it wouldn't matter if they couldn't actually sail a spoon round a coffee cup, let alone a schooner round the Caribbean.

They provided the local boys with endless excitement because they ran aground so often on the coral reefs surrounding the island. Then the guys would all jump into their boats and race for the floundering vessel because the first one to get a rope on it could claim pieces of eight for towing it off the reef.

I used to daydream about a Nickie substitute turning up on a tourist charter. A meeting of minds, two people together laughing at the absurdity of the whole place. The pair of us sniggering at the ridiculous swimsuits, the rich kids slumming it, the Americans drifting in by mistake, and the Barbie girls wearing make-up on the beach.

But it never happened. The only female who ever turned up on her own was Sylvia, and she turned out to be a Shark.

The typical Shark is found all over the world: a tough-skinned old blonde with a fin between her shoulder blades. But for some reason they're particularly prevalent in the Caribbean. In fact, the place is infested with them. You can spot them a mile off. Brillo pad peroxide hair, a leather-deep tan, all-weather lipstick, sugar-pink bikini and enough plastic flowers to sink the Titanic.

But Sylvia was brunette. And fat. Oh all

right. Buxom. Curvy. Probably more Sophia Loren than Hattie Jacques; but she looked like a poxy mountain to me. All heaving bosoms, butter-soft skin, doe-eyes and flashing white teeth. Unlike your normal straightforward Shark, she didn't flutter and kitten, she sort of glided heavily and silently through the depths. Like a whale. A huge, malevolent man-eating whale with bits of seaweed growing on her spine.

Now the Pirate is not and never has been a millionaire, but he's not exactly a pauper, either. So he didn't escape Sylvia's tender notice. She floated round his bank balance, sniffed at me with her piggy little nose and and decided that he would do nicely and I was irrelevant.

I was in Betty's one day, emailing Nickie, when she drifted lazily past my chair and asked if I was on holiday.

'No, I live here . . . ' I said, hitting send and leaning in front of the screen. I hate people reading my emails.

'Mmm. How lovely for you,' she said without smiling. 'How did you come to live here?'

'Well, I er . . . married someone.'

'A local?'

'Er, no . . . a tourist operator.'

That's what I always said, because it was

slightly true — if you ignored the smuggling of packages on and off the day cruises, the connections with dodgy strongmen from Venezuela, the clanking crates in the office, and a financial set-up which would make any normal businessman's eyes pop.

'Really. Which one, dear?' Sylvia's eyes were scanning the surroundings, ensuring that she wasn't missing the slightest morsel of drifting plankton while she calculated the cost of my clothes — probably about $4.50. Or maybe less. She then, with one withering shudder, made it clear that she thought I wasn't worth much either.

Oh God, how I hated that woman! I couldn't stand anything about her. Her voice, the way she looked me up and down, the way she called me 'dear' . . . From start to finish she set my teeth on edge.

As she meant to, of course. Because, looking back, I think she was probably just as bored and lonely as I was — I mean why else would she spend so much time deliberately winding me up? It was merely her way of passing the time.

'Excuse me, I'll be back in minute,' I lied. 'I think someone's calling me to the phone.'

To be honest, I thought that would be the end of it. I logged off, told Betty to put her Perrier on my tab and went back to the office thinking I'd never see her greasy fat arse again. But she turned up at the complex later that afternoon wearing a micro bikini that might have been stapled in place, it was stretched so tightly over her blubbery flesh.

She was enquiring about prices for day cruises and as fate would have it, practically fell into the arms of the Pirate. He was just rolling in from the jetty as she drifted into the shade and swam right into him, murmuring insincere apologies.

'You okay?' he asked, grabbing hold of her enthusiastically, and swaying from the impact.

'Darling man, you saved me. I might have broken my arm. I am so grateful, you must let me buy you a drink. I insist. No, please let me introduce myself: Sylvia, and you are . . . ?'

You could practically see the mud churning up from the seabed as her gills went into hyperventilation mode. Vomit, vomit, vomit.

I watched from the open office door as the Pirate looked her up and down appreciatively and smiled, showing all his nice white false teeth. 'I the Captain,' he announced. Then he squeezed her massive soft arm and took her off to the bar for a Pernod.

She caught my eye over his shoulder, lazily lowered her eyelids at me, and gave me a long slow triumphant smile showing all her rows and rows of horrible sharp fishy teeth. A

Shark. A Shark in disguise.

Not a problem, I told myself. Not at all. I got the Tippex out, re-cooked the books and slipped another hundred dollars into my bikini top. Fuck her. Fuck him. Fuck the pair of them.

'You know what she does?' I emailed Nickie, 'to keep her revolting tan paint-perfect, she threads herself onto a spit and cooks herself on the beach. She's probably got a battery-operated spit-turner out there. The only thing she doesn't need is basting, the fat oily cow.'

'Yeah and I bet the spit bends double under her weight,' said Nickie, loyally.

'Yeah, she must weigh a ton,' I typed furiously. 'You should see the size of her hips. Keeping that lot covered up must be keeping the entire American cotton picking industry in profit.'

'Frilly beach skirt?' asked Nickie.

'Looks like a walking circus tent,' I assured her.

'Wrinkles?'

'Far too fat. Her skin is stretched as tight as pig guts over a cooked sausage.'

'Sounds like a dog turd,' said Nickie.

I cracked up. 'Yep,' I giggled. 'A grilled one. Inner thighs exactly the same shade as shoulders. You can almost see those little diamond patterns from the grill . . . '

'I bet she has them surgically removed every winter,' said Nickie.

'Shouldn't think so,' I said. 'Probably just sands them off with a Black and Decker before getting herself re-plastered.'

'Bet she buys special ultra-pong scent to drown out the stench of char-grilled flesh. Have a look in her bag,' chortled Nickie.

'I can't find her bag,' I told her. 'It's disguised as a plastic rose factory. She's sprouting all over: beachwear, towels, bags, sandals, lighters, cigarette packs, sunglasses, Alice bands and you can hardly see her horrible black hair for plastic rosebuds; she's dripping with floral designer accessory sets. You know, the Armani spit-roast timer with the matching Ambre Solaire spatula and grill tongs.'

Ripping her to shreds with Nickie calmed me down, but the next morning Sylvia was back. This time asking for the Pirate's advice about investing in a yacht. And that afternoon she wanted to know about buying property in the Caribbean, and the day after that it was learning to sail, followed by queries as diverse as investing her alimony, phoning New Zealand, avoiding death tax, handling her divorce, and chartering a light aeroplane, although frankly, chartering an industrial waste carrier would have been more pertinent.

I used to update Nickie on her activities by email, reporting back on her salivating over suggestions of fried fish, or steak in pepper sauce, pasta with cream and mushrooms, pork chops, roast chicken, lasagne, mousaka, Spanish omelette, French toast, mushrooms à la Grec, Irish coffee, Belgian chocolates, Swiss cheese . . . and finally, having discussed every single item in detail, ordering 'carpaccio de mangue — no, no, nothing more, and please take everything else off the table. Yes, including the salt and pepper.'

'Too tempting,' replied Nickie. 'Just imagine if they left the salt and pepper on the table. After a few minutes she'd be ripping the tops off the condiments and desperately shovelling them down her throat with her false nails. Pounds and pounds and pounds of salt and black pepper showering her shoulders . . . '

'Mixing with the suntan oil . . . '

'Forming a marinade . . . '

'Because otherwise she'll be too tough for the spit!'

'Burn her! Barbecue her!'

'Shoot the fat cow!'

'I know the type: makes a huge fuss out of only ordering water.'

'She has a very strict timetable,' I said. 'You know, keep-fit at dawn, face mask and two sips of hot water for breakfast . . . shopping for fake roses until it's time for her horrible mouldy mango lunch . . . '

'Preferably somewhere with music so no-one can overhear her stomach rumbling,' said Nickie.

'Yes, and she can't go to restaurants with director's chairs,' I added with zest, 'in case her great lard-arse buttocks rip the canvas seats and she falls straight through and cracks the floor tiles.'

'Nah, she'd just bounce.'

'God I hate her!' I typed. 'I could murder the bitch! Put a bullet through her.'

'You'll need a silver one,' said Nickie.

There was no end to her intrusions, and all the time she was cranking her horsehair eyelashes up and down and asking why such a sexy man was hiding his, er, talents in such an isolated place. She probably even said 'Ooh, you are enormous!' The Pirate lapped it up.

She drove me nuts. At first I just wished she'd leave, then after a while I longed for her to fall into the drainage system, but before long I just wanted her dead. My finger itched to pull the trigger for once and for all. Even now, I can't help it. Just the thought of her makes my blood boil.

I know, I know. The world is full of women trying to hook rich men, and so what if loads of men leave their wives for a tart with big tits and no brain. She wasn't even the first woman to flirt with the Pirate. He's the sort of man that attracts flirtatious women. But she didn't even stop when I was around. She didn't give a shit. She was clearly a professional, working her way round the world from one alimony settlement to the next.

'The amount of time she's been at it,' emailed Nickie, 'I dread to think where she started. Not just the gutter, the sewers.'

'Lower,' I said. 'Much, much lower. When she got as high as the sewers, she mistook them for Buckingham fucking Palace.'

'Bet she congratulated herself on feeling so at home,' emailed Nickie.

God knows where she really came from. By the time fat-lips installed her plankton-fed kilos on our island, you couldn't even guess her nationality any more she was so determined. And desperate. She was ready to settle for anyone with money left to squander.

Perhaps if Nickie had been there too, it would have been all right. I mean, I might have seen the funny side of it. As it was, I got more and more heated up with every day that passed. I was on the point of getting the gun out. A million times, I nearly did it . . .

And meanwhile — either oblivious to my murderous intentions or confident that I wouldn't actually have the nerve — in the privacy of her dearly-bought hotel room, Sylvia gobbled chocolates, slathered on more cream, grilled herself on her balcony and phoned her divorce lawyers before throwing up, making up, and dressing up every evening.

She usually circled the bar at the Shells, sniffing round her prey with the occasional twitch of her killer tale and gazing hungrily at the menu with her beady little eyes. Which, I suppose is how she had stayed out of my direct orbit for so long, but once she'd drifted into my orbit she reduced me to a gibbering heap of incandescent fury with her antics.

She specialised in that nauseating 1950s baby-doll stuff . . . promising blow jobs, breathing over cocktails and somehow never quite delivering because 'I like you too much. You see, if I did that, I'd probably fall in love with you and then where would I be, Daddy? Poor little me. All broken hearted. No, no . . . just friends. Oh well, one little kiss then, oh please . . . oh my God, you're enormous! Don't touch me! You're driving me crazy. Aaaah, here's my taxi-boat. Until tomorrow, my darling.'

Jealous? I wasn't jealous. Why should I be? Well, looking back perhaps I . . . but that's really beside the point . . . I mean looking back perhaps I'm glad that Sylvia came along because without her maybe me and the Pirate . . . maybe we'd have just gone on forever arguing about my passport and never really sorting anything out. At least this way, it's all over, and we all know where we stand.

Because that's what happened. Sylvia went too far. I caught her and the Pirate sticking horrible slimy olives into each other's mouths one afternoon and just thought I'm damned if I'm going to play gooseberry to my husband and that greasy whale in lipstick.

It was time for action.

8

It was dawn. Through the porthole I could see the sun rising across the sea, making it blush with pleasure. I was just coming out of the shower and the Pirate was brushing his teeth. He passed me a towel with his free hand and I twisted my hair up into it. He was gurgling happily and leering at me so I thought it might be the moment.

'I was thinking of making a trip,' I said casually, leaning against the sink. 'Now that the worst of the season is over. I thought I might go and see the boys. I really miss them you know.'

'Yeah?'

'Mmmm . . . I could surprise them. You know, just turn up and see how they're doing.'

'You wanna go now?'

'Well, pretty soon. There's no point in waiting.'

'You wan me to buy you a ticket?'

'No, I don't mind paying for it myself. I mean, you said you'd pay me for working in the office . . . You don't have to do a thing. I can sort it out.'

'How long you wanna go for?'

'Oh I don't know. Not long. A couple of weeks, maybe.' I was smiling at him. He was actually going to let me go. With a rush of relief and affection, I kissed the nape of his neck. He smiled, gave me a quick hug and went off to get dressed.

'So I'll find a flight, then?' I asked, following him.

He eyed me for a minute or two and then shook his head. 'No. Boys will be here soon anyway. If you want, we take trip together. Maybe Venezuela.'

'But I don't want to go to Venezuela!'

'Okay, we go to Europe, see your lezzy girlfriends. Maybe I take you to Greece.'

My heart sank. I would have to shoot him after all. What alternative was there? He was never going to hand my passport over just for the asking. And if I took the keys out of his speedboat he would probably turn up in the office just as I was opening the safe. I'd have to put a bullet through his brandy keg.

Well he was hardly going to let me tie him up nicely, was he? Well think about it — I mean, hi there, would you mind sitting still with your hands behind your back for half an hour or so, while I work out how to tie you up so that I can break into your safe and shog off with the contents . . . I don't think so. And after my experience with the office, locking him in obviously only worked for about five minutes. He didn't look like Houdini but he obviously knew the same tricks. It would be pointless attempting to lock him into his cabin.

Still wrapped in my towel, I flopped down on the bed, moodily watching the Pirate search for a pair of swimming trunks.

'On the chair,' I said. 'Clean shirt in the cupboard.'

He stumped about for a bit and then went off to make coffee. I didn't bother to get dressed. I just lay there on my back with my hands behind my head. I wasn't going into the office today. I needed time to think.

'You wanna coffee?' he said, coming back. 'Why you in bed? You ill?'

'Nope.'

'You sulking, boudeuse de Paris?'

'Nope.'

He came back a few minutes later with a cup of coffee and a ginger nut.

'What's this?' I said scowling at the biscuit.

He shrugged. 'Dunno. I thought you English, maybe you like English tings, so I order them.'

I wrinkled up my nose at him, but I ate it anyway. He grinned and sat down beside me on the bed.

'I know you like them. Twins tole me. Now, you coming to office?'

'No, I'm staying here. Planning how to shoot you.'

Just voicing it gave me the shivers, but it made him laugh and he went off, full speed ahead in the Venus, singing some terrible sea shanty.

I stamped into the galley for the rest of the biscuits, telling myself that I needed brain food. The galley still wasn't exactly well stocked, but things were definitely better in there. One fridge held drinks and the other had various bits of picnic stuff in it, you know, cheese, cold meat, the inevitable boiled eggs along with some yoghurt and salad, and jars of jam, mayonnaise, pickles, mustard, ketchup, that sort of stuff. We didn't often eat on board, but we did occasionally come back for a bread lunch. Usually when the Pirate felt like having me for pudding. I grabbed the rest of the coffee and went up on deck to do some serious thinking.

I could wait for him to go away on one of his mysterious trips, but then I only knew how long he was gone for when he came back. I mean, just because I hadn't seen him for a few hours, it didn't mean he wasn't lurking about somewhere. And I could easily make him appear. All I had to do was start picking the locks in his desk and he'd walk into the office sure as sharks were sharks. As long as he was alive, he'd be behind me somewhere ready to bounce out of a bush and wave our marriage certificate in my face. I realised that I'd actually have to do him in. Get him permanently off the planet.

What can I tell you, Philippa? I wasn't really going to do it. I had just been plotting to shoot him for so long that it had turned into a habit. Especially when I was pissed off — and I was seriously pissed off with whale-arsed bloody Sylvia.

So as I went downstairs to get dressed, I vented my frustration by playing with the idea of pushing him overboard. I could do it as he came up the ladder, I thought. There's always that split second of imbalance as he transfers his colossal weight onto the deck. Just one sharp shove and he'll go splash into the sparkly deep. I'll have to push him with a broom of course — so he can't drag me down to the lobster pots with him in a death-grip.

I smiled to myself, and started brushing my hair.

But. What if he manages to swim ashore? Or bribe the lobsters to tow him to safety? Or yell loud enough to get help? Or in some way refuses to be pushed? Or what if he grabs the broom and takes off into the palm trees

236

squawking like a gross old parrot silhouetted against the outline of the rigging?

Hmm. I frowned over this one, chose a nice pair of earrings and pondered the prospect of feeding him to the crabs. If I poison him first, and then cut him up before chucking him overboard in little pieces . . .

I jiggled my head so I could see the earrings glint in the sun. But if he was poisoned, wouldn't all the crabs die and float to the surface, surviving just long enough to croak 'Treasure poisoned the Captain!'

I stuck my tongue out at the mirror. Also, chopping people up must be exhausting, not to mention messy, just imagine all the deck swabbing you'd have to do — in the middle of the night, too.

I started brushing my teeth and dallied with the idea of bulldozing him into a heart attack. They do that in films all the time. Young blondes often give old husbands heart attacks like that. The idea withered in the bud. Not even a coach load of nympho starlets could bulldoze the Pirate to death. In fact, he'd probably relish their attempts. Or turn the tables . . .

I spat the toothpaste out.

I'd obviously have to put a bullet through his thick skull. Or his fat bottom. Or . . . well, through any bit of him, really. The sudden mental image of the Pirate full of holes made me blench. I'd have to do it with my eyes closed. Which would mean shooting at close range so that I didn't miss.

I hurriedly ate another biscuit. Shooting at close range presents a further difficulty, I thought to myself as I grabbed a carton of juice out of the fridge. How can I get close enough without him noticing that I'm grasping a gun in both hands and pointing it straight at his nose? With my eyes shut.

I giggled hysterically and orange juice went up the back of my nose. But even snuffling and coughing over the sink I still couldn't abandon my black fantasies.

I'll have to do it in the dark. Perhaps he won't notice the gun then. As for Sylvia the walking scumbag cow, she'll be welcome to pick up the pieces, if she still wants them. Well, you know. The dead pieces. I'm not leaving her with anything still capable of bulldozering. But why should I bother shooting her? She's so fat and greasy that a bullet would bounce off anyway.

Oh God, I thought, wiping my eyes and throwing the empty juice carton into the bin. What if I get hurt by a bullet ricocheting off bloody Sylvia the walking whale? Where will that get me? Exactly. Into hospital, and I hate hospitals. I'd just have to toss her headfirst into a bin (an outsized one) and make a break for the airport.

Having decided all that, and feeling ready for action toot sweet, I rootled through the lockers in my cabin for a swimsuit. It was too hot for sitting about in a towel by that time, and if I sat around in the buff the Pirate would surely see me through his telescope and (lunch time or not) come back for pudding.

Anyway, I said decisively, there's no point hanging about. Make your break for the border before your husband and his fat-arse mistress ship you off to a nunnery or a loony bin, or . . . have you disposed of!

Shit. I hadn't thought of that before. Determined to get my oar in first, I dragged a top and some shorts on, clipped my hair up and scrambled into Little Star as fast as I could, heading for the computers in Jack's place.

But once I got there, needless to say, I couldn't book a flight over the Internet because I didn't know my credit card number. I could have kicked myself for not remembering that, and for a minute I was stumped. So I checked airline routes, prices and ticket availability. Then I had a look to see what inter-island services were available, but to be honest I didn't find much.

Philippa, you probably think there are loads of ferries buzzing round the Caribbean between the islands — I did myself — but there aren't, because the Caribbean isn't one country so there's no integrated transport system. I know, I looked. Really looked.

By the time I'd spent two hours surfing the web, drinking coffee and smoking cigarettes, I knew I'd have to wing it. There were plenty of flights to the UK. Just not from any island anywhere near ours. All I had to do was get to an international airport without anyone spotting me. All? Right.

I left Jack's and walked along the beach kicking at the sand and making little golden clouds around my ankles. With any luck, I told myself, no-one would realise that I'd done the Pirate in until after I'd done a runner.

It was tricky though. I hadn't worked out all the details of exactly how to kill him and I was still slightly hazy about disposing of the body, since I hadn't decided whether I was going to kill him in self-defence, or whether mysterious robbers were going to kill him, or whether he was simply going to shoot himself in the nose. On the other hand, perhaps we would both just quietly disappear beneath the turquoise foam. A lovers' pact.

I arrived at Betty's and paused to inspect

the shark enclosure. It was between the restaurant and the beach, fed by a sluggish pump and inhabited by a posse of slightly green flat-headed sharks and because the concrete walls were a good half metre thick, you could walk on top of them all round the enclosure.

Watching my reflection on the water, I pushed these various problems to the back of my mind, along with the minor detail of listen-and-click safe breaking and the missing bar of key-imprinted soap. Of course I'd be able to sort it out, I told myself, and threw my shoulders back. After all, murder isn't rocket science. I mean, have you ever looked at mug shots of murderers? Frankly they don't look like major contenders for Brain of Britain, do they?

I stared at the sharks, lazily flicking their tails in the dark green water, and went on plotting. Just in case the rozzers did get on my tracks, the morning after the killing in question I would leave the island on the ferry: an oily tramp steamer which called at the island once a week delivering gas bottles and stale vegetables. It wasn't the sort of boat that appealed to tourists because there was no free rum punch and you couldn't buy bikinis on board, but it did take passengers (usually only locals and hippies), so it would be easy

241

enough to walk up the gangplank and conceal myself behind a roll of chicken wire or a crate of water melons.

I would take the ferry all along this string of islands, right to the end one. After that, I would probably have to get someone to run me over to the next large island. Either in a speedboat, if I could find someone willing to do it, or I could probably pretend to be a stupid tourist left behind by another day cruise and tag a ride on a day charter. If all else failed, I could simply impersonate Lard-arse and blonde my way onto some boat or other by telling the crew, 'Ooh, you are enormous!'

What do you mean, wouldn't I have cracked up?

Then, from the next large island, I would be able to get a charter flight straight to the airport island. I stood sideways so I could admire my elongated shadow on the sand, and it occurred to me that I'd need luggage. A Lard-arse outfit as well as something practical to travel in and probably some food. I'm sure I read somewhere that murder makes you terrifically hungry. Like skiing. And breast feeding.

So I'd need to pack some sandwiches. Ham. And some ginger beer. In fact it would be quite fun, I told myself brightly. After nearly a year in the Caribbean, I'd never been anywhere. It would be great to go shopping in the markets. I'd heard that there was a spice market on one of the islands and thought it might be the ideal place to get some souvenirs for Nickie and the twins. Well, not that any right-thinking eleven year-old wants a miniature faggot of cinnamon sticks as a Caribbean souvenir, but . . .

I jumped off the wall, doubled back and walked away from the complex, thinking I would slip round behind the shacks and perhaps buy a Coke there. I certainly wasn't going anywhere near the office. Nope. I was on strike.

I calculated that it would take around a week to get there. Not the quickest journey in the world, but if I got on board the ferry unseen, it would probably be foolproof and no-one would follow me because everyone would think I'd left with some tourists or with one of the Pirate's cut-throat cronies. That was the obvious way to leave the island, after all. Either that or they'd think I'd also been shot in the nostril and dumped overboard. Or else kidnapped. Ha!

As the morning dragged on the kidnapped idea grew on me. In fact it became my favourite scenario. I could set the whole thing up to look as if the Pirate had been shot in the vain attempt to prevent my being hauled off onto a rival pirate ship against my will.

I liked the irony of it. Perhaps I could cut out some speech bubbles to lay beside his body. Things like: 'Un-hand my wife, thou dastardly coward!' and 'Fear not dearest — only the stars can separate us!' And if I could find another corpse from somewhere, especially a sinister-looking one, I could do another speech bubble reading: 'Stand aside my bully, whilst we kidnap the wench!'

Having arranged the stiffs, I'd have to get over to the office and break into the safe. I didn't have the faintest idea how I was going to do this either. I mean, it's all very well watching Butch Cassidy and thinking, well that looks simple enough, but when you're actually faced with doing it yourself, it's quite different. Apart from anything else, there wasn't any sign of the Sundance Kid and I didn't have any dynamite. Or a train. Wasn't there a train in Butch Cassidy? Or was it a bicycle?

Anyway, the point is I decided to have a contingency plan regarding the safe. If I couldn't open it and get my papers back, I'd have to nick someone else's papers and impersonate them. Someone like Lard-arse.

She'd probably be exercising with her earmuff loudspeaker things on at that time in the morning. I'd be able to creep up, shove her into a skip, nick her paperwork and piss off pronto. In which case, I'd have my work a bit harder cut out. I mean in terms of being on the run. Because obviously Lard-arse wouldn't like being shoved into a skip and would make a stink about it. Well, she would also stink. Having been in the skip, I mean . . .

Anyhow the point is it was all very exhausting and confusing, working out the details. You know, stuff like, would it be better to ditch the gun before nicking Lardie's passport, or would it be better to hold onto it in case I decided to risk death by ricochet rather than be pursued round the Caribbean by a killer brunette?

Throwing my empty Coke can in the bin, I walked back down the lane and came out at the shark enclosure again. It was like that on the island. There really wasn't anywhere to go. If you wanted to walk, you either had to get a boat to somewhere else, or follow your own footsteps round in circles.

I didn't know what to do with the murder weapon and I hadn't resolved the soap question, either. Well, not that I had a tablet of soap, but the issue of whether I should try to get one or not . . . with imprints, I mean.

And what I should do with such a tablet were I to acquire one.

But in the end I was overtaken by events: Lard-arse came strolling along the other side of the shark enclosure. Probably a sentimental visit to her birthplace. Or was she merely visiting her sisters under the skin?

She flashed me a filthy smile, and picked her way round to my side of the enclosure in glittery pineapple flip-flops and a floaty wrap-over skirt. I badly wanted to push her in, but contented myself with shoving my hands into my pockets and standing my ground. If she wanted to get past, she'd have to scramble down onto the beach. Either that or get in with the fishes.

'Hello,' she husked.

'Hi. Still here, then.'

'Oh yes, I'm having such a wonderful time I decided to stay on for a while.'

'Oh.' I didn't know what else to say. I don't mind a nice clean slanging match, but I'm a total klutz at verbal fencing and barbed wire playground games. 'Oh,' I croaked. 'Right.'

'I've met such a wonderful man here,' she mused, turning profile so as to give me a better view of her bloated rosy nipples. She shifted her weight onto one foot, and stuck her enormous hip out. She looked like Jessica Poxy Rabbit she had so much tits and ass hanging off her spine.

'A real sweetie,' she went on, half under her breath. 'Such a darling, but his wife . . . oh dear. A total savage. Treats him desperately badly. I gather she only married him so that he would educate her sons — can you believe that?'

'Really?' I said looking her in the eye, and clenching my fists. She didn't flinch. Just met my eye blandly.

'Really, darling. I've met her. It's all true, I promise you. I'm so sorry for my poor lamb.'

'Oh really?' I was going red in the face with the effort of controlling my temper. She gave the glimmer of a smile.

'Absolutely. In fact, that's why I'm staying on. I plan to rescue him.'

That was it. One step too far. I braced my weight, softened my knees, swung both my fists backwards and sent her flying into the slimy green water with a smashing two-handed blow between her shoulder blades. The splash as she shot through the water was tremendous and several tourists sitting nearby screamed.

One of Sylvia's flip-flops had come off and was lying at my feet. I picked it up and skimmed it across the water so that it bounced twice and hit her full in the face as she tried to stand up.

The pond wasn't more than three or four foot deep, but the water was fetid and oily with a lot of mud at the bottom, mainly composed of food which had been thrown in by tourists, shunned by sharks, and left to rot. Poor Lard-arse's careful hair was ruined, and I do believe one of her diamond earrings had gone missing. Her cousins were beginning to circle round as she started splashing towards the side and Betty came running with a long stick.

No, Philippa. They weren't those massive Jaws-type Hollywood things, only just little nursery sharks, barely a metre long. Over-fed ones at that, but Betty wasn't taking any chances, so she flailed around with a long pole, and Lard-arse splashed and the tourists screamed.

'What happened?' Betty called over to me.

'I don't know,' I shrugged. 'I think she er . . . went too far. Slipped up.'

Betty shook her head at me. She clearly wasn't impressed. Lardie didn't give me another glance. Having been hauled out of the pool (shuddering artistically), she flicked her hair over her shoulders, and leaned against a brace of waiters. Having been wrapped up in a towel and repeatedly asked if she was okay and offered everything from band-aids to brandy, she accepted a nice soothing glass of Perrier and headed straight to her hotel room. Presumably to repair the waterlogged plasterwork and plan her revenge.

Don't get me wrong. I wasn't scared of her. I didn't run away from that olive-faced, leather-skinned, gimlet-eyed old cow. Or her promised war. And I didn't run away because the Pirate fancied the arse off her either.

I just realised that it was time to leave. Things had gone far enough. I had enough money to pay my way, I'd collected several whole pages of useful phone numbers, and there was enough ham in the fridge to make my getaway sarnies. All I had to do was work out how to get onto the ferry unseen.

I strolled back along the top of the shark enclosure wall, noting with satisfaction that most of it was wet, and mulled the problem over. Everyone knew me, everyone knew what I looked like, even at a distance. How was I going to get on the ferry?

No! No they didn't. People recognised my yellow hair and my clothes. Nothing more. It was simple. In trousers and with a scarf round my head, no-one would recognise me. I could be anyone.

I ducked off the beachfront between a couple of shacks and strolled into what passed as a souvenir shop on the island. They sold loads of scarves so I sorted through them, but couldn't find one big enough to cover my hair completely and in the end I nicked a dark red, printed, mini-pareo tourist skirt which would work as a scarf.

Skipping back along the beach, and giving Betty's a wide berth, I felt pretty pleased with myself. Even the shopkeeper wouldn't recognise his skirt once it had become headgear. And the dried blood colour was disgusting enough to look old and dirty already.

Back at Jack's I grabbed a cold bottle of juice and untied Little Star, feeling that I'd had an extremely successful morning after all.

For the rest of my getaway outfit, I just went through Bettina's cleaning rags on board the Sun. There was a pair of dark blue trousers at the bottom of the bag — way too big for me, and with part of one leg missing. Presumably left by a visiting pirate with a stump. It didn't matter. I chopped the other leg off to match, reflecting as I did so that this was almost like practising for chopping up a corpse. Which I might well have to do. But definitely not with dressmaking shears. Well, unless I went for the kidnap scenario, of course.

I dragged my brain back to the task in hand. I could hold the trousers together with a safety pin. All I would need was a shirt or something and I'd look just like all the other ferry passengers. As long as I pinned the scarf on properly. I didn't want any long blonde tresses fluttering in the breeze.

I tried it all on in my cabin and climbed on the berth to get a look at myself in the small mirror screwed onto the opposite wall. I looked great. The trousers were so large that they made me look even skinnier than usual, the shirt was uneven and the combination of the two was excellent, extremely world-traveller and hippyish. Frankly, I looked like a man. Dead chuffed with myself I climbed off the bunk, stripped off my disguise and folded it carefully into a carrier bag.

That afternoon, I took the bag over to the office. Mike was pottering about there, but he didn't notice when I shoved my bundle down between the filing cabinets before wandering off again with a delightful bubbly excited feeling in my stomach. I was ready to go!

I know, I know, Philippa! But I didn't really mean to go through with it. It was all still just a Famous Five adventure. I was thinking more about running away than shooting to kill.

That evening we had drinks with Lardie. I can't imagine she wanted to see me, but she obviously wanted to see the Pirate and she was probably hoping to make me walk the plank in return for her swimming lesson. So she turned up about five minutes after her hair and make-up entered the bar, trailing yet another silk shawl, smothered in designer plastic flowers and drenched in amber scent.

But I didn't care any more. Not that I'd ever cared about her in the first place of course, but every time I looked at her I kept seeing her flying into the shark pit, and imagining her arse bulging out of a skip and that made me laugh. Then I started embroidering, deciding to cut half her hair off while I was at it. Or shave off one eyebrow, or perhaps force her at gunpoint to open thousands of toothbrush wrappers until she broke all her nylon nails. I was so taken up with these daydreams, that I hardly noticed anything she said and certainly couldn't be bothered to snipe at her.

In fact I was rather sweet to both of them. In a preoccupied sort of way, you understand. Maybe that's why the Pirate got rid of her.

'Sylvia, thank you for joining us. We see you later? At Betty's maybe?'

Lardie looked like she'd just inhaled a stale kipper, but managed to stretch the leather skin around her mouth into the semblance of a smile. 'Maybe, darling. Maybe not. Who knows? I might forget the time.' She shot me a steely glance, directed her gaze full onto the Pirate and added huskily, 'No, don't kiss me darling, you'll only stop me sleeping!'

I rolled my eyes. The cow was old enough to have witnessed the death of the dinosaurs, and she was carrying on like a teenager trying her wings out on the assistant stage manager. How vomitous. As she strolled off, tossing her hair and trailing a paradise print shawl behind her globulous buttocks, I trod on the hem and it ripped loudly.

'Ooops!' I said sweetly.

She didn't miss a beat. Just let the torn silk slip through her fingers and fall to the ground, leaving it lying there like Peter Pan's shadow as she strolled away.

The Pirate grinned and raised his eyebrows. 'You coming to eat?' he asked.

He was unusually quiet that evening, and I was sure it was because he didn't want me around any more, cluttering up the beach for him and Wobble-Arse. But I didn't give him a chance to tell me I could have my passport back. No way. Now I'd got it all planned out, I didn't want to start changing it all again. I mean, I was thoroughly looking forward to toshing old Whale-Woman in the skip, and I'd already bought a bottle of ginger beer for my picnic.

So I told a series of bad jokes, asked a

selection of idiot questions which were guaranteed to set him off on his favourite monologues, and ate a huge dinner. You know, just in case it was true about murder being like skiing. And breast feeding.

Then we went back to the Sun. 'Don't you want to go to Betty's?' I said. 'I thought you were going there tonight?'

'No. You and me, we have little talk.'

'Oh well, I don't know if I'm up for talking tonight,' I sighed. 'I'm exhausted, you know. All I really want is an early night.'

He didn't reply, just handed me into the Venus and drove us out to the boat. The moon was shining across the sky making a path right down through the water, and the night was warm and still. Behind us lights twinkled along the shore and the faint echo of music carried across the sparkling sea. The air was soft and still, scented with wood smoke from the barbecue huts on the beach.

We drifted up against the Sun and while the Pirate tied the speedboat up, I climbed the ladder onto the deck. The first thing I saw was a broom leaning against one of the hatches. This was my chance. All I had to do was grab the handle, wait until he just started to transfer his weight onto the deck and lunge forward with all my might. I looked at my hands in the moonlight and felt pretty pleased with myself. They were remarkably steady.

'Wha-tyou-doing?' demanded the Pirate, walking past me. 'Come and sidown!'

I put the broom down, and hesitated. If I sat down with him, he'd start talking and then he'd get his oar in before mine. I had no intention of joining the ranks of those pathetic wives who leave their husbands for adultery. For being a kidnapper and a pirate? Yes. For shagging some tart with outsize tits? Being a plain, boring, ordinary Standard Issue Class A Bastard? No way.

So I decided not to sit down with him or give him any chance for a chat, because whatever he said was liable to confuse the issue.

'I'm just going to get some drinks,' I called. 'What do you want?'

'I just take a beer, if you got any,' he said.

'Okay, no problem, I'll have a look.'

I went downstairs and started opening and closing all the cupboard doors in the galley, banging them all loudly as I did it. Hopefully he would think I was looking for glasses, when in fact I was retrieving my cash. I gathered it all together and, wading through the sea of newspapers on the floor, dumped it on my bed and went back for the gun.

Working quickly, I rifled through the porn

vids until I found the one with the man's bottom on the spine, and hiked it out of the shelf. Yes, just behind it was the hiding place. I pulled out a few more cassettes, removed the wooden cover and slid the gun out of its hidey-hole. Then I shoved the videos randomly back in their places, just so as to leave no gap on the shelf — and went into my cabin to load the gun.

I unzipped my sponge bag, opened the packet of cough sweets and tipped the bullets into the palm of my hand. Shit! They were all covered in sugar. I didn't have time to wash and dry them, but I certainly didn't fancy sucking them clean. I dusted off as much sugar as I could and loaded the bullets into the revolver. I'd just have to hope that the teensy weensy bit of sugar left on them wouldn't gunge up the works. Or doesn't it matter about having sugar in a gun? Is that only car engines, Philippa? Or, no . . . I expect you've never really . . . no.

I'd practised loading it before, so that bit went quite well. I didn't drop any bullets on the floor, and I didn't get the stupid thing stuck when it was only half-closed . . . you know how guns do that? Or maybe it was only that gun that did it . . . just sort of went stiff when you tried to close the bit where the bullets went in so you had to hit it on the doorpost.

Anyway, as I was saying, it was fine and I even managed to close the thing with a satisfactory snap, when the cabin door opened.

'Wha-tyou doing? I waitin for you!'

The scene is etched on my mind. I'll never forget it. There was me sitting on the bunk surrounded by bullets and cash, there was him in the doorway demanding what the fuck I was playing at.

I twisted round with my heart beating and pointed the gun at him. Unfortunately I'd managed to get sugar all over the handle, so it was horribly sticky. I changed hands so I could wipe the thing with the hem of my skirt, and lick my palm clean. In fact, that took a bit of time, and I had to do quite a lot of changing hands and palm licking, until the thing stopped being sticky. I do hate a sticky gun, don't you?

And all this time he was eyeing me up, which was not at all my plan, because I didn't want to shoot him in my cabin and get blood all over my dollar bills, but he was between me and the door and there was no other way out of the cabin.

I couldn't have got away from him by climbing out of the porthole because how could I have climbed out of it backwards, which I would have had to do in order to keep the gun pointing at him? And anyway, if I'd have climbed out of the porthole, I'd have fallen into the sea and got the gun wet. I poked it forward, scowling viciously. 'Move back from the door! Now!'

He leaned against the doorframe and folded his arms.

'So wha-tyou gonna do now? Shoot me? And then wha? Take my boat and run away with Mr America from the Shells?'

I rolled my eyes at him. 'No. I told you this morning. I'm going to England.'

'How?'

'Well, how d'you think? On a bloody escalator? I'm flying of course.' Pointing the gun at him with both hands, I told him exactly what I was going to do: 'I'm going to the UK, and nothing is going to stop me.'

'What d'you mean, you going to the UK? How d'you fin-tha-fuckin-gun?'

'I found it behind your horrible porn videos.'

'But why was you looking there? What was you doing?'

'I was looking for my passport of course!'

'But it's not on the boat. I fucking told you, it's in the safe!'

'Yes, but I couldn't get into the safe so I

was looking here in case you were lying, or in case I could find the keys to the safe.'

'I don-keep them here!'

'I know!'

'What do you know?'

'I know you don't keep the keys here!'

'How dyou'know?'

'Because I've been through the whole place, that's why! What do you think? You lock me up on the HMS *Sinkquick* and you think I'm going to spend three days painting my nails and hoping you'll come and set me free soon? Are you mad? Of course I searched the place!'

'So you found the keys, then?'

'Of course I did. The other week when I took your speedboat.'

'But you left them there?'

'For Christsake! Stop thinking I'm stupid will you!'

'I don-thing-kyou're stoopid,' he said, laughing. 'You a crazy woman!' Then he took a pace towards me. I brought the gun up quickly and pointed it at his nostril.

'Get back! Get away from me now! I'm warning you. Don't even think about it!'

He raised his hands and took a step backwards. 'Okay, okay. Calm down.' He looked at the gun in my hands uneasily. 'Is it loaded? Do you know how to use that thing?'

'I don't know if it's loaded,' I said. 'I might have done it wrong. But I've just put six bullets in it and I don't think the sugar will make any difference. As for using it, I think you just point,' I said, demonstrating, 'and pull this thing here, like in the movies.'

'All right, all right, I believe you! Put the fucking gun down!'

'Shut up!' I told him. Things weren't going to plan. I hadn't counted on having to talk to him before I knocked him off. I'd been planning something much less personal, you know, open the door, shoot the gun, close the door, easy-peasy, lemon-squeazy, that sort of thing.

'And what sugar? What sugar you got in the gun?'

'It came off the cough sweets,' I said crossly. 'Now, walk backwards. Slowly.'

'Cough sweets? What are you talking about?' His eye lit on the cardboard packet on the bunk bed and he made the connection straight away. 'You had the bullets in the sweetie box?' he asked, his eyes alight with laughter. 'What a fuckin woman!'

'Look, just get into the galley,' I told him, although I was trying not to laugh too. 'Just get in there and shut up! I've got to think.'

He backed into the galley with his hands up and a huge grin on his face. 'Where d'you get all that money?'

I shoved the gun at him menacingly and told him to get the ham out of the fridge, and he still didn't stop asking stupid questions and making smart-arsed comments. 'You gotta plane ticket booked? How you gonna get into the safe?'

'Shut up, and get the ham out of the fridge!' I ordered him.

'Okay, I doing it! Look here's your ham.' Then he did a double-take. 'Ham? We never have ham! Wha-tyou got ham in here for? Wha's ham gotta do with it?'

'Just shut up!'

'An wha-tyou gonna use for money? You ain't got enough on that berth. That won-ge-tyou far. What about visas? Wha-tyou gonna do with the gun? And wha-the hell's the ham for?'

'Shut up! I've got other money, the visas won't be a problem, it's all planned out . . . it's for sandwiches . . . '

I kept on trying to explain it to him, and trying to think straight, but he kept asking things like when I'd decided to do it and what I would have done if he'd taken the gun away, and was I really serious about shooting him, and did I have a proper plan, apart from the ham sandwiches?

He was staggered, but not at all afraid. But

I couldn't really concentrate on all that any more. By that time, it simply seemed to me that if I got a nice picnic organised, everything would be fine.

I kept looking at the ham sitting on the table in its plastic wrapper, and worrying that it was going off, and he kept on saying fucking hell whata woman and I kept on trying to think what to do next, and then he made another lunge at me. I saw him coming towards me with his hands reaching out in front of him, and he was trying to grab the gun off me. I backed away from him into my cabin, but he followed me in through the door and I knew he wouldn't stop until he'd wrenched the gun out of my sweating hands.

So I closed my eyes, pointed it straight at his left nostril and pulled the trigger.

9

Of course I missed. The bullet slammed into the door, tore right through it into the locker behind and buried itself in a collection of porn mags.

'Jesus Christ! Wha-you doin?' exclaimed the Pirate, and tried to wrench the gun out of my hand. I kicked him and must have scored a lucky goal, because he collapsed on the floor clutching his most precious possessions. I scrambled up into the bunk above my head, and was crouching there aiming the gun at him, when suddenly he looked up and exploded into laughter.

'What a fucking woman . . . you ain't wearing no panties!'

I wasn't? Shit. How on earth had that happened? I thought I had them on. Where had they gone? I twitched my skirt down crossly.

'So? So what?' I demanded. 'What's so funny?'

I was furious with him. I mean what has wearing knickers got to do with knocking someone off? No, I don't mean that, I mean, does it matter whether or not you wear knickers when shooting your husband? Of course not! I've never seen any rules mentioned in the movies about it. Listen up: there is no underwear code for committing hubby-cide. I mean, give me a break!

So there he was curled up on the floor groaning with a combination of pain and hysterical laugher — and there I was on the top bunk clutching my skirt in one hand and a revolver in the other, peering down at him through a fog of gun smoke. The place stank of cordite. To be honest, it was a bizarre situation. I was stumped.

'Wha-tyou gonna do now?' he gasped, and curled up in more hysterics.

'I don't know,' I confessed. 'But one more false move and I'll shoot you again!'

'Why don-tyou tie me up?' he suggested, trying to keep a straight face. 'Thass wha-ti would do,' he added. 'In your situation tha-tis!' He lost the battle and went off into fits of laughter again.

'It's not funny!' I said. 'I'm going to kill you, you know.'

'I don-cair. You are worth anything!'

Damn the man. The gun was getting heavier and heavier and making my wrist ache by this time, so I pointed it towards the window and fired off another couple of rounds, hoping it would be lighter with less bullets in it. The noise was deafening and the glass shattered in all directions. I ducked myself, and the Pirate, who hadn't seen me taking aim because he'd been laughing too much, twitched with fright.

'What the fuck!'

'Move! Get in there! Now,' I ordered. 'Into the galley. Shift it!'

He tried to stand up, but I waved the gun at him again. 'No, on your knees! Crawl!' Amazingly, he dropped onto all fours and I realised that for the moment at least, he really believed that I might shoot him — if not on purpose, then by accident. I was in the driving seat, and he was strapped into the pram. Excitement zinged through my body.

He crawled slowly out of the cabin and into the galley, his pendulous belly swaying from side to side, his shorts all rucked up over his bottom, exposing the soft white flesh of his thighs.

'Keep moving!' I said. 'Into the workshop.'

I dropped down off the bunk and followed him at a safe distance, keeping the gun pointed straight at his retreating buttocks. I had to find some rope, I thought. Or perhaps some chains or wire. I thought chains would be quite good. I could imagine them making a wonderfully satisfactory jingling noise.

'Wha-tyou gonna do?' he demanded,

chucking the words over his shoulder. 'Make me walk the plank?'

'Walk? You must be kidding! I'm going to make you crawl on your fat belly, you slime bag. You stealing, thieving, kidnapping, lying, cheating, piece of pond scum. You don't deserve to walk!'

'When did I lie to you?' he demanded indignantly. 'I don-lie! I never lie!'

'Don't argue with me, you cheating scumbag!'

'A-ha! You jealous of Sylvia, thas-wha-tall this is about! Sylvia!'

'Not a hope in hell, baby! I don't care who you fuck. The pair of you are just plankton as far as I'm concerned, and you're welcome to each other! But not until I've got my passport back. Now crawl! Go on, get! Or do I have to shoot you in the arse this time?'

He crawled a bit further into the workshop and then stopped again. He was panting and rubbing his knees.

'You gonna kill me baby, with this thing. My knees is hurting.'

All the bulldozering that man did, he had knees like leather. But he did look puffed out, and I suppose the planks were quite hard. I sighed loudly.

'Okay, turn round and sit down! No, on the floor. That's right. With your back to me!'

As he obeyed, I edged past him and grabbed a roll of parcel tape. The very thing. In school I'd been quite nifty at arts and crafts. I made him turn round and then I tossed the tape at him and ordered him to tie his ankles together because I'd had a sudden inspiration that once I got him more or less immobilised, taping his hands together would be easier.

'Right, now your knees,' I ordered. 'Tape them up!' He obeyed. Perhaps if I hadn't been so nervous, I'd have noticed that he had gone quiet. Then I might have been more on my guard, because he was almost always plotting devilry when he went quiet and angelic-looking.

Once his legs were tied up, I made him put the tape round his right wrist and throw me the reel. I didn't trust him one centimetre, but he co-operated without a murmur. I caught the reel with my free hand, still aiming the gun at his nose with the other, and ordered him to put his hands together and make like a goldfish.

'Do a what?'

'Like a goldfish.'

He just looked at me. 'Like this!' I yelled putting my hands together and wiggling them. 'Like a bloody goldfish! Didn't you ever go to school? Didn't you ever learn the wheels on the bus?'

'Like a goldfish,' he said, deadpan. 'Like this, you mean?' and he obligingly put his palms together and made little fishy swimming motions so I could wind the tape round his wrists without getting anywhere near him. When it was done and he was well and truly oven-ready, I taped his mouth up and tied him to the mast where it penetrated the cabin ceiling and thrust down through the deck into the hull.

Once I'd finished, I checked the knots were tight and stepped back to admire my handiwork. Yes, I'd well and truly cooked his goose. I gazed at him with satisfaction, and his dark eyes shone back at me over the parcel tape gag. That was him silenced.

I leaned against the door jam and considered my next move. I'd definitely put a large spanner in his works. On the other hand, I still had to raid the safe in the office. And judging by his Houdini impersonation last time I'd attempted to confine him in a secure environment, it wouldn't take him long to get free once I stopped holding him at gun point. I didn't want him coming after me. Or did I? No, of course I didn't. Having got this far, I was determined to go all the way.

He was lounging against the mast,

watching me. For the moment, he didn't seem to be struggling to break his Sellotape bonds. I glanced around the workshop. Once I was off the boat, he'd be free of his handcuffs in an instant and there were plenty of tools and knives around to help him escape. Shit! I'd better throw them overboard. One-handed, still keeping the gun pointed at the Pirate, I gathered his tools into a plastic crate and dragged it into the galley.

It was hard work getting the damn thing up the stairs with a gun in one hand, but I finally managed it. Then I listened intently. Was he moving about down there? I couldn't hear anything, so I put the gun down on the deck for a minute and tipped the contents of the box into the sea before snatching the gun up again and going cautiously back downstairs.

But he was still gagged and bound. I went round the boat looking for anything else that might help him escape. I started with all the kitchen knives. He never used them anyway. How many knives does it take to boil an egg, for God's sake? Then I thought I may as well get rid of the forks, and tin openers, and other metal things. Then I added the rest of the cutlery to the Out Tray because it was so horrid — all bent and stained.

Going through the cupboards, I saw a saucepan that I'd always hated (cream enamel with a dark green rim) so I included that in the pile too. It took several trips up and down the stairs to get that lot collected up and ditched. By the time I got back to the workshop after the last lot of kitchen utensils had turned into crab toys, I was sweating and out of breath.

He'd already managed to lick and spit the tape off his mouth, but I didn't care. He was still securely tied up, and I was too busy to attend to details.

'Wha-tyou doing now?' he demanded.

'None of your business,' I panted.

'Come here . . . '

'No.'

'Come on, Camille, I'm sorry. I was wrong, okay?'

'About a lot of things. How dare you tell that Lard-arse cow that I married you so you would put the boys through school?'

That wiped the smile off his face. 'I never said that, Camille. I never talk about you skids to her. Never.'

'Kids, not skids! What's wrong with you? Kids are children, skids are what happens when you mix oil and rubber.'

'No, no baby, skids is what happens when you slip up. You know that!'

I refused to laugh. I just shook my head at him. He obviously still thought I was just a joke. I went round the boat looking for anything else that might help him escape and chucked all that overboard too: wire, string, nail files, tweezers, first aid kit, mobile phones, his horrible laptop and the radio.

He saw me bashing it about with a hammer, trying to get it loose from the bulkhead. 'Christ, Camille! Not the fucking radio!'

But at that moment the wood splintered and it came away in my hands. I stumbled up the stairs with it, the Pirate still shouting 'No, not the fucking . . . '

Splash. I leaned over the railings and watched the inky sea swallow it up.

And then for good measure I chucked a whole load of other stuff into the sea too. Just while I was at it, you know. Theatrical reflex, perhaps. I suppose I just thought that since I was spring cleaning, I might as well make a really thorough job of it. So I trashed the other stuff I'd always hated: his pathetic porn videos, his ancient dusty out-of-date maritime magazines, all the salty, sweaty sheets and towels that defied laundering, all his horrible cheap shampoos and left over bits of body milk, his revolting soap-encrusted shaving brush, his ancient atrophying underwear, the lot.

It took hours, and in the end I gave up

carrying the gun around with me. He clearly wasn't making the slightest effort to get free. He was just sitting there grinning. I ignored him. I just stuck my nose in the air and went on gathering up all the offensive, disgusting detritus of his amoral insanitary lifestyle and throwing it overboard.

'What a fucking woman! I never thought, I never knew you . . . fucking Christ, all this time . . . ' he chortled, as I staggered past him with a pile of porn. If his hands hadn't been parcel-taped I bet he'd have been applauding. I glared at him but he just laughed again, but the more he laughed, the more I ripped the place apart.

And when I was finally out of breath, shaking with total exhaustion, and the place was utterly, totally trashed, he looked at me and said 'Wha-tif someone come-son board tonight? You know I invite Sylvia?'

I gave him my most contemptuous, withering glance. 'I'll tell her it's not the moment, tell her we're busy, tell her we're fucking doing . . . fucking!'

'And if she won't go?'

'I'll shoot her in the arse,' I said brazenly. By that time I didn't care; it had all gone way too far. But he knew I wasn't going to kill him or anyone else. I knew it too.

He nodded, and then after a moment he

asked, 'You gonna make me sleep here on the floor, then?'

'Well, I'm not untying you!' I said. 'What do you think I am? Stupid or something? If you can't manage to get yourself to bed . . . ' I shrugged contemptuously, but he still flicked me a wink.

'Come on, baby. It's late. You goin no-where now. We both gotta get some sleep and I can't sleep here.'

I sneezed and rubbed my nose. It was true. I was tired. But if I went to sleep, he'd pull some trick or other. And if I untied him, he'd definitely get the gun off me.

'Listen. Just cut me off this mast. You leave me tied up, but at least then I go to bed and lie down.'

'No tricks?'

'I'm tired, baby. I'm an old man. Gimme a break.'

I remembered his story about the forged notes and how he'd played the old man card then, too. If I undid that tape round the mast, I'd have to tie him to something else. Otherwise he'd probably hop all the way up to the deck, jump into the sea and swim ashore like a lumpy eel and I'd wake up in the morning surrounded by policemen. Or pliroma.

I looked round for something to cut the

tape with, but of course I'd thrown all the bloody knives overboard and I couldn't find anything sharp or metal either. In fact, the Sun was practically stripped to the hull.

'You'll have to use your teeth!' grinned the Pirate.

'Not on your life,' I spat. 'I'll shoot through the fucking tape. Hold still.'

'No! Camille, wha-tyou doing? Don-do vat! You'll sink the damn ship!'

'What?'

'You shoot straight down like that and you'll rip a hole in the hull. You wanna drown us both?'

I couldn't cut the tape off, I couldn't shoot through it, and I certainly wasn't going to break my nails trying to pickle up the end of the tape. I realised that he was right. I'd have to bite through it. Carefully keeping the gun out the Pirate's reach, I got down on all fours and crawled in past him so I could get my teeth into the tape.

He rubbed against my bottom, tickling me. I wiggled impatiently. 'Stop that, or I'll leave you here all night!'

'You gotta sexy arse!' he murmured, but at least he stopped shifting about so I could get the tape between my teeth. Finally I managed to bite through the section that was tying him to the mast and pulled it off, making him yelp where it had been stuck to his skin.

'Don't be such a baby!' I said, witheringly.

'Just come ere and feel what kind of a baby I am!'

'Nope. I'm staying right here with my friend,' I answered, patting the gun. 'Time for bed, baby.'

'Oh yes, I'm ready!'

'Shut up and wriggle!'

He managed to get across the floor eventually, cursing and swearing and sweating like a pig, humping himself about like a lobster with all its claws and legs tied together. But he couldn't get onto the bed. He just lay propped up against it, his skin shining in the moonlight, grinning at me.

I looked at him, and he looked at me, his dark eyes gleaming with excitement.

'And now what we gonna do?' he said softly. I looked away. The bastard was still up for it. Un-be-friggin-lievable.

What? You want to know, do you? Did we? Please! I'm not going to tell you all the gruesome details — and anyway he was my husband, wasn't he? What do you think I am? What's wrong with you? Oh, all right then, yes. Yes, we did. I couldn't resist him. Never could. I dragged him onto the bed and he was laughing as he rolled on top of me . . . his mouth searching for mine, the weight of his body moving slowly, rubbing against me, making my pulse race.

And no, since you ask, in spite of the fact that I was the one holding the gun, and that he was bound hand and foot, he was still the same old bulldozer boy. The minute he touched me I was just as helpless as ever. What can I tell you? I wanted to kill him, but my body would have crawled through the Sahara for just one touch of his tongue. It still would, come to that.

I know, Philippa. So pathetic, so weak, so amoral. But at least that time I didn't let myself be totally bulldozed. My plans were dented but not entirely blown. I knew he wouldn't sleep of course. He never fell asleep before me. But for once I managed not to sleep either, and a couple of hours later I lashed him securely to the double bunk, made my sandwiches, packed them into a carrier bag with my ginger beer, and left the boat.

Yes, I went through with the plan. I crept upstairs in the early dawn, closed and locked all the hatches, checked that there were no remaining life rafts or emergency dinghies left on board, climbed down the boarding ladder into Little Star and tied the Venus onto the bar at the back. Then I cut the ropes securing the boarding ladder and let it sink slowly into the emerald depths of the Caribbean Sea. The Pirate was absolutely stranded on the Sun with the mist swirling and not a soul in sight.

Halfway across the bay, I cut the outboard motor of the dinghy, climbed into the Venus and took the keys from their hiding place. Then I slipped them into my pocket, scrambled back into Little Star and regretfully scuppered the speedboat. It would have been madness to leave it behind for the Pirate and I could hardly tie it up at the office jetty or everyone would have wondered why it wasn't out at the Sun.

I stood up in my dinghy for a second and watched the speedboat drift gently down through the clear waters to the reef where it settled comfortably, looking like a broody hen. How sad. Still, I told myself, it wouldn't be long before someone salvaged her. She wasn't lying far down, just deep enough to be out of sight from the shore.

Once I got to the office jetty, I moored Little Star in my usual spot, walked calmly into the complex, opened the office door with the keys from my pocket, stepped into the gloom, bolted the door behind me and set about breaking into the safe. A piece of poisson.

The first key I tried opened the cupboard door and once that was open I didn't need any more keys. The Pirate hadn't locked the safe. It was open. I rifled through the contents, checked that my papers were there, and then scooped the whole lot into a carrier bag. It would be fascinating, sorting through that lot later on. Then I slammed the safe shut, spun the dial, and closed and locked the cupboard door.

All I had to do now was get out of the office and onto the ferry. It didn't take long. I stripped off all my filthy sweaty clothes and realised that I still wasn't wearing any knickers. Damn. I could have kicked myself. Why hadn't I thought to put spare knickers on my list? But there was no help for it. I'd just have to hope my trousers didn't fall down.

I climbed into my disguise outfit, got the scarf tied up over my hair and checked in the mirror. No problem. You couldn't see a single blonde tress. I tugged at it and a corner pulled loose and flopped over my face. Perfect. I checked the shirt and sawn-off trousers, congratulating myself that at least I'd remembered the safety pins. I was dressed and things were going exceptionally well.

I wiped the gun hastily on my shirt-tails, and emptied the bullets out of it. I'd have to get rid of them later. I wasn't about to leave it loaded. Not given the likely mood of the

Pirate if he ever found the damn thing.

I wrapped it up in the clothes I'd just taken off and slipped through the door into the passage outside. Heaving up the second paving slab along, I took the hidden cash out of the gap underneath it and slung the gun in. Then I dropped the slab back into position, stamped it flat, and closed and locked the barred gate and the inner door. That was that. So far so good.

I lifted the drawers out of the desk and pulled my hidden greenbacks out of their hiding place. Then I replaced the drawers and retrieved the money from under the lino. I tucked the big denominations into my bra and put the smaller ones in my pockets.

The rest, there was about two hundred dollars I suppose, well I just shoved it into the carrier bag with the other papers. I didn't have time to waste counting it and hiding it properly. Then still taking care not to make too much noise, I checked the office to make sure I hadn't left anything behind. It was fine. I'd got the cash and my papers, had hidden my clothes and the gun, and was ready to stroll off the island just carrying a plastic bag of papers in one hand and a picnic in the other. Perfect. Then I saw the keys lying there and slipped them into my pocket.

It was rapidly getting light but as I

narrowed my eyes and gazed out of the window across the bay at the Sun, there didn't seem to be any movement on board. I took a couple of deep breaths and then, forcing myself not to scribble, I wrote a note for the pliroma.

'The Boss ate too many oysters last night and he is sick today. He is sleeping now but he will be in the office later. Please do not disturb him. I have gone to find Robert. See you later, Treasure.'

I stapled the note to the outside of the office door, then picked up my carrier bags and looked around me. I hadn't forgotten anything. In fact, there was nothing to give away the fact that I'd ever been in the office at all that morning. Stepping outside, I snapped the padlock back into place and then, instead of heading through Marie-Rose's bar and onto the jetty, I strolled out of the complex by the back way and headed off up the dirt track.

Carefully scuffing my sandals and keeping my eyes on the dust under my feet, I made my way up to the big quayside where the ferry was just docking and stood behind a small group of deadbeats waiting to board her as passengers. It was just 7.30am and the sun was already burning though the sea mist on the horizon. I was nearly off the island. I was nearly home and dry.

It went like clockwork. I waited as the sun rose and beat down on us, kept my eyes down, didn't speak to anyone, and followed the others onto the ferry just before 8.00. I shuffled slowly onto the burning iron deck as the filthy old tub cast off, and its ancient engines shuddered into life, churning up the island's sewage as it went. The stink was incredible.

I didn't touch the rail. It was too hot, and anyway I wanted to keep my pale arms out of sight. But once we were clear enough of the quayside; once we were far enough out to sea that no-one on shore would be able to distinguish my face, I looked up and out at the island where I had been held prisoner for so long. It looked beautiful. Truly a little jewel with its diamond white sands, emerald palm trees and turquoise water.

There was still no sign of any activity on board the Sun, nothing was moving at Marie-Rose's bar. No-one had found my note suspicious. The Pirate wasn't chasing the ferry in a borrowed speedboat. He wasn't jumping up and down on the quayside. In fact, he didn't even seem to have got off the Sun yet. I dropped the keys and the spare bullets one by one into the sparkling sea. I'd finally managed it. I'd beaten the Pirate at his own game. I'd won. He was beaten. I was free.

But the sea breeze made my eyes sting.

10

It took far longer than I had calculated to get to an island where there was an international airport and during the whole journey I was convinced that the Pirate was on my tail, probably hand-in-hand with Lard-arse.

I was so paranoid that I went to absurd lengths not to be noticed. I didn't buy any new clothes, I didn't stay in any tourist joints, I slept on boats and ate junk from takeaway stalls. I travelled on tramp steamers, bribed local fishermen, walked from one scummy port to another, and spent my afternoons dozing in the shade, or hanging around in dodgy bars.

I looked a mess. Naturally I didn't manage to grab a shower or wash my hair so I was dark with grease and sweat. I was filthy, I was ragged, I was knackered. In fact I really did look like a deadbeat. Having forgotten the factor 100 I was not only brown with encrusted dirt but I was also sunburned and had a series of blisters on the tops of my shoulders. Just to complete the look.

When I finally arrived at the big island I couldn't even get a room in a normal hotel, I looked so rough. All the way I'd been dreaming of an air-conditioned room and a large tiled bathroom with endless hot water, bubble bath, soft towels and clean mirrors, but I ended up sharing a clean but cramped outdoor cold-water shower and perhaps it was just as well. I mean, staying in a flophouse probably kept me out of the Pirate's vision, because Nickie told me later that he had people looking for me by then.

Anyway, I bought some new clothes and sandals from the market on the first day along with a large bottle of shampoo, and spent the next two days sleeping and showering in my cheap hostel until I was presentable enough to pass muster in normal shops.

On the fourth day I trailed round the travel agencies in the heat looking for the first possible flight to Europe and finally managed to book a ticket to London. As the guy waited for the machine to process my newly retrieved credit card my heart pounded. Was there any money on it? Would it still work?

Thank God. The payment went through without a hitch. Next I bought a sturdy gold chain to wear round my neck, quite a long one so I could thread my wedding rings onto it. I didn't want to wear them, I didn't even want to keep them, but I didn't want to lose them either. Don't ask me why.

The rest of the week I spent buying things in the local market to fill up my new suitcase because I didn't fancy turning up at the airport with no luggage. Yes, even after two weeks of liberty and independence I didn't want to draw attention to myself. Just in case. I filled in the next few days waiting for my flight by lying on my bed feeling the sweat roll off my body and soak the sheets beneath me and wondering what Lardie and the Pirate were up to. Not that I cared, of course.

By the time I went to get my flight, I was sauna-clean and dressed in typical tourist clothes: white shorts and a T-shirt emblazoned with a tacky marijuana message. My skin was mahogany with fake tan, my hair was plaited into a mass of beaded rats' tails and I was wearing blue sunglasses. I was fairly certain no-one would recognise me and apparently no-one did because I wasn't queried.

Sitting on the plane I had a nasty moment though, because at the last minute the police sent sniffer dogs up and down the aisle. But perhaps they were looking for drugs. Anyway, they didn't sniff at me. UK customs did, but that was probably just the horrible tourist plaits. They didn't stop me though. I just sailed by looking as if I was expecting to be met by a nice reliable chauffeur and they let me go.

I took the Piccadilly line all the way into the West End and emerged shivering into the bright lights of a Friday night feeling completely weird to be back in London after so many years away.

It hadn't really changed, although a thousand and one little details were different, but the sense of déjà vu added to my sense of living in a dream. Every time I closed my eyes I felt like I was still in the Caribbean and was surprised when I opened them to find myself back in the UK.

My legs aching and my head spinning, I walked slowly along Shaftesbury Avenue and turned left up a side street into Soho. Aunt Lottie has a tall narrow Georgian place just up there behind the Windmill, where I used to stay in the school holidays — when Daniel forgot to send me airline tickets or Harriet was giving birth — but it had been years since I'd been to see her.

I stood on the pavement and looked up at the house. Nothing had changed. It was as shabby as ever. From the names beside the bells, even the tenants hadn't changed. The basement was still occupied by the same shaggy architect, the ground floor still housed a dodgy theatrical agency. The first floor bell

285

was still blank, so I guessed Lottie was still letting that floor to touring dancers by the month.

The top two floors, filled with dusty sofas, ballet memorabilia, pot plants and faded red velvet cushions, are Lottie's. She lives there with a variety of cats, entertaining an even larger variety of floating men friends who take her to private clubs for lunch and afternoon drinking sessions.

Standing back, I peered up through the orange London gloom. It looked as if there was a light on up there. I trod up the steps, rang the doorbell and in response Aunt Lottie leaned out of a top window, her white hair billowing crazily around her head and a Chinese wrapper clutched around her shoulders.

'Darling!' she exclaimed. 'Come in! Oh, my God, Milly! How are you? Wait a minute, I'll just find my keys.'

I lurked on the pavement and a few minutes later she leant out again. 'Catch!'

I stood well out of range until the keys landed. Then I scooped them up, let myself in and started up the creaky stairs.

'Milly, is that really you?' she called down over the banisters.

'I'm sorry . . . ' I panted, stumbling up the last few stairs to the landing. 'I suppose I should have hugged her or something, but that last climb upstairs had finished me off and I just stood there. She gave me a sharp glance but didn't comment on my red eyes or mad plaits.

'Just come in,' she said, and steered me towards a sofa. She bundled a pair of tabby cats off it and plumped up the cushions. 'Put your feet up, dear. I'll see what we can do in the way of refreshments . . .'

She disappeared into the kitchen and I sagged heavily onto the red velvet and stretched out with a sigh.

'Would you like some pilchards?' she asked popping her head round a dusty velvet drape which served as a kitchen door.

'Mmmm . . . I'm not actually very hungry.' I couldn't even open my eyes.

'Oh well,' she said, bringing a saucer of them out anyway. 'Puss might like them. See if you can tempt him, darling. He's getting old you know.' She picked up an enormous ginger cat, and plopped him on my stomach. 'There you are, Baby. Milla will feed you.'

I stared at him groggily and he stared back at me. I was obviously lying on his sofa. A few minutes later she came flitting back with a glass of mulled wine in a tarnished filigree holder and a crocheted cat blanket.

'I'll just put this over your feet, dear.'

My eyes closed heavily, and opened again as she came back with a cup of Russian tea and a minuscule box of chocolates from Fortnum and Mason. I pushed Puss off, put the pilchards down on the floor for him, and wondered whether to tackle the tea or the wine first. I closed my eyes, waiting for my head to stop buzzing, and fell instantly asleep.

Aunt Lottie woke me the next morning with the information that she'd run me a hot bath. Quacking softly and aching in every limb I staggered to my feet and disappeared to the bathroom. When I emerged from the steam disguised as a towel-wrapped lobster, she was perched on the edge of a collapsing armchair in the sitting room.

'I've made breakfast for you, dear,' she said. 'Just for a treat.'

On one of her wobbly antique tables was a tray set with a clutter of fragile china, a large silver teapot, a boiled egg in a cosy and the tiny box of chocolates.

'If it's too early in the day, don't think you have to eat the egg,' she said, pulling a face.

'No, it's fine.' I poured myself a cup of tea. 'Perfect. I hope I didn't wake you up last night . . . '

'Not at all. As you know I never go to bed before three.'

'I'm sorry to just turn up on you . . . '

'I thought you would, sooner or later. You are all right, dear. Aren't you?'

'I'm fine.'

She shrugged, her thin shoulders making little mountain peaks in her silk shirt. 'I don't know. Perhaps I was wrong,' she said. 'But I thought you'd be better off . . . you know, when your mother died. Boarding school seemed like such a good solution. At the time. It was my idea, you know.'

'What d'you mean?'

'Oh well, it's sometimes seemed to me as if you blamed Danny, thought he didn't love you enough or something . . . he absolutely adores you, you know. Always did. Took a lot of persuading, to let you go after your mother died.'

I didn't say anything, and she pulled a face. 'Age catching up with me,' she said. 'Introspection, doubts, all that sort of thing. I don't know why I'm sitting here chit-chatting. I really ought to go and clean out the cat litter. I just worry about you sometimes. You seem so terribly . . . determined not to let anyone love you.'

I hadn't a clue what to say. I just sat there with my teaspoon half sticking out of my egg.

She laughed. 'Sorry, darling!' she said suddenly. 'Too dire, so early in the day too! But I'm out to lunch so I haven't got much time.' She raised her eyebrows. 'When you get to my age the face needs all the help it can get. I'll have to go and put some slap on. Could you possibly change the cat litter for me? I'm running a bit late and Edward will kill me . . . '

'Sure . . . '

'Good girl. But first, bring your tea up and talk to me. I want to hear everything.'

Upstairs in her cluttered dusty bedroom, I lolled on her enormous un-made bed and Aunt Lottie pushed a cat aside and sat down at her dressing table. She already looked completely made-up to me but as I watched, she applied several more coats of lipstick and, shoving piles of faded silk flowers out of the way, dipped a fluff brush into a pot of rouge and dusted it comprehensively over her face, neck and cleavage.

'Come on, out with it!' she said watching me through the mirror.

So I gave her a condensed version of the last few years of my life, while she applied several more coats of black mascara.

When I finished, she shook her head. 'What a catalogue of wrong-headedness! I've got to go, but you're completely batty. You'll never settle for respectability. You're genetically unfitted for it. Look at me, look at Danny, look at your mother — running off with a sax player — I mean, you've got it from both sides. Oops, is that lipstick on my teeth? Or chocolate? You might as well accept it. You're a swan my dear, not an ugly duckling. A very beloved swan.'

She held her paper-thin hands up to the light and inspected her nail varnish. 'Not too chipped, are they? Don't say a word. I'm late. My taxi will be here in a jiff. No, don't argue with me. I've got to go. I have to call in at the butcher and buy some yummies for the cats. If I do it after lunch, I'll forget and then they won't be happy tibbies. Make yourself at home, do what you like but you must absolutely promise not to run off before I get back. Cross your heart?'

I promised, and she slung a moth-eaten fur coat round her shoulders, sprayed herself generously with scent and climbed elegantly down the steep stairs, being careful not to catch her high heels in the threadbare carpet. Just as she was about to disappear round the bend in the stairs, she looked up and shook her finger at me.

'Just one more thing! You can take this much from an old woman: this husband of yours — you're mad if you think he doesn't love you. Men only marry women they adore.'

The front door slammed, and from the

window I watched her enter a black cab, gracefully drawing her ankles in after her like a princess. She gave me a tiny wave as the taxi drove away.

Downstairs I investigated the kitchen and wasn't the least surprised to find that the fridge contained absolutely nothing except cat tins and wine. Puss and his feline flat-mates came pattering in, so I scooped a selection of cat food into the bowls on the floor and went out into the hallway to deal with their litter.

That done, I sat down on the sofa intending to make a list of things to do and fell asleep again. I was desperately tired.

Aunt Lottie got back from lunch late that afternoon clutching a dripping bag of cow intestines and declaring that she was incapable of moving any further that day.

'Too much calvados, darling!' she said dropping into an armchair and kicking her heels off.

I put the cat food in the fridge and switched the kettle on. 'Too tired even for a civilised little supper with me?' I asked from the kitchen. 'My treat? To say sorry?'

'Well, darling. Perhaps if I had just a very small glass of champagne I might revive . . . Is there a bottle in the fridge?'

In fact, she drank several very small glasses

of champagne, redid her lipstick, powdered her nose and then, her eyes sparkling, reached for the phone and booked a table while I went upstairs for her fur hat and coat.

We went to an old fashioned Russian restaurant on the corner of her street where all the waiters bent down to kiss her and she ordered without reading the menu.

'Now, there's only one more thing I want to say to you and then I'll stop being a tiresome old bore and shut up,' she said firmly as the waiter retreated with our order.

I did elaborate yawning at her. She was incapable of shutting up.

'Yes, Auntie Charlotte.'

'I want you to visit me more often, bring the boys to see me although where they can sleep I don't know. Perhaps with the dancers? And stay in better touch with your poor father and just . . . well, realise you have an extremely nice and loving family. Danny does have an email address you know. There's nothing to stop you using it.'

'Yes, but . . . '

'I really don't think I have the strength for the details. Daniel would be thrilled to see you, darling. That's all. Just go and see him. Take the twins. He loves you so much. Do you know, I think that darling boy over there is making eyes at me? Candlelight! Such a comfort to the decaying beauties of this world. They're all dancers here you know, the waiters. That's why they move so well. And have such well-defined buttocks, of course.'

She then kept up a stream of inconsequential chatter, only once dropping her guard, long after midnight, when just before drifting up the stairs to bed she brushed my cheek and said, 'I'm so glad to see you. Such a pleasure! Don't wait so long next time. No, don't say anything. I really can't bear discussions. Where's Puss? Come on, little man, come to bed with Lottie.'

The next morning I took her a cup of tea in bed before I left for the station, and kissed her forehead to wake her up. Her thin eyelids fluttered open and in the daylight, without her make-up I realised that she really was getting quite old.

'So thoughtful, dear . . . but I might just go back to sleep if you don't mind,' she said drowsily. 'Come back soon.'

'Okay,' I whispered.

'Sexy waiter . . . ' she said and smiled, obviously already drifting back into sleep. I watched her for a moment, but she showed no sign of regaining consciousness so I trod silently over to her dressing table, selected a dusty un-used red lipstick and wrote 'Thank you for everything. Love you lots, Cxxx' on the mirror.

Then I crept out of the house leaving Puss and his friends to yawn, stretch and curl in blissful torpor on Aunt Lottie's satin eiderdown.

11

I slept on the train down to the south coast, and at the station climbed wearily into another taxi. Aunt Lottie had given me food for thought, but to be honest I wasn't ready to think. She was well meaning; she loved me; I loved her. But I was still in action-man mode. Action-woman. Super-woman, idiot-woman . . . whatever.

'Where d'you say, love?'

I handed the driver a slip of paper with the address on it.

'Oh yes, I know,' he said, nodding. 'Been somewhere nice, have you?'

'Yes, been on my holidays,' I said. 'Spain. It was really hot.'

Holidays! Life with the Pirate had hardly been a holiday. While the driver rambled on about his fortnight in Majorca, I wondered what had happened after I left. Had he managed to get himself free or had someone found him? Had he already started divorce proceedings?

'Here we are, love. What number did you say?'

'Number 16,' I said.

'Oh yes, here you are. Looks like they're

having some work done, don't it?'

I stood on the pavement as the taxi drove away. The front garden of Nickie's house was occupied by a skip piled high with old timber and building rubble. The front door was painted scarlet and the windows were hung with stripy blinds. I shivered. England seemed furiously cold after the Caribbean although it wasn't raining and in fact it wasn't a bad day. There was even a pale sun sulking about in the grey sky.

'Milly!' squawked Nickie, flinging the door open.

'Hiya,' I grinned, and we hugged each other like a pair of footballers.

'Come in, come in,' she said, dragging me through the front door. 'I'm so glad you're here. I hoped it was you when I heard the taxi. I was sure you'd turn up sooner or later!'

We grinned at each other, and she shut the front door. 'Come through to the kitchen. Yes, this way,' she said, picking an armful of coats up off the floor and hurling them over the banisters. 'Is that your luggage?'

I shuffled further into the hall clutching my suitcase, and gazed around. Very arty, very designer, very Nickie. Lots of colours. Like a posh teabag box.

'I brought you some spices from Martinique,' I said, rummaging hopelessly, bags breaking open and things falling all over the floor. Nickie picked up a pair of trousers and held them up.

'What on earth are these? Not exactly Jean Muir, are they?'

'Oh, those. Getaway disguise.'

'Of course. Why didn't I think of that? A getaway outfit. I should have known! And you're keeping them because?'

'Had to fill the case up. Here you are. Fresh nutmegs and a batik thing.'

'Fab! Great colours. Thank you, darling. Come through, come on. The kitchen's through here. What do you want? Caffeine? Hydration? Alcohol?'

'White wine if you've got it,' I sighed, and sank down at her kitchen table which was pine, stained crimson. The wooden chairs around it were all stained different colours; scarlet, orange, green, yellow. The walls were roughly washed over with yellow ochre and instead of kitchen units, Nickie had brought her old chestnut-wood kitchen dresser and cupboards over from France. The floor was covered in reclaimed quarry tiles and rag rugs. The whole room looked like an advert for romantic French living.

'Beautiful kitchen,' I said, looking around. 'You are clever.'

'Yes, it worked out quite well,' she said. 'I

quite like those cupboards against the print on those curtains, even if it does fight a bit with the crimson. Hmm . . . I might have to change that, damp it down a bit. But not until I've got the rest of the place sorted. I haven't even touched the bedrooms yet.'

She tossed a packet of pistachio nuts onto the table and produced a bottle of white Bordeaux from the fridge with a flourish. 'Spoils of war!' she said. 'At least I've got something to show for my respectable marriage!'

'A large stash of dry white?'

'Precisely, my dear. Not to mention the nuts.' She hauled the cork out of the bottle, slopped the wine into two tumblers and sat down at the table. 'Now, I want all the details! What happened?'

So I filled her in and she nodded and said, 'Yes, that would do it . . . that would explain it.'

'Explain what?' I asked, with a sense of foreboding.

'You've obviously driven him demented. He's been phoning pretty much night and day from some clinic or other. A secure unit in a mental health facility, I expect. Completely incoherent. Last time he rang, he was babbling about guns and radios. Seems to think you might have drowned, says he wants to rescue you. Er, from yourself. Here, have a pistachio.'

'What! Rescue me from myself! That's a good one.' I grabbed a handful of pistachio nuts and started shelling them maniacally.

'He says you need looking after.'

'Looking after! That fat-arsed, slack-bellied, pig-bottomed, weed-encrusted remainder of a memory of a dried-up pond scum DNA sample! I hate him!'

'Yes, well of course you do. He is your husband. What else are husbands for? Or are you divorcing him?' She filled our glasses up. 'Cheers.'

I gazed at her, imagining the Pirate faced with a divorce petition. He'd hit the roof. He'd shout and yell, wave his arms about and throw things, but he definitely wouldn't tick the box marked easy-peasy Japan-eezy I agree let's divorce quickly. He'd make a fuss. A huge, colossal, massive fuss. Just on principle.

'No, he won't even divorce me,' I sighed.

'So are you going to make it up with him?'

'Hardly! You don't seem to get the picture, Nickie. It's serious. I tried to kill him. I was that close to murder. That close. I mean I left him with his feet taped together at one end of the bunk, his hands taped behind his back, and about two reels of parcel tape wound round his mouth so he couldn't call for help.

See what I mean?'

'Your marriage is going through a sticky patch?' she said and started cracking up like a hatching chicken.

'Not even a wet patch. I tried to shoot him, Nickie!'

'Oh, yes, well I've tried to murder the sailor several times,' she said snorting with laughter and wiping her eyes. She drained her glass and slapped it down on the table like a gunfighter giving up his gun belt at the Crazy Horse Saloon. 'It does them good. Keeps them in line. There isn't a man alive that doesn't need to be frightened now and again. Makes them respect you. Perhaps you're just expecting too much? He's only a man, after all. Here, have some more wine.'

I pushed my glass forward for a refill and tried to explain. 'I don't think you're in the picture, Nickie. The guy abandoned me on a boat, he nicked my stuff, he wouldn't let me leave . . . '

She choked with amusement and I felt half inclined to sulk but then she wrinkled her nose up and pulled one of her crazy faces. 'And you stole some important papers? You stole a boat? And you pulled a gun on him? And you taped him up?'

'Well, er sort of. Look, the gun was just, er . . . borrowed. And the papers, well some other papers just got sort of mixed up with my stuff when I opened the safe so they just came along with me. But the speedboat. No. I didn't steal his speedboat, I just er . . . scuttled it a bit.'

'Huh?'

'I sank it,' I said. 'So he couldn't come after me in it.'

'But hadn't you just left him tied up on the boat, getting intimately acquainted with five rolls of parcel tape?' she said, going off into giggles again. 'So there was no way he was coming after you, was there?'

'You don't know him, Nickie! When I locked him in the office . . . '

'Er . . . ?' Nickie sniggered. She clearly wasn't even trying to take me seriously. I filled our glasses up again and tried to explain.

'Well he found me trying to break into the safe because I wanted to find out what he'd done with my passport and then he came in and we had this huge row and I locked him into the office.'

'Er, yes. Extremely romantic. Very loving. Almost Stepford Wife stuff, in fact,' she said, grinning at me.

'Well he was furious.'

'So would I be, if I found you breaking into my safe!'

'Not because of that, because of the prawns. I threw a box of frozen prawns all over him.'

Nickie laughed and slugged back her wine. 'You crack me up,' she exclaimed. 'You accuse him of all this stuff, but you're just as bad. Sounds like the pair of you are well matched!'

I grinned, knocked back the rest of my glass and re-filled the tumblers.

'Well, he deserved it,' I said, tilting the bottle sideways to check that it really was empty.

'Probably,' she agreed. 'He's a man, after all, isn't he? Deserves everything he gets.'

'Certainly does.'

'Here's to us!'

'String in your chin!' said Nickie as we clinked glasses. 'Are you going to read his emails?'

'Not right now,' I said. 'Why, what do they say?'

'In just a few words? He wants you back, and says to leave the boys in school so as not to disrupt them. And he wants his speedboat back.'

'Hasn't he found it, then?'

'Clearly not.'

'I thought he'd find it straight away.'

'No, I think he was under the impression

that you'd tried to take it over to some other island and got yourself drowned. He had the navy out looking for you.'

'Oh, my God.'

'Apparently they've been looking for you all over the Caribbean. But then the police found your name on some flight list to London, and he started phoning me here.'

'But how did he get your number?'

She shrugged. 'Photocopied your address book? Spied on your emails? Used an intergalactic long-range address-book probe? Read your mind? Hired a private investigator? Was receiving signals from a high-tech chip implanted secretly into your left heel? How should I know?'

'Oh well, as long as he doesn't turn up here,' I said.

'What are your plans? I mean, you're welcome to stay here, but the place is a mess, and . . . '

'No, don't worry. It'd be great if I could stay here tonight. I'm just too knackered to do anything else today. But I'll find somewhere else tomorrow. Perhaps one of those furnished flats on a short term lease?'

'You're planning to stay here, then? In England?'

'For the moment. I don't know what else I can do. Fiona's still living in the house in

France. Running some sort of pottery co-operative. But it must be going well because she's been paying rent into my bank account.'

'Has she indeed? It must be profitable, then. You know I think she's really getting her shit together these days. She even lets Max ring me once a week.'

'Huh?'

'I know. But he's my dawg and ah lerves him. She rings up every Saturday and holds the receiver to his face so I can hear him snuffling, and he can hear me going 'biccie, Max, bic-bic!'

I gazed at her. Her eyes were actually glittering with sentimental little tears. Was her dog more important to her than . . . well, than her kids? Her husband? Her house? Me? Why was she talking to me about her dog?

'Only one more month to go and she's bringing him home. I just can't wait.' A twinkly tear rolled down her cheek. 'I love him so much!'

She caught my eye and had the grace to wipe her tears away and sniff back the rest of the salty flood. 'Sorry Milly-Moll. I know you're not a dog-woman. But I really miss Max. I just miss him like hell.'

'Well, thank God that Fiona lets him phone you once a week, then!'

Nickie pulled herself together. 'Yes. Thank God for Fiona. What would we do without her?'

I met her eye. Strange. We'd always laughed about mad Fiona but here we both were, relying on her to sort stuff out for us.

'Yes, anyway,' I said gruffly. 'So I can't go back to France. Not if Fiona's still potting in my house. And God knows where Daniel and Harriet are — could be still in Moscow for all I know, and anyhow they've got enough on their hands with Mischa and the littles.

'Huh?'

'My father and his girlfriend. Their kids. Mischa's the nanny. Yes, a Russian. A man. Balalyka. Anyway the twins are in school here. Also, there's more chance of getting a job here than in the Languedoc, so . . .'

'What are you going to do about the boys?'

'I don't know. I haven't seen them yet. I'll have to talk to them about it, but I shouldn't think I can afford to go on paying their school fees so I'll probably have to shift them into a state school. But I've got to find somewhere to live first. And a job.'

'So you're not going back to the Caribbean?'

I looked at her aghast. 'Are you mad? Do you know what he'll do?'

'You don't think he's learned his lesson?

Here, do you want something to eat? You must be starving. You look bloody thin, you know.'

'Oh don't. The Pirate was always telling me to eat.'

'Now . . . what have I got here,' muttered Nickie raking through the fridge. 'Cheese, sausage, ah, here's some chicken korma — I'll heat it up for you.'

I didn't think I could eat but in fact I was starving, and gobbled my way through all Nickie's leftovers while she cooked dinner. It all tasted great to me, even the zero-fat fruit yoghurt.

'You know, I think I might be able to help you on the job front. There's a guy at work called Gus. He's always complaining that his wife can't get decent secretaries for her office. She runs an indoor plant agency.'

'A what?'

'Here, have some olives. They get contracts to supply and maintain tame jungles in big offices. You know the sort of thing. Lots of Swiss cheese, yuccas, rubber plants. I could have a word with him if you like.'

'But I'm not a secretary.'

'Well, you can type, can't you?'

'Sort of. But I'd be useless at filing or making coffee. I mean, last time I worked in an office they were still using telex machines.'

'Oh, you'll pick it up. You just need to get some office clothes and look willing. I'm sure you'll be okay.'

'Office clothes?'

'Yes, you know the sort of thing; knee-length skirt with a nice elastic waist so you don't get wind from sitting down all day. Neat blouse, cardigan and a pair of comfortable shoes.'

'Oh, my God.'

'I'll come shopping with you, if you like.'

'Is that what you wear to work?'

She had the grace to blush. 'More or less.'

'Shouldn't you be at work today?'

'Jesus, Millie! Look, I've had your husband on the phone solid for three weeks.' She stopped stirring then and turned on me, waving a wooden spoon. 'He's filled my inbox with demented e-mails, and was phoning me at work approximately every thirty seconds, and the IT guy had to block all my incoming mail because he was jamming up the office server, and when Interpol arrived in the office to interview me about a missing person my boss hit the bloody roof.

'Pirates on two continents have been searching for you. You're bloody lucky that the school kept them away from the kids. I've been off work all week because when he realised you were probably in the UK, your husband told the police you might turn up here and they were threatening to camp out on the fucking doorstep.'

'Oh God, I'm sorry Nickie. It didn't occur to me that anybody would be looking for me apart from the Pirate. I'm really sorry.'

'Well, I suppose it's not your fault. You really do owe me one, though. Thank God it's only the police and not the taxman. I'm going to have to phone, by the way, and let them know you've turned up. Here, have some cold beans.'

'Oh God, I'm really sorry,' I mumbled guiltily.

'Don't be. It's been rather a Godsend, actually,' said Nickie and flashed me a sparkly pout over her shoulder.

'What?' I said. 'What have you been up to? Come on, tell!'

'No-thing! Just getting myself invited to exhibit my work at the most prestigious gallery on the south coast,' she said, flushing with excitement.

'This is brilliant!' I said. 'When, where, how, tell me! Hang on. Stop. Getting yourself, you said. Do I detect something else afoot? Could there be a . . . man in here somewhere? Nickie! What are you up to?'

She flicked her hair out of her eyes with a wicked pout and lounged against the counter

. . . 'Nothing,' she said in a husky voice. 'I'm a respectable married lady and if a gallery owner with spectacularly good taste and even better connections in the art world, just happens to think that my take on modern sexuality is utterly inspirational and, what's more, accomplished with impeccable technique . . . then it's not my fault is it?'

'Is he good looking? Is he a hunk?'

'Our relationship is purely cerebral, Millie!'

'Ugly as sin, then?'

'Just a tad . . . balding.'

'Nothing a wig couldn't fix.'

'Millie, you're horrible. Anyway, I'm not going to bed with him . . . '

'Just allowing him to appreciate your inspirational modern sexuality?'

She grinned at me and turned back to her cooking pots.

'Time to come home, Treasure!' shouted the Pirate.

'Shit!' I yelled, leaping to my feet, sending my glass flying and knocking nuts all over the floor. 'Why didn't you tell me he was here?' My heart was tangoing from one side of my chest to the other, and I felt like I was going to faint. Nickie jumped too when I yelled, and then after one look at my terrified face she broke into uncontrollable hoots of laughter. In between guffaws she waved her wooden spoon at me and shook her head.

'No! No! Not him! Parrot!'

'What? What are you on about! Stop it, Nickie, stop it!'

But it took some time for her to stop screaming with laughter, and when she tried to speak, she choked and that set her off again. I slapped her on the back and passed her a glass of water but it was hopeless, her legs had gone wambly and she was sitting on the floor laughing like she'd won the pools.

'Come on, woman. Pull yourself together! What the fuck was that?' I demanded.

'Parrot!' she gasped, mopping her eyes. 'He sent you a parrot!'

'That was a parrot?'

'Yes, a Pirate parrot! It shouts all the time.'

As if it had overheard her, the parrot suddenly repeated 'Time to come home, Treasure!' in an exact imitation of the Pirate.

'Good grief!' I exclaimed. 'Where is it? How did it get here? Where did it come from? I mean, you're not telling me the postman delivered it? A parrot? He sent you a parrot?'

'I don't know how it got here. It just arrived in a taxi.'

'Rudolph!' I muttered. 'Bloody Rudi the Red Nosed Parrot Smuggler! Just you wait till I see him. I'll kill him! How dare he send you . . .'

'But it's not for me,' grinned Nickie. 'He sent it to you!'

'Me? What am I going to do with the damn thing?'

'How am I supposed to know? Teach it to say Not Tonight Josephine? Send it back? Keep it, cuddle it, love it . . . whatever you like.'

'Sell it.'

'I don't think so.'

'Why?'

'You haven't heard what else it says.'

'Tay-kit-off! I don-cair!' shouted the parrot.

'The worst thing is the kids,' said Nickie, wiping her eyes. They've been teaching it to sing 'There's a hole in my buttock, dear Lisa, dear Lisa . . . '

'Oh God!'

'Then fill it dear Henry . . . With a cork dear Henry, dear Henry . . . '

'How disgusting!'

'You haven't heard the rest of it . . . You know what kids are. They think it's the funniest thing since the word nipple was invented.'

'And they're teaching that to the parrot?'

'Can't stop them.'

'Where is it?' I asked, and she staggered to her feet and led me through into her sitting room. It was half decorated, the walls washed with terracotta and the furniture standing about on bare floorboards.

'I couldn't finish painting with that thing standing there,' said Nickie, gazing at a birdcage the size of an aviary. Inside was an enormous, disreputable parrot. Various multi-coloured feathers were in the process of falling out, it had a bald patch on one shoulder and one foot looked as if it had been stuck on crooked. As we advanced towards the cage, it cocked its head at us and swivelled one eye in circles, the scaly skin of its eyelid showering the cage floor with parrot dandruff.

'Ger-rum off!' it shouted. 'Ger-rum down!'

'OmiGod,' I breathed. The parrot raised its tail and a large dollop of parrot poo fell onto the cage floor.

'Christ, what a stink!' I exclaimed.

'Shh!' whispered Nickie. 'He'll repeat everything you say!'

'Oh my God!' moaned the parrot. 'Christ! Oooh! Oh my God! Oooh yes! More! Don't stop! Oh yes, yes, yes . . . arggh, ooof, whoa, yeah, ooooh, don't stop, I'm coming! Aaarg, aaarg, aaarg!'

It swayed on its perch, happily reproducing orgasm noises and rolling its eyes at us. I gazed at it in horror and disbelief.

'That's why you can't sell it,' she said.

I just stood rooted to the ground. Nickie put her finger to her lips and pushed me towards the door.

'Oooh!' moaned the parrot again. 'Pretty fuckin polly! Time to come home, Treasure. Christ, what a stink! I'm coming!'

Slamming the door behind us, Nickie looked at me, and mopped her streaming eyes again. 'And before you ask, no I can't keep it for you! The kids have been inviting all their friends round to listen to the bloody thing, and I'm just waiting for some po-faced parent to start asking awkward questions. And I had to cancel Muthar's visit. I mean, can you imagine her coming face to face with that? An orgasmic parrot, for Gawd's sake!'

Back in the kitchen again, needing reinforcements, we attacked the cooking sherry.

'Here, have some of this,' said Nickie. 'I bought it because Muthar likes trifle . . . '

At that moment the phone rang. 'I'm not here!' I said quickly. 'Whoever it is, I'm not here!'

'Yes, okay, hang on,' said Nickie into the phone and then tucked the receiver under her arm. 'He just wants to know you're safe,' she whispered at me. 'Give him a break!'

I made furious throat-cutting signals, mouthed 'No!' and shook my head, but she did it anyway.

314

'Hello? Yes, she's here. Just arrived. No, she's fine. Not hurt in any way, just tired. No, I haven't phoned them yet, I was just going to do it. No, she won't speak to you, she . . . '

I yanked the phone plug out of the wall socket.

'Hello? Hello?'

'You cow!' I exclaimed. 'Why did you do that? He'll probably turn up here now.'

'He just wanted to know you were safe. I won't let him into the house if you don't want me to, okay?'

'What, you think he's going to just stand there on the doorstep a-ringin the bell like a nice boy? You're mad. He'll just walk straight over you and leave you lying on the doormat. Flat. With footprints all over your tits.'

'I'd like to see him try!' said Nickie. 'Stop panicking. He's not even in the UK.' She lifted her glass. 'Come on. Here's to us!'

We clinked our glasses of cooking sherry together and emptied them, and then I said, 'It was his fault, anyway.'

'Course it was,' said Nickie. 'He's a man, isn't he? Have you got any cash? Shall we go out for some champagne?'

I love Nickie.

12

I stayed at Nickie's but I was so tired I don't remember much else about that evening. Her family came home, the police came round, I answered questions and ate humble pie, the police went away, we ate supper and I went to bed.

The next day I went off to the boys' school where I had a seriously sticky interview with the head teacher. I mean, at one point I thought she was actually going to give me lines: I must not go awol in the Caribbean, to be written out 500 times and handed in before morning assembly. But finally she ran out of steam, I scoffed down yet another helping of humble pie and the boys were ushered into her study. I fell on their necks with squeals of joy, stroking and patting them as if they were a pair of wriggling puppies as they yelped and tumbled around me.

They didn't seem the slightest bit surprised that I was in England, accepting without question that I'd just fancied dropping in to say hello. They'd grown enormously and were full of enthusiasm; vying with each other to tell me about riding tests, rowing competitions, sailing, their top marks in geography and Spanish — which they were doing instead of French because they already spoke it fluently. I listened and laughed and hugged them again, stroking their heads and gazing into their happy faces as they prattled away about their friends, their drum lessons and the drama group. They had settled in like fleas on a cat.

Finally, having promised to take them out on Saturday, I left the school full of determination to keep them there if it was my last act on earth. It would be awful to move them into another school when they were so happy and obviously doing so well.

The problem was money of course. I had no idea if I'd be able to earn enough — if I'd even be able to get a job at all with a peculiar cv, no qualifications and about the same amount of work experience as a mushroom skin. But I comforted myself with the thought that Fiona's rent for the house in France had mounted up considerably, I still had a reassuring roll of American dollars in my suitcase and I hadn't used up all the overdraft facility on my own bank account yet. I had time to think of something.

Once back in town, I bought myself a mobile phone and a local paper, and settled down to scan the small ads.

It took two days to find a furnished flat over a betting shop in the town centre. It was intensely dull — cream paint throughout, brown and oatmeal furnishings, disgusting aluminium window frames — but it had two bedrooms and it was vacant. I paid the deposit, signed the tenancy agreement and moved in immediately.

Sitting in my porridge-coloured kitchen that night, I finally read the Pirate's e-mails. Nickie had printed them out and brought them round after work.

'Jesus, this is vomitous!' she said. 'Who on earth put all this revolting cream paint in here?'

'Landlord, I suppose. Probably thinks it's classy.'

Nickie raised her eyebrows and pulled a face. 'Well, I suppose you can always paint it . . . '

'Not unless I want to lose my deposit.'

'Oh. Might be worth it, though. This is disgusting!'

I shrugged. 'Oh, I don't care. Do you want a drink?'

'No, I can't stay,' she said still eyeing the walls, 'I just wanted to give you Philippa's phone number, and find out if you've got an email address yet? No, I've got your mobile number. Oh, and I brought these for you . . . '

She dragged a sheaf of papers out of her raffia shopping bag and pushed them into my hands. I gave her a filthy look, but she just smiled brightly.

'I've got to go now,' she said, beating a rapid retreat as I scanned the top sheet of paper with a gathering frown. 'Have to take the monster to tennis. I'll ring you later on your mobile.'

Nickie clattered off down the stairs and I sat at the formica kitchen table and flipped through the Pirate's emails. He wanted me to contact him, he wanted me to come home, he wanted the boys to stay in school. He apologised for his 'mistakens'. He said that the twins' school fees were already paid until the end of June. 'So don't mix twins in this, that is only to hurt them for nothing.' He said I was the only woman he'd ever met that was as strong as him. He said we belonged together, that we were perfectly matched, that I shouldn't throw my life away. He said I owed him at least a phone call.

Thoroughly exasperated, I threw the whole lot in the bin. The man was mad. Not just off his trolley, but so far off it, he probably didn't even know what a trolley was . . . 'Bloody man,' I muttered crossly at the mud-coloured sofa. Because yes, the Pirate's world was quite literally a trolley-free zone.

By the morning, I'd made my decision. For the time being the boys would stay at their school, but as day pupils not boarders. We would all live together in the mealie-mouthed flat. As for the fees, well I'd cross that bridge when I got to it. Once I'd got a job, I could always earn extra cash teaching piano or French or something.

So I trotted determinedly round the employment agencies filling in forms and attempting to convince them that I was an employable proposition. I took to wearing my wedding rings again in an effort to look more respectable. I even bought a floral knee-length skirt, and claimed that I could type. Which I could. Sort of. One finger at a time. It didn't matter. I was so full of enthusiasm that I enjoyed filling in clean white forms and sitting in neat typing chairs doing baby maths and English tests. I prided myself on ticking the boxes incredibly neatly without making any nasty smudges.

Which is where you came into the story, Philippa, so I won't go over over all that. Nickie introduced me to Gus, he introduced me to you and you were either desperate or mad — oh no, that sounds horrible. You were divine. You were wonderful. You gave me this job and I love it. I like working for you. I like the other people, I like the office. I really like working in a shifting jungle of plants coming and going. I especially like going off to the greenhouses to do stocktaking and make progress notes on the rescued plants. Thank you, Philippa. You really are a star! I mean it.

Anyway, the boys had moved home a week before I started working for you, and after a week or so, when there had been no sign of the Pirate, I relaxed and started enjoying my new life. He was still emailing me twice a day of course, but I didn't bother to check my email that often, and if I saw anything from him I just deleted it unread.

I was way too busy to think about him because I was playing house — well, playing flats, actually. Nesting. The flat was a furnished one but none of the stuff was very nice, and there were loads of things missing — lamps, rugs, vases, pictures, all that sort of thing. So I spent a lot of time wandering round Saturday junk markets, poking about in thrift shops, and gazing at expensive window displays.

Adjusting to living with the boys took time, too. They'd changed, grown-up I suppose. They were no longer my little babies, they were young men who locked the bathroom door, left stinky socks on the floor, and called me 'mother' instead of 'mummy'.

I bought a second-hand car and revelled in getting up early to drive the twins to school. I know it sounds mad, but I loved the whole business. I used to get up extra-specially early to shower, wash my hair and get dressed properly so that I could take them to school with my make-up on straight and my eyes shining with excitement.

I'm probably the first person in our entire family to do the school run. I can't imagine Harriet doing it. I shouldn't think her kids even go to school. I bet she and Daniel are home educating them — sitting in some recording studio in Berlin teaching them Italian and music while Mischa drinks vodka and they all argue over repertoire.

It rained a lot, which pleased me too because the silver English rain was cold and fresh rather than warm and sweaty. There were muddy road works and diversions, rude drivers and roads blocked by accidents, but I adored it all. I could hardly wait to get out of the house in the morning and see all the glittering puddles, the stormy faces, the frost on the cars and the misty exhaust fumes wreathing round the glowing street lights.

I used to turn the radio up and sing along with all the tunes. I only knew about half of them though, so where I didn't know the words I just yodelled harmony lines. The twins thought it was hysterical and skidded about on the back seat howling with laughter. The first day or two, I parked the car near the school and walked the boys to the gates, loving the sensation of breathing in cold air and thoroughly enjoying the ritual of calling good morning to all the other parents — but I got warned off.

I was being seriously un-cool, said the twins. The other parents were from the lower school. Kids from the upper school didn't suffer the indignity of watching their parents cluster round the school gates, they walked to school by themselves. So after I dropped them off I got into the habit of having coffee in town, reading a newspaper and feeling incredibly organised and together. In the afternoons I strolled round the shops buying things and then I had the pleasure of doing the school run all over again in the afternoon.

And the day I started work for you, Philippa, well it was just brilliant. Oh! The thrill of being in a large office block with lifts, nylon carpets and a canteen for lunch! It was all so nice. Totally nice. All the men wore clean suits and ties, all the women wore neat skirts and pretty tops. I bought a great pile of them myself, and some cutie-pie shoes to wear with them. Of course, after months of wearing nothing but flip-flops the shoes were excruciatingly uncomfortable, but the look of them was compensation enough. I even had my hair cut into a Mary Tyler Moore bob with a fringe and flick-ups. The clicking of my heels just went so nicely with the stiffly curled hair and the pale pink lipstick that I used to find myself laughing out loud for sheer joy on my way to the coffee machine on level 2.

The flat was easy-clean. It had a hoover and a dishwasher and lots of white plastic surfaces which only needed a puff of spray-on foam and the flick of a J-cloth. I was tickled pink. I used to spill things all the time and then wipe them up again just to prove how easy it was.

Shopping for food was great too. We would drive through a wonderland of sparkling pale-grey rain, park in a tarmac heaven and push a gigantic trolley into this enormous, brightly lit paradise of hygienically wrapped food packets. The twins dashed about happily filling the trolley with rainbow-coloured boxes and jars and tins while I clicked along the floor in a daze, stroking things with my perfectly varnished shell-pink nails. I loved that place. The floors were so clean and the staff wore nice shiny jackets, and smiled all the time.

I got settled into a routine that I'd only

ever dreamed of before: up early to play with the hot water in the sparkling, tiled bathroom, followed by games with frosted cereal flakes in the gleaming white kitchen, a little waltz along the pavement to the clean shiny car, half an hour's worth of school run and then off to work, tippety-tap, stopping on the way to pick up a sandwich from a lovely bakery done out in plastic to look like a cottage loaf.

Tripity-trip into the freshly hoovered office, watch my bracelets skitter across the polished fake mahogany of my desk, answer the phone brightly, type a few things neatly, clean my computer keyboard with special little cleansing pads, eat my sandwich, make some coffee and then run down to the photocopy department for a chat with Janice before skipping off to collect the boys from their after-school homework club.

On Tuesdays and Thursdays I ate lunch in the canteen, on Wednesdays I bought a magazine, and on Friday evenings we either ordered pizza using the shiny new telephone or went shopping for little dishes of ready cooked food that you could heat up in our brand new, totally clean microwave. Ping.

After supper we watched the television together, and once the twins were in bed I usually sat on the sofa and flicked through magazines for an hour before going to bed myself. Usually with a real china cup and saucer full of expensive herbal tea. Naturally I'd stopped smoking.

At the weekends, I drove the twins to a series of school cricket and football matches, where I enthusiastically agreed with the other parents that the weather was closing in and that the new development behind the post office was taking ages to complete. Making up for lost time, I also took the boys to see endless films in the new neon-lit multiplex, and to eat American food in cafeterias where even the plants, being plastic, could be disinfected.

It was bliss. Everything was clean, everything was well organised, everything ran like clockwork. I had a brand new pale leather handbag full of tasteful personal accessories and a matching purse with gold clasps that made my nails shine when I undid them. I was clean all the time, and I didn't have a single mosquito bite anywhere on my body. In fact, I didn't have a mark on my body, not the slightest scratch. Not a bump, a bruise, a bite, a scrape, a graze — nothing. Just clean smooth skin anointed nightly with a new bottle of almond body milk. My clothes were all smart and neat and ironed, my hair was always clean, I never found myself dripping with sweat only two minutes after getting out of a cold shower.

My rapture lasted until the phone rang one evening.

'Camille, is tha you?' rasped a familiar voice. 'You there?'

'Yes, I'm here,' I said at last. 'What do you want?'

'I wan chew to come home.'

'I am home.'

'No, you ain't. How can you be at home in fucking plastic-land? I know you!'

'No, I don't think you do. I'm loving it here. And it isn't plastic-land.'

'Don-tell me you like those plastic-people! Don-tell me you having fun over there!'

'No, I'm not! I mean, I am! Look, I'm just living a normal life like everyone else. I do the school run, I go to work, I . . . '

'What? You working?'

'Yes, I work in an office . . . '

'But I need you in office here!'

'Look, I'm sorry, I've got to go.'

'You gotta man there?'

'I've got to go.'

'Camille, Treasure!'

'What?'

'Email me! Promise! Please!'

'I'll think about it,' I said, and put the phone down.

I had every intention of forgetting to think of him ever again, but I dreamed of him all night and the next day as soon as I got into work, I watched my beautiful nails fly over my glittering new keyboard in the office: 'Why do you want me to email you?' they typed.

I sighed and shook my head as my wayward fingers clicked on send. At that point, I clacked smartly off to the coffee machine — before they could start dialling his phone number.

After that it was different. He emailed back with an account of Robert trying to persuade Teffi to drink water instead of beer, and I sent him a frosty description of the flat. Then he sent some pretty funny football jokes to the boys and before I knew it, I was back in the old tango. He'd become the most interesting, vital, funny, stimulating part of my day and, as it had in France, the rest of my life began to fade out of focus in comparison with the scorching heat of his personality, his zest for life, his outrageous pronouncements, and his breathtaking sense of fun.

But this time I was forearmed. I knew better than to take him seriously and when he started flirting I ignored him.

'You beautiful woman,' he typed.

'I bought a juice-maker today,' I typed back primly.

'You don't need no machines to make juice,' he declared instantly. 'You are only juice in my life.'

I didn't answer that one, so the next morning he sent me a recipe for raspberry crush, and swore blind that he would be blending it all weekend, hoping that we would be drinking raspberry crush together — even if we were half a world apart.

I mailed him back saying I didn't believe that he'd ever drunk anything including fruit in his entire life and asking if he'd finally drained the Caribbean dry of Pernod.

He promptly responded that his life had been turned head over heels a few months back and that a lot of things had changed since then. I told him to pull the other one and accused him of being a common Jack Tar smuggler.

Not at all, he said. I was imagining things. The piracy thing was merely the result of living in the Caribbean. If he lived in Spain, he said, he'd be a bullfighter.

And I'd barely stifled my giggles over that one when he sent me a whole thing about Plato and the search for truth, which was actually really fascinating and we exchanged quite a few emails on that subject, but he was soon back onto sex again.

'I want lick you from your toes upwards. Very slowly.'

'I must remember to buy some light bulbs on the way home,' I typed with trembling fingers.

Nickie phoned from time to time, but she was seriously busy putting her exhibition together and when I tried to tell her about my beautiful new school-run life, she kept saying 'Yes, yes, yes, I know. You'll get bored with it sooner or later. You weren't bred to the treadmill! Look at yourself! You just aren't provincial. You're punishing your father, if you ask me.'

She was painting like a maniac, said the gallery owner was her new muse, and to hell with finishing the house.

'But I thought you didn't want to prostitute your art,' I said. 'In France, didn't you say it was too stressful, making money out of it?'

'Ah, but it's different now,' she said. 'I mean, you know, I'm inspired. You must come to the opening.'

Daniel phoned too and I instantly suspected Aunt Lottie of having been on the rampage, but perhaps that was unfair. When I told him what I was doing, he invited me to stay with him and Harriet.

'We'll be here in Vienna for at least six

months and we've got a huge apartment in an old mansion block, so there's plenty of space. Harriet will teach the boys for you. Do they speak German? You can't work in an office, cherub. Total gloomsville. You'd better come and stay with us. Sort yourself out. I'll get the piano tuned. Don't worry about tickets, I'll buy them . . .'

Harriet chimed in with the offer of another husband. Over the phone line, I could hear her in the background saying, 'Yes, but Daniel, Stanislav needs someone! And at least he wouldn't make her work in an office . . .'

The pair of them are completely off the wall. Utterly doolally. Not just barking, they are actually wagging their tails and snuffling up each other's bottoms. But they care. They really do. I mean, they really do want me to be happy. They love me. And I love them too.

I didn't want to hurt his feelings, so it took some time to talk Daniel out of sending me tickets but I did it in the end, and sincerely promising to come and see them soon I rang off, blurting out 'big hugs' just before I put the phone down.

I also wrote to Aunt Lottie; a long incoherent missive apologising for being hopeless, promising to improve, and explaining that I loved her more than she could possibly imagine. In reply she sent me a postcard of Eros with 'Ne change jamais, cherie' written on the back of it in scarlet ink. And a whole row of kisses, so I knew it was all right.

When I told Nickie about the Pirate's plastic-people she laughed. 'He's so right!' she said. 'So bloody right! Do you know in our office we actually discuss how many cups of tea we drink each day! And this morning they were counting how many tries it takes everyone to get into their parking places in the office car park! Can you imagine that?'

I could easily imagine it. After all, we were having exactly the same conversations in our office. Plastic chat in a plastic world. Nice, clean, shiny chat, hygienically-wrapped and guaranteed not to disturb the calm flow of a well-regulated life.

'Don-tyou laugh no more?' demanded the Pirate. 'When was the last time you was really alive? Haven't you murdered anyone yet?'

'Oh fuck off,' I typed back crossly, and chipped my nail varnish on the keys.

I got bored with reading women's magazines. They all had the same articles in them every month. And I'd gone off the jars and packets from the supermarket; the contents didn't taste very nice. I started fingering limes outside the corner shop, and once I even found myself transfixed outside a fishmonger's because the window display was got up to resemble a Caribbean beach. I tore myself away from it but only a few yards further up the pavement fell prey to a travel agency advertising paradise breaks with optional day-cruises.

Not that, frankly, any of it meant anything. I certainly would never again believe even one syllable that any man uttered — especially Short Fat Balding Sex-Maniacs who Lived on Boats and Shouted A Lot — and as for giving up my dreary job for a precarious but luxy lifestyle in the Caribbean, well huh! Not a chance. At least I'd built myself a stable life on the English south coast, something sustainable and realistic.

'Stable life is for fucking horses!' swore the Pirate.

The twins needed me too, I told myself — and sent him a pithy essay on parental responsibility.

'Yes,' emailed the Pirate. 'They need you to drive them everywhere, that's what they need you for!'

I shrugged and sent him a hyperlink to a parenting site. I knew my boys. Of course they needed me. All children need their mothers. They'd only become so independent through having been boarders. And through me being a fairly hopeless mother since the word go, I suppose.

I shrugged, unwrapped a chicken pie, put it in the oven and started re-painting my nails. They'd be home soon. They were getting a lift after rehearsals for the school play, and then they'd crowd round me where I lay on the sofa, tease me lovingly and say how glad they were to be together with me again.

Of course they wouldn't burst into the flat, hurtle straight into the kitchen and raid the fridge. Of course they wouldn't fling themselves into armchairs and glue their noses to some disgusting police programme. Of course they wouldn't sigh and say that the boarders were staying up late to run lines for the show, which would have been useful for them too. Naturally not. They adored being with me.

We were so terrifically happy, the three of us in our cosy little nest. We simply didn't need anyone else. We laughed and joked and made homemade pasta together. Well. No, we didn't actually get round to making it, but I suggested it and I would have done it if the twins had wanted to. I had all the instructions ready, cut out of a women's magazine. As it was, they were busy, and they were right. They were too old to play mud pies in the kitchen with mummy. But we went out together. Sometimes. With them walking two paces behind me and pretending that they were out alone. I didn't have to get out of the car when I picked them up from school any more. In fact, I wasn't allowed to stop the car outside the school any more. I had to park on the corner and wait.

We were, as I say, utterly, blissfully happy. Totally. In paradise. Yes.

I had started to bitch to myself about the cold in the flat, the traffic jams, the boredom of my job, the stupidity of my work mates, the narrow-minded attitudes of the people I met around town, and the amazingly dreary conversations I had about wallpaper and summer holidays. I told myself that this was normal. Bitching was what normal people leading normal lives did. But if the truth be told, I was screaming up the walls.

'You're mad,' said Nickie. 'I don't know why you insist on staying here, grinding on with a dead end job when you could be glamming around in the Caribbean. In fact, I think it's your duty to get your arse back there, so you can invite me out to stay for a couple of months. I could just do with a bit of torture by luxury.'

'I thought you were the Queen of Domestica these days.'

Nickie shrugged. 'Hmm. Well, I was. I am! But you know, every girl needs a bit of space in her life, and an artist needs emotional stimulation.'

'Who says so?'

'Gallery owner,' she croaked with a show of nonchalance which didn't deceive me for a nanosecond. I raised my eyebrows, stuck my hands on my hips and just looked at her. In response, Nickie indulged in an orgy of shrugging and pouting and blushing. I shook my head at her.

'And the implications of this leetle fleeng, pray tell?'

She gave a delicious sparkly little giggle. 'No, no, silly. He's married with kids, same as me. And I love the sailor, I do. He's fantastic. He's just, you know . . . married to me.'

'As opposed to Mr Gallery who is married to someone else?'

'Precisely,' nodded Nickie. 'And I just thought, you know, a break together . . . '

I had to laugh. 'Like, a couple of months staying with me in the Caribbean?'

'Mmm, yes, that sort of thing, yes . . . '

'Which is why you want me to go back to my insane and terminally furious husband?'

'No, I just . . . '

'So that I can provide you and your squeezy-mop with a decent alibi for a two-month shag-fest?'

'As a bourgeois housewife, I admit I am a

failure,' said Nickie, making a pathetic attempt to mourn her lost respectability and succeeding only in glowing with sexual fulfilment.

'Can't wait to see the exhibition. I imagine it shows all the inhibitions which have now become ex . . . or is the 'ex' just for x-rated?' I asked her bitterly. There's nothing more irritating to the newly-celibate woman than the sight of her best friend radiating well-being, talking in sexy little giggles and starting every sentence with the word 'He' . . .

'I am just a slave to physical rapture,' she sighed.

I mimed sticking my fingers down my throat. 'And the kids . . . ? Yours? Mine? The boys . . . '

'Well, frankly as far as I can see, yours were just as happy being boarders. You could easily . . . '

I shook my head at her. 'Not even for you, Nickie. I'll never go back. Not a hope in hell. I'm finished with him.'

'Apart from the emails?'

'Oh well, that's different, I'm just being civilised. He is my husband, after all.'

And that's the way it stayed until just last week. Last Friday in fact, when Janice bounced into the general office saying I had a visitor. Every head, including mine, instantly swivelled towards the door but I was the only one whose heart skipped a beat. Advancing purposefully towards my desk carrying a large bunch of orange and white lilies was the Pirate.

I must have gone all kinds of colours. I hadn't a clue what to say. I mean, apart from anything else, he looked so incongruous, so exotic. So fit and tanned. The Pirate — well, to be honest I wasn't even sure that it really was him, he was so seriously scrubbed up — was wearing a cream shirt, immaculate pale brown trousers and leather shoes. Not a swimsuit in sight, no earring, no sweat, no parrot.

I mean, Janice saw him. You ask her. He was brushed and polished, bright-eyed and well slept. He actually looked normal. Even a bit thinner, maybe. He was still short of course and his hair was still receding, but it was as clean and tidy as the rest of him.

No, don't get all excited. Because no, the sight of the Pirate all scrubbed up and re-vamped didn't suddenly melt my icy heart. In fact, nothing melted. I just sat there looking up at him like a banana: stupid, bendy, squidgy round the edges and decidedly yellow. All the others sat there too, gazing at me with fascination.

'Treasure!' he said standing beside my desk.

'What are you doing here?' I mumbled, fiddling with my hair. At the desk facing mine, Cathy's eyebrows were going up and down like pistons.

'I take you for lunch!' declared the Pirate loudly.

'I, er . . . ' I tailed off. The silence was complete. Nobody in the office was even pretending to work. They were all just watching the show. I glared at Cathy. She pulled a face, propped her chin on her hand and smiled.

'Here!' he said, thrusting the flowers at me. 'For you! Let's go. Come on.'

'Don't worry, I'll put them in water!' chirped Janice, holding out her hands. 'Such lovely flowers!' And behind the Pirate's back she mouthed, 'Who is he?'

As if he'd heard her, the Pirate swung round on his heel and surveyed the office with a sharky gleam. 'I take my wife to lunch!' he announced. 'What is problem?'

No-one said a word; they were all transfixed. Even Simon didn't say a word, and some of them actually looked shocked. Suddenly I could feel laughter welling up inside me. They found this shocking? If only they knew!

I glanced at him. His eyes were sparkling with unholy amusement. Any minute now, he'd do something really outrageous, like throw me over his shoulder and charge off towards the lifts yelling for pliroma. I bit my lip, but then he caught my eye and we both burst out laughing.

He grabbed my hand. 'Okay, bye-bye!' he said between guffaws. 'Come on, Treasure!'

He pulled me out of my typing chair and I stumbled to my feet clumsily knocking my coffee over. A pile of papers slithered off the filing cabinet fluttering through the air in all directions.

'Here, you!' he said to Janice. 'Take this!' He tossed the lilies at her and petals showered the carpet like confetti. The flowers landed in Janice's arms and she just stood there holding them and gazing at us.

'Excuse me!' said Simon looking affronted.

'Fuck off,' said the Pirate amiably. 'Come, Camille we go!'

I just had time to grab my bag as he put his arm round my shoulders and dragged me out of the office, both of us stifling mad giggles. I'm sure Janice told you about it.

We ate at The Angel, that big old hotel on the sea front, yes, the one with the French chef and the fantastically long wine list. The Pirate had booked us a table in a window alcove where we had a wonderful sea view but couldn't be overheard by other diners.

Characteristically, he ordered for both of us, stabbing at the menu and bullying the waiter over the wine list. I didn't care. In fact it was a relief. I adore having someone order for me. Daniel always does that too.

Once the wine had arrived along with little plates of amusegueule, he leant back in his chair and surveyed me at his leisure. I followed suit and stared back at him hard. He didn't even blink.

'Well, santé, I think,' I said at last.

'Here's to you,' he said, and we clinked glasses in the pale English sunlight. His shiny new wedding ring matched mine. I wondered how long he'd had it — not that it mattered any more. We sat in silence, each one of us sipping wine and waiting to see what the other would say. I cracked first.

'So how's Sylvia, then?' I said, taking a tiny pastry tartelette containing half an olive and a sliver of anchovy.

'Sylvia? Are you mad?'

'Don't tell me she's left you already?'

'She never existed,' said the Pirate waving her aside with an elegant gesture. 'She was nothing. Just a pawn. Tha's what I was gonna tell you that night . . . '

'So who picked these clothes out, then?

Don't tell me you went shopping for this lot on your own.'

'That was Marie-Rose . . . '

'Yes. It was always her, wasn't it?' I said. 'She let you out of the office, didn't she? She found out that I was at The Shells that night, didn't she? I bet she even found my address in the UK. She's the one, isn't she?'

'She's . . . ' said the Pirate, but I cut across him.

'I don't know why you didn't marry her in the first place,' I snapped.

'Yes, it was her,' he nodded. 'She got me off the Sun too. And she found out what flight you took to London. She's a clever girl. She's looking after the business, while I'm away.'

I realised I was gouging trenches in the starched white tablecloth with my butter knife and put it down quickly.

'How long was it before she found you on the Sun?'

'Around midday she found me. I nearly died.'

'What?'

'You didn't leave me no water. My kidneys didn't like it much. I spent two weeks in a clinic in Florida.'

'Oh my God! I'm so sorry! Is that why you're so thin?'

'That's why I sent you the parrot.'

'What, because kidney failure affected your brain?'

'Nah. Revenge for the clinic. I hate fuckin doctors.'

'Me too.'

'I know, I know you do. You're like me. But they patched me up okay. I even learned some more English. So what you do with the parrot? You still got him?'

'Good grief, no! I sent him to a parrot rescue centre, but they didn't want him. Can you imagine what he would have taught the other parrots? In the end I had to pay them to keep the wretched bird. What I really wanted to do was send him to Sylvia with a card saying he was from a secret admirer.'

He grinned and popped a minuscule pastry heart into his mouth. 'You a smart woman, you know that?'

'Oh well . . . '

'Yeah well. Marie-Rose been having a go at me. Said I was a fool, tole me I had forgotten what civilisation was like, tole me I had to clean myself up.' He swirled the wine round his glass. 'She like you a lot you know. She always on your side. Said I was an animal. Said I got what I deserved.'

It was my turn to swirl wine. 'Yes, well, I went a bit over the top. I'm sorry I trashed your boat. Was it a mess?'

He shrugged. 'I don-cair. Marie-Rose like it. Said she wanted to do the same thing a million times over. What you do with the gun?'

'Threw it into the sea,' I lied without missing a beat. 'Along with the bullets, and your keys.'

'Bloody women, you all the same!' he said peevishly. 'That thing cost money, you know?'

'So I'll pay for it,' I snapped.

'No, I don-want money. I don-cair about money. Money is a psychological thing, anyway.'

'So what are you here for? What do you want? Why don't you just go home and live happily ever after with Marie-Rose, since she's so wonderful?'

'I just want to talk to you. Honest, no bullshit. You driving me crazy.'

I reached for my handbag. I'd sooner go back to the office than continue this cat and mouse gourmet lunch. I was beginning to feel like cat food myself: brown and slimy with little bits of soft minced carrot hiding under my liver.

The Pirate threw his hands into the air. 'Okay, okay. She's my daughter,' he said.

'What? She's your what?'

'Marie-Rose is my daughter. It is better if people don-know it, tha-sall. Is not so safe to be with me. Clepsi-clepsi. Thieves.'

'How can she be your daughter?'

'Come on, Camille, you know. I started young, I didn't know I had a daughter, she came looking for me, found me and stayed. Simple.'

'What do you mean, you didn't know you had a daughter?'

'Happens all the time. Young girl come to Greece on holiday, have nice time with local boy, go home on next flight. This was little French girl, sixteen, seventeen. We was only kids. I din-know. She never wrote me or nothing. But Marie-Rose, she grew up and she din like her Paris family . . . lots of money, nothing to say. So she ran off, came to fin' me. She's good at finding people.'

The waiter arrived with filets of sole wrapped into tiny thin flower shapes and positioned the plates carefully before us. He fidgeted with the table, refilled our glasses, adjusted the position of the breadbasket and left again.

'Okay, all right. She's your daughter.' It made total sense to me that Marie-Rose was his daughter and I do like things to be logical. Which explained the happy bubble of laughter in my throat. It absolutely was not relief.

'That still doesn't explain what you're

doing here,' I said sternly. 'What do you want?'

'Is it good, this fish?' asked the Pirate.

'I don't know, I haven't tried it,' I said and picked up my knife and fork. It was good. The fish was fresh and tender, tasting of sunshine and seawater, lapped with creamy sauce that tasted like wild herbs and tangy dried lemons.

'Mmmm, this is delicious!'

'Das your problem,' said the Pirate, 'You don know as much as you think you do. You see? You say you hate food but you do like to eat if is good.' And getting back into his usual bossy stride he added, 'Come on, mange! You too thin!'

In spite of myself, I smiled as we ate the beautiful fish, tore the fresh bread apart, dipped it into the sauce and enjoyed the sensation of eating good food. I didn't even mind him being right. What the hell? What was the difference whether I was a foodie or not?

We stared contentedly out at the glittering sea until the next course arrived. Hare in red wine with slivers of dark plums and halos of black olives with tiny green beans tossed in olive oil. We ate that too, our eyes meeting from time to time in shared pleasure. It was followed by crispy green salad, a fabulous cheese board and diminutive pots of dark chocolate mousse.

Okay, laugh Philippa. Famous me who can't be bothered with food. Why shouldn't I enjoy a meal once in a while? Especially when it's that good. I tell you, Philippa, you and Gus ought to go there for lunch, if you haven't already been . . . but I expect you have. Yes.

Anyway, as the waiter cleared the table and murmured about coffee, I sighed happily. I felt fat, full and fabulous. I propped my chin on my hands and stared at the Pirate. He picked up a coffee spoon and stabbed it into the sugar bowl.

'You look beautiful,' he said at last. 'Beautiful. I like your hair like that. Lovely.'

'Thank you.'

'And how are you-skids?'

'They're fine.'

'Still in same school?'

'Yes, but just as day boys. They live with me now.'

'Yes, I know. You got my papers? From the safe?'

I nodded. I still had them even though I wasn't entirely sure of their contents.

'You read them?'

'Not all of them. Only the stuff in English and French. I can't read Greek, you know that.'

'I teach you if you like.'

I glanced up at him suspiciously. 'What for?'

'You my wife,' he smiled. 'I don-cair if you know everything.'

I shrugged. 'What is there to know?'

'Nothing. You seen my will, you seen my birth certificate, you seen my papers. What is there to know?'

He was staring a challenge at me. I stared back. If the papers I had stolen were bona fide, he was far less of a loose cannon than I'd thought. They had included visas and permissions, properly drawn up accounts, marriage and divorce certificates, life insurance policies, shipping documents, insurance policies, and a will which was a neat share out between me and his children. But were they bona fide cod? Or red herrings?

'What were those crates in the office?' I demanded. He smiled at me, spread his hands out in the air and shrugged expressively.

'You told me they were T-shirts,' I said, raising my eyebrows. 'But I moved a load of them one time and they clanked. So don't lie to me. They definitely were not T-shirts. What were they? Guns?'

He blushed and shrugged. 'Nothing,' he muttered and I wasn't sure if he was acting or not.

'What were they?'

'Shh!'

'Tell me!'

'Oh, all right! Bloody woman! They tin openers.'

'What? Tin openers! What were you doing with six crates of tin openers in the office?'

He looked sheepish. 'I got em cheap in Venezuela. Soldem to a mate in Jamaica. He got catering supplies firm. Jus a leedle bit of trading. Make a bit of cash, you know.'

'Tin openers!' I repeated. I wasn't in the slightest bit convinced. I mean, give me a break. Who in their right mind smuggles tin openers? I'm not that stupid.

He brushed the subject aside. 'You beautiful woman,' he said. 'You got beautiful eyes. Green, like a cat.'

'What do you want?'

'I want you.' He put his hand over mine, where it lay on the table. 'I want you back.'

'No. I can't do that. The boys are here, my job, the flat . . . no, I live here now.' Tailing off, I just looked at him like a hamster: little eyes, bulging cheeks, pink hands rubbing round in circles.

Suddenly he sighed and shrugged bad-temperedly. 'All right, all right. I love you. Is that what you want? I fucking love you.'

I boggled at him.

'I can't live without you,' he whispered. 'Okay?'

I was completely flabbergasted. It was the last thing I'd expected him to say.

'Before,' he continued. 'I just wannid to fuck you, but you . . . you crazy woman. Swimmin ashore, stealing a speedboat, pulling a gun on me . . . you crazy woman and I love you.'

'But . . . ' I was deeply suspicious. I knew he was up to something. He smiled, took my hand and laid it on his chest. Approximately over the place where ordinary mortals keep their hearts. 'Here. Cross my heart! Truth. I never lied to you.'

'You don't love me,' I stammered.

'I do. I loved you a long time. But you din wan it. I try to tell you that time on the beach . . . and again afterwards, more than once, but you never wanta know. An if I tole you when you was leavin you'd have shot me . . . '

In spite of myself I grinned. 'True. I probably would have done!'

'You were so sexy pointing a gun in my face!' His grip on my hand tightened and he gave a great guffaw of laughter. 'With no knickers on!'

'Shh! Everyone's looking!'

'I don't care! Let them look! They're only jealous cos my wife is a beautiful woman.' He lowered his voice, and leaning across the table, looked straight into my eyes. 'Hey! Treasure! Look at me.'

I shook my hair out of my eyes and looked at him.

'One thing. Jus-twun-thing. Why you email me?'

My lips twitched as I looked at him. I didn't love him, absolutely not.

'I don lie to you,' he reminded me, and I wondered if that was true. He'd stolen from me, cast me adrift, left me alone, hurled abuse, generally pissed me off and bullied me about . . . yes he'd done all that but he didn't usually lie. He either refused point-blank to tell me something, or he told the truth. Except about the tin openers, and probably about his papers. I was seriously sceptical on both counts.

'The truth,' I said. 'You want the truth?'

He nodded.

So I told him.

'You are a stupid old bastard,' I said quietly. 'I was half in love with you before we even met, but you didn't trust me, you forced me to stay in the Caribbean and you shouted at me, and stole my passport, and you were horrible to me in front of everyone, and you're so bloody bad tempered . . . I mean, you practically turned me into a murderer . . . '

'And now?'

'And now it's too late. It's all over. So you might as well leave me alone.'

'Come! Come with me!' He stood up, his table napkin falling to the floor, and held his hand out to me. I put my hand in his, he pulled me to my feet and led me out of the dining room. As we left he nodded at the waiter who raised his hand in a discreet salute. Even here, he didn't pay restaurant bills. I felt even more doubtful about the tin openers.

We walked out of the hotel, across the road and down some concrete steps onto the shingle beach. There, he walked a few paces into the shelter of a breakwater where he swung me round to face him and took me in his arms. He looked at me for a long moment and — I know! I know I should have pulled away, stamped on his corns, done anything except . . .

He grabbed me and I let him. Against my better judgement I even pressed closer to his great powerful chest as his mouth closed on mine; my knees started their jelly imperson-ations, my pulse raced, my heart thumped . . . all the usual reactions. I was quivering all over. My body was still ready to crawl across the Sahara for one touch of the Pirate's little finger, and there was nothing I could do about it.

'Come on!' he urged. 'Say it, tell me!'

'Say what?'

'I love you, Camille, and you love me. We belong together. You won't find anyone man enough for you in that stupid fucking office and you know it!'

I tried to pull away from him.

'No!' he said, pulling me back and kissing me again. 'You're mine!'

'Stop bulldozing me!' I complained.

'Or you'll what? You gonna shoot me?'

'I might even do that,' I said, laughing nervously. By that time my heart was trampolining up and down on my diaphragm and I realised that I was scared to death. Attempting to murder the man was child's play compared to admitting that I might just be head over heels in love with him. Might.

He laughed and pulled me into a bear hug. 'Carthimou, querida, you were made for me. I love you with all my heart. Come home . . . '

'What? To live on your crummy boat again?'

'No, I don-care about the Sun.'

'Liar!'

'I want you. So if you wan apartment on mainland with la fuckin' clim, que sera sera.

If you wanna come to Europe every summer, que fuckin' sera. If you want to bring the skids and we hire someone to teach 'em, or you teach 'em, or whatever you want, I don-cair. I just want you home. With me.'

'No. You kidnapped me.'

'I'm sorry for that. Really. I was wrong. Marie-Rose, she told me I was wrong, she told me I was mad, but I thought if I could only make you stay long enough, you would come to love me.'

'But why else do you think I married you?'

'You never said it. You wouldn't let me say it.'

'I didn't want to. I didn't want to love anyone.'

'But you did, din-you?'

'Let me go!'

'And you love me now? Don-you?'

I looked up at him and tried to pull away again. But he was having none of it. He held me firmly by my shoulders, his fists digging into my flesh.

I looked at him, at his newly cleaned teeth, his evenly tanned cheeks and greying hair. No, Philippa, he doesn't look the least like Errol Flynn. He isn't young, or tall or handsome. He doesn't have dimples or a smile that would amuse Queen Victoria.

On the other hand, he's intelligent and

witty; he's powerful, erotic, passionate, generous and loyal. He makes life fun, we laugh together, we understand each other. And he has beautiful velvety brown eyes.

'You fuckin' difficult woman,' he said, shaking me impatiently.

Yes, he is foul-mouthed, autocratic and irascible. If I went back to him, within minutes he'd be bossing me about, shouting, calling me names, arguing, insisting on getting his own way. Yes. But at least he'd never want to discuss how many cups of tea he drinks per day. Or parking techniques, or spider plants, or road works, or getting lumps out of custard.

'Camilla?' he whispered.

I looked straight into his lovely eyes and smiled. 'I love you,' I said, and he pulled me into his arms with a triumphant guffaw. 'I always have and I always will.'

The words left my mouth like huge flapping seagulls clambering into the sky and I suddenly felt totally liberated. I love him and I don't care what the future holds.

He will always be Errol Flynn to me.

★   ★   ★

And that's it really, Philippa. I married a pirate, and I'm going back to him.

Which is why (and I'm sorry I've been so long-winded about it) which is why I won't be coming back to my job tomorrow morning.

Best regards

Camilla.

PS Sorry I didn't come back to work after lunch on Friday.

We do hope that you have enjoyed reading this large print book.

Did you know that all of our titles are available for purchase?

We publish a wide range of high quality large print books including:
Romances, Mysteries, Classics
General Fiction
Non Fiction and Westerns

Special interest titles available in large print are:
The Little Oxford Dictionary
Music Book
Song Book
Hymn Book
Service Book

Also available from us courtesy of Oxford University Press:
Young Readers' Dictionary
(large print edition)
Young Readers' Thesaurus
(large print edition)

For further information or a free brochure, please contact us at:
Ulverscroft Large Print Books Ltd.,
The Green, Bradgate Road, Anstey,
Leicester, LE7 7FU, England.
Tel: (00 44) **0116 236 4325**
Fax: (00 44) **0116 234 0205**

THE LIFE OF REILLY

Paul Burke

Sean Reilly seems to have his life sorted: gorgeous wife, beautiful house and lucrative career as a voice-over artist. But he craves the sort of romance and affection that he no longer receives from his wife. Why is it, he wonders, that once married, women want men to change? Whereas men hate it when women change. Lucy Ross, 'caught single' after breaking up with her long-term boyfriend, is also looking for romance when she meets Sean. She doesn't want him to change; she wants him the way he is. So could the life of Reilly be sorted after all?

WISH YOU WERE HERE

Phillipa Ashley

When Jack proposes to Beth at the end of a holiday romance, she doesn't think twice — she knows he's The One. But on their return home, Jack walks out with no explanation. Eight years on and a twist of fate finds Beth a new job — working for Jack — forced to face the man who broke her heart every day. But she really needs this job. Compelled to spend time together, the mystery of Jack's disappearance unravels. But are they both carrying too much baggage to try again — or could they finally be in the right place at the right time?

I TAKE THIS MAN

Valerie Frankel

When Jersey Girl Penny Bracket is left standing at the altar by fiancé Bram Shiraz, she doesn't know how to react. Her mother, Ester, on the other hand knows exactly what to do — track Bram down, knock him unconscious with a bottle of Dom Perignon and imprison him in the attic of her mansion. Now this may seem extreme — but Ester's got some serious questions for the fugitive groom . . . plus she needs someone to write all the return labels for the wedding gifts. But can she find out why Bram got cold feet before everyone else discovers what she's done?